I'll Never Be.

A. L. Fox

A. L. Fox

ISBN: 979-8-218-23573-4

To my first love, and to my forever love.
Without either, my heart would not love the way it does.
And to love itself. For always *being there for me,*
even when I had wished for you to just leave me be for forever.

Contents

CHAPTER ONE.

SUMMER 2009.

Rapid City, South Dakota is not a place for teenagers. It is a place for families and the elderly. It's somewhere where Tina and Jimmy can bring Jimmy Junior and Franny, along with their two Golden Retrievers—Sassy and Penny (are we sensing a theme here, or is that just me), and the six of them can run around like chickens with their heads cut off for four days before driving their burnt orange Subaru Outback back over to Utah. Rapid City is the kind of place where, in another world, Tina's seventy-five-year-old dad Harley, can move to and no one will have to worry too much because it's relatively safe and big, but not too big to be stressful.

Rapid City, South Dakota is not, however, the kind of place where the Trystan's of the world can run freely—repercussions be damned. There's always a Jimmy in his SUV rolling his eyes and telling his wife about the crazy teenagers that reside here.

I am sixteen this summer. I'll be seventeen in a few months, but it already feels like I'm there. I can tell this next year of life is going to be one for the books. I can feel it in my bones.

I just got done serving time.

Hard, lonely, well-deserved time.

I was grounded for what felt like an eternity, but really was only three weeks. I got caught smoking cigarettes and my mom, as rad as she is, did not love that news.

Unsurprising.

It was my first major offense. Aside from going over my cell phone minutes or arguing with my little brother, I have been a fairly "chill kid" as my mom put it whilst lecturing me intensely in the dining room of our fairly modest Rapid City home.

Now that my parole-mother has released me, I'm finally able to drive my beautiful, burgundy-ish Dodge Stratus again. Salsa, I call her.

It's the best my sixteen-year-old brain could come up with, don't judge too harshly.

I have missed her dearly—my Salsa. She very much gives "basic seventeen-year-old" vibes. The zebra print seat covers, the matching steering wheel cover so that my fingers don't freeze off in the South Dakota winters. And to prevent third-degree burns from the summer sun.

Getting back my freedom is a huge relief. Having my stepdad tote me to and from work was beginning to be embarrassing. And it really put a damper on my after-shift flirting—always having Craig there to pick me up right on time.

I've worked at McDonald's for two years now and let me tell you, it is a pool of cute boys with little adult supervision. Adults that actually give a shit, that is. And though I am no stranger to the smoke-break-flirt-session, that is about all I have really done in the romance area of my life. Typically my flirting isn't very target specific, going to anyone who is remotely nice to me. I've been called a "tease" a time or two. But lately, there has been only one boy on my radar.

Jared Barns.

Jared is.... Handsome. Almost annoyingly handsome. And kind too. The audacity he has to be quite attractive and also genuinely nice is unreal. He recently turned eighteen which makes him that much more alluring. An "adult" if you will. Not long-ago Jared got promoted to a low-on-the-pole manager position and I don't know how he does it but black clunky non-skid shoes picked out from a fast-food attire catalog, black cargo pants, and the button up shirts that remind me of a bag of Skittles... they could never look this good on anyone but him.

Sometimes I just stand there and watch as his tanned arms work while he flips hamburger patties or pulls baskets of fries from the grease vats. I'll notice his forehead glistening with sweat. And while I have never been a girl who admires perspiration... I'm never upset when I notice his. I'll watch the muscles on his arms, the ones that start at the base of his fingers and lead up to covered biceps, peaking out over his collar on his neck... I know they have been formed from his years of running track and helping on his family's ranch.

What? A girl can appreciate the finer things.

Jared's smile is one for the books too. It's all bright and straight and big, lighting up his entire face and meeting his eyes every time. His hair is the color of the most perfect cup of coffee—that sort of beautiful brown, making your cup almost more cream than it is coffee. It sits perfectly atop his head in a short style that gives off a military sort of haircut but grown out, makes me want to run my fingers through it. And then, my most favorite part—*his eyes*. They're the kind of blue that you can't put a name to. They look like those marbles one might use to play Mancala with—that kind of glassy and shiny blue. And just like him—they're bright and beautiful.

The cold of the stainless steel table bites into my elbows as I lean on it in the drive-thru, holding my chin up with my fist and absolutely gawking at this boy—no, man.

His eyes meet mine from across the table, and I can't help but wonder if I might get the chance to look into his glowing, gorgeous blue's for a really long time.

It's not every day that I get a front row seat to what I would define as the "Smoke Show" that is Jared Barns working. Sometimes he's around a corner or I am in the back. This particular McDonald's is a giant rectangle, all angles and walls. The front of the store is all large windows with silver frames. The standard red and yellow seats with round and rectangular tables placed methodically throughout. There are soda machines on one wall, and a counter with a few black computer monitors separates the front from the back of the building. Behind that is the ice cream machine that more often than not gets adorned with an "Out of Order" sign. Coolers aplenty line almost any and all remaining wall space. The farther in you go you have the drive-thru area, *my preferred station,* with way too many sauce options that always need restocked. The fry station, where I love to watch Jared work, is oily, salty, and warm from the bright heat lamp above the metal catcher. It sits next to one side of the double sided "work line" that houses the hot food and cold condiments. Beyond all of that is the dry-stock area and large sink, the walk-in fridge and freezer, and the manager's office that comfortably fits two small people. Further back is a prep table and another drive-thru window that gets skipped eight out of ten times even though the person in here taking the order says "pay at the first window." It might sound like just another fast-food restaurant—and sure, it is. But for me it's my favorite fast-food restaurant. One I will surely remember the layout of for years to come—moments of time mapped out in every nook and cranny.

It's as I am gazing at the aforementioned muscles rippling down Jared's arms that a black car pulls up with a blond-haired man that desperately needs his fix of that super special, extra fizzy McDonald's Coca Cola. And just like that I am brought back to reality, staring put on hold for the job I'm supposed to be doing.

It's near the end of my shift now, the Friday night flying by. I was told to work on prepping more salads before heading home, so after gathering all of my bowls and boxes of lettuce I make my way to the prep table near the back of the store. All of the walls back here are a bright white with stainless-steel covering anything that would otherwise be wooden or plastic. Easier to keep clean I suppose. Laminated pieces of paper with salad, parfait, and oatmeal recipes that I have memorized hang from Velcro stickers above the large, silver table.

I stand here now, palms of my hands braced against the cool metal, with salad mix and black bowls scattered all around me as I allow my gaze to roam over to a rather fine specimen a few yards away from me.

Am I staring at Jared? Again?

Shamelessly.

There is just something about the way he wraps a hamburger with such precision, and the fluidity of the way he pulls the trays of chicken nuggets out of the hot shelves, the finesse he has when re-stocking every box and wrapper and condiment... It's like watching your favorite sport, only a little shiny from the oily sheen that you gain from just entering the building.

As I continue my perusing, working my way up from his large hands to his tan face, his bright eyes connect with my near black ones. I startle, accidentally knocking a bowl of lettuce off the table while trying to play it cool. Clearly, I need to reevaluate what it means to "be cool" because the way Jared is looking at me has me feeling anything but. He smiles his perfect smile, lines bracket it almost like dimples, and a faint chuckle that sounds like magic personified, escapes his throat. His whole presence threatens to take me out at the knees. I know I've been absolutely caught ogling, but I don't look away. I let him see my cheeks turn red and I allow him to relish in the fact that I was most certainly checking him out.

It isn't like it's new.

I don't duck my head. I don't look away to avoid his amused gaze. My eyes stay locked on his and for a brief moment we both just look at each other. Neither of us move. Neither of us acknowledge the small bit of laughter coming from a coworker, my best friend Beth if my ears are correct, witnessing this... whatever *this* is.

Jared and I simply just... connect.

It's only when our manager comes out of the office from behind me, demanding to know why there is lettuce at my feet, that either of us look away from the other. My smile only grows at the butterflies swirling in my stomach. I look up as Beth sidles up next to me, placing lids on bowls. She winks and giggles, her eyes bright and knowing.

Oh, seventeen is going to be so fun.

CHAPTER TWO.

Jared and his older brother didn't go to their dads house this year like they normally do for the summer. It has been working to my advantage, though. The three of us have become friends over the last few months—bonding over irritating bosses and coworkers and general gossip. Beth, busy bee she is, left me to my own devices outside of work. I made do. The boys and I have been going to the movies or sitting together during our breaks. Some days we drive around after our shifts end to get food that we didn't take part in making. I assume the reason for no-Texas-trip is of a personal nature and while it saddens me that there may be some turmoil there for them, you won't catch me complaining about the boys staying put and befriending little old me.

Just looking at the boys next to one another and you would know they are brothers. Kerry is a couple years older than Jared and will be done working at McDonald's in just under a couple of weeks—moving on to bigger and better things. He is very much looking forward to his new job in bicycle sales. He has the same chestnut hair as Jared, but Kerry keeps his a little longer—not quite shaggy but not shaved. His teeth are also perfect and white, his stature tall and lean. Kerry is far goofier than Jared—more class clown than silly goose. His eyes aren't as catching and bright, but that could just be a me thing. Where I see and hope for Jared to be more than just a friend, Kerry is just that; a friend.

When the three of us were on our break at work a couple of days ago Kerry invited me to their house for an annual softball luncheon that their mom and stepdad put on as summer comes to an end. Gauging Jared's reaction to the invitation and seeing his enthusiasm, I quickly said yes.

Kerry for Wingman of the Year.

The drive to their ranch is about forty-five minutes from my house. I've got my Kristina DeBarge CD playing on the digital radio my stepdad had installed for my birthday last year.

I don't often have a reason to venture outside of town, so being on the open road is doing wonders for my soul. The sun today is shining bright, barely a cloud in the light blue sky. Early September in South Dakota can be unstable. Going from soggy and cold to warm and sunny, you never know what you're going to get around here.

The black asphalt highway curves and slopes and winds on the way to my destination, faded white and yellow dashes blurring as I go. Rolling green hills, crumbling faded red barns, and an assortment of large and small houses provide a rustic view on either side of the highway. A flock of sheep every now and then, herds or multicolored cows—it's all very country out here. Everything is so green and vibrant this time of year. Soon the leaves will start to turn, and the grass will wilt, forewarning a temperamental Midwest fall.

Having never been to Jared's, all I've got to go by are some vague directions written out for me on a piece of printer paper in blue pen. He scribbled them down at work in his very boyish handwriting last night before he left, saying "can't wait to show you the place!" with a wave of his calloused hand and a flash of his big smile. And while I relished in the close proximity to which he stood near me as he wrote down these instructions—"a left at the 3rd dirt road then a right on to Sugar Creek Rd. Go 2 miles" blah blah blah... these directions are proving to be quite challenging to know where in the fresh hell I am going.

I even asked him last night, "How am I supposed to know when it's been two miles, Jared?" The boy simply laughed his magical laugh at me like he thought I was kidding.

I was not. At all.

Turns out I am directionally challenged. Who knew?

Eventually when I hit The Badlands, a National Park home to South Dakota, I know I've gone too far. The next-to-useless piece of thermal paper is literally saying so. Like the damsel in distress I have zero problem being, I dial Jared on my pink Motorola Razor to tell him I need help.

I start to mentally prepare myself for what exactly I'm going to say to him, wanting it to sound perfect and cute, like it even matters. My heart rate kicks up a bit with the anticipation of talking to Jared. It does this every time I see his little white car in the parking lot at work. Or when I see his name on the schedule. Or when I hear his name. Or simply think of him.

Gosh, I have it bad.

On the second ring his deep, smooth voice graces the line.

"Hey Tryst. All good? Where ya at?"

I can feel my face warm just at the sound of him.

Get it together, Trystan.

"Jared?" I clear my throat and then tell him in one breath, "I'm lost. I'm like, IN The Badlands and I think I shouldn't be."

He laughs at me, and I simply die inside. Not from embarrassment but from sheer desire. I want to hear that laugh every day for the rest of my life. To not only hear it—but to be the sole reason and cause for it.

"I'll find you. Stay there," he says followed by another small laugh as we say goodbye.

*He'll find me. *swoon**

Fifteen minutes go by before Jared shows up, Kerry in the passenger seat, in a faded cherry red, rusted Ford two-door pick-up. They both give me happy waves while shaking their heads in amusement. And while I can't hear them, I can see their laughter from here. I follow their lead back on to the main road, knowing full well neither of them will let me live this down.

I just know I will be so razzed for this getting lost bullshit later.

As we take a few turns and go around some dirt road curves, it is now crystal clear to me that I am not meant to be in charge of navigation. I was *way* out of my way.

We pull up to their house a few moments later, and I find myself a little taken aback at how charming and picturesque it is. It looks like the kind of scene you see in a Hallmark movie. I come from humble beginnings—nothing lavish or extreme. Very much suburban but like, middle class suburban.

This ranch looks anything but.

The first thing I truly notice is the incredibly detailed black metal gate that opens from the middle. When closed it covers the entire width of their driveway and the top looks like it sits about five feet off the ground. In a beautifully strong sort of font, if that is even a thing, it has their last name "BARNS" cut into it on one side, and on the other it says "RANCH", occupying a third of the space towards the top of the gate. Filling in the rest of it, underneath both words, are cowboys and cows and horses and there's even a windmill, making this sort of picturesque landscape scene. The image it paints is one of serenity and hard work and I can't help myself as I walk back down the driveway to check it out more closely after parking my car behind the boys' and saying hi to them quickly.

From behind me I can hear footsteps crunch on the gravel driveway and as they come to a stop I hear Jared tell me in a shy sort of tone, "I made that in shop class as my senior project."

I spin around in shock, my eyes doubling in size.

"I'm sorry, you *made* this?!" I gesture widely to the gate.

He laughs at my surely stunned face, shaking his head and seeming a little embarrassed.

He's humble and I find that far more attractive than I maybe need to.

Jared runs one hand over the back of his neck with his eyes cast down to where his feet move the beige dirt and rocks around. I've never known him to be shy, but perhaps he doesn't get complimented often? Or maybe he doesn't enjoy them? I make a mental note to find out which it is and applaud him more.

Everyone should know there are people in their corner.

"I can't believe you went to a school that was capable of letting students do something this huge and cool," I comment.

After another minute of taking it all in, I turn back to look at Jared and am a little taken off guard to find that he is looking back at me.

I swallow and take a step towards him, feeling extra bold, leaving a couple feet between us.

Things have definitely shifted between us in the last week or so. The flirting has picked up on both our ends. The small touches when either of us must move around the other at work. The constant eye contact even if one of us is talking to a group of people around us.

"It's beautiful, Jared. Truly, I am blown away. Obsessed," I say with total honesty, letting a large, unbridled smile show.

He smiles in return, the lines in his cheeks creasing. Not little indents like dimples but long, curved lines that frame his smile. With a tug of his head he tells me it's time to go to the makeshift softball field and start the game. He leads the way and I follow, my head looking a million directions and taking it all in.

He leads me from the entrance of the driveway, showing me their house on the left. It's lovely, from what I can see. Some sort of "L" shape with dark green shutters on the few windows I can see. White siding with a gray roof—very farm-esque. There is a small concrete patio with a single yellow-ish Adirondack chair in front of the white front door. It looks exactly like what I had been picturing for a ranch homestead. Beyond the house is a rusty, red cow chute, a large white Quonset, various pickups and very few cars littered throughout the gravel lot. Between all of the buildings and equipment is wide open spaces.

Cue "The Chicks."

Jared takes me to the large Quonset, "the shop" he calls it, his brown cowboy boots kicking up the red tinted dirt the whole way over. His light blue-jeans remain surprisingly clean as the dust swirls in the air up and around his calves. His navy-blue T-shirt hangs loosely off of his strong shoulders. Like the incredibly observant and only slightly creepy person I am, I have noticed he wears blue often. Blue jeans. Blue cotton T-shirts outside of work and varying shades of blue button-ups at work. Blue eyes.

And boy, oh boy, does he look good in all of that blue.

There are quite a few people here, not a single one being someone I have met before. I'm not exactly comfortable with strangers, but I'm not *totally* uncomfortable either. I don't know if it's my age or my insecurities right now, or if I'm a little bit of an introvert-meets-extrovert, but I'm positive that if Jared were to leave my side, I would shrink into nothingness here. I would become an actual wallflower. Roots would dig themselves into the metal siding of the shop and begin claiming the space as our new home. Luckily, and to my mild surprise, Jared doesn't leave me to fend for myself. I don't know why I thought he would—we are friends after all. I haven't seen much of Kerry, who did in fact disappear as soon as we got back. I have yet to be formally introduced to their parents because they have been busy hosting their party, but I've been perfectly content walking around next to Jared, or sitting at one of the picnic tables set up inside this building. There's been a lot of talking and laughing between us, getting to know him more. Sometimes one of his parents' friends will come up and sit with us briefly. The exchange feels fairly routine after the fourth or fifth person; Jared introducing me to whoever it is and me shaking their hand and smiling as they look at Jared with a look that feels like it might be about me.

Yes, encourage it. Get him there, thank you.

One of the more notable people that dropped by was Granger. I assume that Granger is around my mom's age—late thirties. He is all dark skin, dark hair, dark eyes, and hands down the most genuinely kind stranger I have ever met. His espresso colored, perfectly curled mustache is equally as excellent as his personality in our short interaction.

"Your *girlfriend* sure is a looker," Granger says while shaking my hand and looking at Jared.

Jared laughs from beside me but doesn't correct Granger on the girlfriend part and I hold in a shriek of excitement over what he might have just silently admitted.

That the crush is mutual.

We became fast friends over the summer but it was definitely more a friendship of convenience kind of thing. At first, at least. It was nothing too serious—not a lot of communicating outside of work, or about things other than work or the people there. In our defense, we both were often scheduled to a maximum number of hours so "work" was all we had going on in our lives over summer break. But this afternoon we have talked very little about McDonald's and its inner operations. It has been absolutely lovely getting to know him little by little. Not manager Jared or quiet movie theater Jared or car ride to Taco Bell Jared. But instead, I have been seeing what I believe might be the real Jared. The guy that has more friends his parents' age than his own age. The one that leads the way to a spot behind a cow chute, hidden from prying eyes so he can smoke a cigarette in secret even though he is eighteen. The Jared that pulls tall pieces of thick grass from the ground and can make it whistle by putting it between his full lips.

As if my crush wasn't already large enough, this day is sure to make me fall even harder. It isn't as though I've hidden my feelings for Jared from anyone. My flirting and pining haven't been limited to our alone time. Kerry, Beth, our bosses, anyone with functioning eyes or ears—they have all been privy to the absolute crushing adoration I feel for Jared. I "like" quite loudly. And now, from the lack of correction to the term girlfriend, it is safe to assume that the feeling is mutual. At least a little bit, anyways.

When Granger called me "a looker" I ducked my head and felt the color fill my round cheeks. I have come into my own over the last six months, sure. Or maybe I have just stopped wishing to be the "size two with blonde hair and blue eyes" girl, and instead have begun to accept myself for what I actually am; Fairly average in every general sense of the word. And I don't mean average in a negative light. I don't find that to be a bad word by any stretch. I am about five foot seven inches tall, the only thing that may not fall into the aforementioned category, and a little broad. My shoulders to my hips give me a vague hourglass figure—albeit a slightly wide hourglass.

My stomach is soft and a little round. I am bigger than most of my friends or the girls I go to school with. Taller, wider, louder. *More.* I always have been though. The comparisons to those around me are constantly battling for the forefront of my brain anywhere I go, yearning to be acknowledged and heard. I've gotten good at doing my best to ignore the incessant nagging. Getting bullied from second grade to eighth makes you aware of these things—the things "wrong" with you. It all sticks with you. A basketball thrown at my face for not being quick enough when I was nine. The entire eighth grade football team "mooing" at me as I walked through the loud halls of middle school. A girl in sixth grade telling my much smaller friend that she "shouldn't be friends with someone like Trystan, the boys won't like that." I wish my skin were as thick as my hair is, alas the comments throughout all those years have stained my soul like the driveway of a car repair shop gets discolored with leaking oil. It's still pretty, the almost holographic coloring, but it's marked nonetheless. *Imperfect.* Not as good looking as it could be. Somehow though, I have found ways to overcome the shitty comments and actions of others. I fortunately made it out of that phase of life without turning to anything self-damaging. I overcame it all, letting the ignorance tarnish bits and pieces but never the entirety of who I am. I grew into my dark frizzy hair, started getting my jagged teeth fixed, and opted for contacts instead of glasses. Sure, sometimes I wear hoodies to cover the "extra" I carry, even when it is most definitely not hoodie weather. But all in all, I'm fine with what I have to work with. I toss around the idea of blue shaded contacts to cover my incredibly dark brown eyes, but never quite push myself far enough down the hole of self-insulting to get there.

There are some things I like about myself. A few things I can appreciate. I have pretty, fair skin. A smattering of freckles covers nearly every inch that young-me bared to the sun. The ones sprinkling my round face are my favorites. My chest and butt are both adequately stacked, and my hair, while frizzy on its own, is quite beautiful and luscious when tamed with proper products and heat.

You have to work with what you have.

Today I've put on my favorite dark wash, flared jeans that make my butt look extra good, and a pair of Justin cowboy boots. They are light brown and round toed. The tops of them reach just above my ankles, little pink embroidered flowers spread throughout the off-white leather. I'm a city girl with the current dreams of dating a country boy. I guess we're both lucky I bought these last fall in an attempt to find my aesthetic.

Jared's my aesthetic at this point, if I'm being honest with myself.

Softball was eventually played, though not by me. I don't do the whole "sports" thing. I spectated and supported those busting their butts in the nearly ninety-five-degree heat quite wonderfully, though.

I am an excellent cheer-er.

The area they play softball in is a literal field. Of grass. I don't know what they normally use it for, I assume it houses cows some months of the year. But from what I heard in idle conversation today it gets mowed down and made into a makeshift softball field once a year.

The sun has started to set after a few hours of ball and food and laughter. The air has cooled slightly, becoming comfortable.

Fickle thing, Midwest September.

Jared mentioned going for a walk around the property to show me around the rest of it. I agreed enthusiastically, setting down my red solo cup of pink lemonade onto the table we had been standing by. I don't think we technically "snuck off" from the rest of the party—nearly everyone is still here talking and laughing and drinking, but we didn't say anything to anyone as we left either. Granger certainly noticed though, his small smirk and obvious wink at me while we meandered by the table he was occupying was evidence enough. Jared's slight chuckle and shake of his shoulders from in front of me lets me know he witnessed what I did as well.

As we crest a small little slope towards the back of their property, splotches of grass and weeds covering every few inches of ground like nature's checkerboard, I'm blown away.

Their backyard is *The Badlands*. As in, THE Badlands National Park.

It's stunning. My eyes sting a bit as they blur slightly, moved so much by the view. My city girl heart always aches for the chance to see something like this in person. This moment isn't like visiting the park on a family outing, going through the entrance and following the road full of other tourists. This is vastly different, the view and the place. The company. I've never seen so many colors at once, and been able to look so far out in the distance from someone's *home*. From where people live and love and laugh and create a life.

The peaks and valleys of the natural hills consist of sand and rock, some dark green pine trees dotting the landscape throughout. The lines of varying shades of color—reds and oranges and tans, they band together on the flat or carved out sides of the land. It's all still visible even with the dimming sun. The contrast of all that sits on the ground, with the multi-colored sky that is cloudless and equally as gorgeous in its own right, is stunning. The setting sun is casting lines of so many different colors as well, it's nearly overwhelming. Apricot, crimson, cerulean, and plum blend and weave and dance throughout the horizon like a watercolor painting, everything bleeding together in a harmonious way. It's breathtaking.

No, really. I think there might be a lack of oxygen getting to my brain.

"It's beautiful, isn't it?" asks Jared, bringing me out of my awed daze.

He places his hand on the small of my back to urge me a couple more steps forward so we're on more of a flat spot of land. I am now positive I was indeed breathing a moment ago, answering the question I was just asking myself, as his hand settles just above the left back pocket of my jeans. I am most certainly not now though. The feeling of Jared's hand there is electrifying and calming, fire and ice, giving me breath while stealing it as well. The feeling of him on me is everything all at once.

It's a hand on your back. Chill.

But I can't. Because Jared Barns is touching me. And the sky looks like a piece of art that could be hung in a gallery, and the air is calm, and even the bugs have excused themselves less they ruin my moment here with this boy.

Jared inches his body closer to mine until we are now side to side, no longer side by side.

After a few moments, not knowing exactly when it happened, I notice Jared has moved his hand from my back and now has it wrapped around mine, like an intimate and unmoving handshake. The feeling is so warm and natural, but also magnetic and wild. And for a few minutes we just... exist. It's beautiful. Not just the view or the boy—but also the feeling that is blossoming in my chest.

"I wish I could stay here forever," I say just above a whisper, not taking my eyes off the horizon.

I wasn't talking about the house or acreage, albeit all beautiful. I was speaking to this moment in time. This comfortable, quiet, still moment with Jared.

The beginning.

From the look I see him give me through my peripheral, I think he understands perfectly what I'm saying.

After the darkness takes over, the only source of light coming from the one tall light post near the Quonset, the silence is comfortable as Jared walks me to my car. He opens my door for me and I take my seat, getting ready to swing my other leg in. He leans down into it, stopping me—my heart along with my movements. With one of his arms on the top of Salsa and above my head, the other with his hand in his front pocket, Jared's eyes connect with mine.

"Go on a date with me?"

I almost choke on my surprise and excitement, reigning it in at the last moment.

Play it cool.

"Ye- yeah, yes. Sure," I stumble, my voice a half octave higher than it normally is.

We stay there—him standing at what has to be an uncomfortable angle and me sitting with one leg out of my car and my body half-facing him. The two of us unmoving, just smiling at each other. Our eyes never stray as we soak it all in. It's as though we know what this is, this moment and this night.

"Text me when you get home, so I know you made it there safely," he says while he knocks on the top of my car twice, smiling broadly.

I nod once, my eyes stay on his and neither of our smiles waver.

My smile doesn't fall the entire forty minutes home. I skip all of the sad songs on Taylor Swift's Fearless album. And when I get home, opening my phone for the first time in what feels like days but has only been hours, I text my best friend.

> Beth. I am in so much trouble.

BETH IS THE BEST

> TELL ME EVERYTHING!

> He's perfect.

CHAPTER THREE.

F ive days come and go after the Barns' softball picnic. Jared asking me to go on a date with him has occupied my mind nearly every second since then. We worked a couple of shifts together through the week and while it did not get awkward, *thank God*, there was another definite shift in the way we interacted.

Where we once lingered if we had to touch, him moving behind me to get somewhere—now we touch for the sake of touching. I'll grip his bicep for fun. He'll pull on a loose strand of my hair. Before, we would talk in a group setting but keep the conversation very topical. Now... he told me how pretty I looked the other day in front of like, four coworkers. And then he winked at me. I almost passed out.

I've only ever really been on a couple dates in my almost seventeen years of life and they were fine, nice even, but I feel like this one is just so different.

Bigger.

Better.

Important.

At my age you would possibly think I'd be a seasoned vet by now. That is simply not the case. Not with the mom I have, bless her heart. Sex, boys, love, relationships—never a topic off limits with Tracy. And as embarrassing as twelve-year-old Trystan found that, I am beyond grateful for the healthy view all of her talks have given me over the years. Though I found her dating rule to be a bit extreme, I can appreciate it now. The societal norm, in my school at least, is a bit more experienced than I.

Tracy Kopfer's Rule For Relations: you are allowed a boyfriend or a girlfriend at age fourteen, not a day before. You are allowed to go on dates with a boy or a girl at age sixteen, not a day before.

That's it. That's the rule I have grown up with.

Now, I'm sure you're asking yourself "what's the point in having a boyfriend or a girlfriend at fourteen if you can't go on a date with them?"

Precisely.

The woman is a genius.

My first kiss, and official boyfriend, was *on* my fourteenth birthday. It was lovely, and admittedly... a little messy. It had been in the works for the months prior, that summer was spent planning for such a blessed day. Shane was kind and good. He had dark hair, nearly black, long and shaggy that hung in front of his hazel eyes. He always wore athletic pants or shorts, and baggy T-shirts. His laugh was one that could literally set your soul alight, cheering up even the saddest of humans. That was Shane though, bright and magnetic. He drew you to him and welcomed you into his life with big cheesy smiles and comfortably squashing hugs. His room sat in the basement of his home—white walls with various horror movie posters on them, all sorts of light blue North Carolina basketball parapher- nalia littered his dresser and shelves. Very much a fourteen-year-old boy's bedroom. A white Xbox sat under a flatscreen television, both resting in front of a worn black futon. An assortment of blankets and pillows, none of them matching anything at all, thrown all around the space. It feels like lifetimes ago by now—that night. That kiss. Shane asked me, his arms snuggly around my waist and mine bunched up between us, "So, you wanna be my girlfriend?" If I could freeze an image of that memory, it would be that moment; his smile large and excited, his eyes focused solely on mine as I nodded my head yes. That boy is still one of my very best friends, and his laugh continues to fill my heart with joy.

My first official date was with a boy I met while I briefly tried out hosting at our local Applebee's. Zane. He was nice and cute, tall and funny. He had muscles like I had never cared to notice on anyone else before. He towered over me just a little bit and was almost two years older than me. I'm sure you can see the appeal. With his light brown hair and bright green eyes, he was incredibly handsome. He flirted shamelessly with me at work, always getting in trouble for talking to me too much at the host stand or not paying attention to his tables enough. I thrived off the attention. Zane had a way of making me feel so incredibly beautiful, even in a restaurant full of gorgeous girls that outranked me in every way. When he asked me out, I wasn't inclined to say no; why would I? The day of our scheduled date Zane had pulled up in his light blue four door car and we were off. He ordered steak and I ordered chicken at Outback Steakhouse. He kissed me when he dropped me off at home later that night. We dated for a couple weeks after that. As quickly as we started though, we fizzled out. No one was heartbroken and it all felt very standard, par for the course.

Aside from those firsts, I've had my fair share of make out sessions with boys here and there. Nothing long lasting, and nothing going much further than kissing.

So, with all of that in the rearview, this date tonight… the stakes feel higher for some reason. It's like my heart knows something my head doesn't. Or perhaps my head does too and it's just trying to keep me from getting too excited. Attempting to stop me from jumping the gun and getting too far in that finding my way out will potentially be damaging.

I'm waiting upstairs now, bouncing between petting our chocolate lab Bear and rubbing my annoyingly sweaty palms on my jeans.

How embarrassing would it be for me if Jared comes inside my house and for some cute, unknown reason, touches my hand and is met with a wet palm?

Ew.

I went all out today in the looks department, taking extra care to look incredible. An extra coat of "very black" mascara, a bit heavy on the emerald, green powder eye shadow from Victoria's Secret making my dark brown eyes pop as much as I can get them to, and a couple solid layers of bubblegum flavored lip-gloss. I've got on my new favorite, slightly fitted long sleeve orange shirt, showing off my boobs enough but keeping my soft middle less exposed. The color reminds me of sherbet, but a very cute kind of sherbet. I put on a black puffer vest over top, leaving it unzipped. My normal dark wash jeans and cowboy boots tie it all together. I even took enough time to have straightened my hair to absolute perfection, which with frizzy AND thick hair is a time-consuming challenge.

I tend to err on the side of dramatically thinking ahead. "Overdoing it" if you choose to look at it that way. So, in my true nature—I can't help but have the thought that this outfit might be one I remember, or more importantly one Jared remembers, for what could be the rest of our lives. The one we look back on in forty years when we tell our kids about our first date and how magically wonderful it was.

Too far ahead of myself. Settle down Trystan.

My mom, stepdad, and little brother are all upstairs with me in the living room, waiting and watching me freak out. They are individually trying to look busy, even my brother. With a first glance at this crew, you would see a typical family minding their own business. A dad messing around on his hand-chosen and crafted computer setup. A mom flipping through the same six preferred channels; the cooking ones, the ones that air musicals, and MTV. And a small child, pretending to mind his own business with his toys in the middle of the room. You would be judging them incorrectly though.

The nosy lot.

My stepdad, Craig, is about as Air Force as you get in the looks department. And personality. He's tall and a little muscular but also soft in the face and belly. He's got short, mousy brown hair cut to exact parameters, light brown eyes. In his civilian clothes he gives off "soccer dad" vibes.

My mom, Tracy, is a bit short—five feet and four inches, and adorable. She *loves* being called that... Her straight, dark brown hair hits the middle of her back and is always a little messy. Her eyes are a really pretty hazel with flecks of greens and ambers bursting out from the pupil.

And then there is my favorite person on the planet. My sweet, little, angel, baby brother Michael. He is perfect. Mikey is twelve years younger than me. Sometimes, with me looking older than I am and him being a five-year-old, if I take him to the store or park or something I get asked if he is my son. Even with him being my half-brother you can still see the resemblance. He has his dad's light brown hair and our grandmas' cobalt eyes. Our faces are similar enough to know we belong to the same tree, even if it's just half the branches. Having a sibling so much younger than you is wild. I love him with everything I have. I would kill, or be killed, for that dude. But in the same breath I would throttle him for eating the last brownie even though I called dibs on it.

I wouldn't call my mom a helicopter mom, but she definitely stays involved in the day to day lives of her two kids. Sometimes a bit in excess. Me being the oldest, I'm privileged enough to be the first to experience these things—dating and such.

Yay me.

So, while I think she's trying to play it cool, I can see in her shoulders that she's a bit stressed. My mom is my best friend, genuinely. I tell her anything and everything. And while we respect boundaries, there aren't many things that are off limits between us. I'm sure she is going back and forth in her head—bouncing between mom mode and the stress that goes with that, and the excitement for me in friend mode. She knows I'll be dishing out almost everything about tonight when I get home later.

I settle on to the blue, cloth sectional couch next to Mikey who is now playing some skateboarding game on the PlayStation, my mom having given up on the focus it takes to choose a show to watch. "Playing" is fairly subjective when you are five, though, so the little skateboarder on the screen is doing about as well on the halfpipe as Mike would do in real life—not very good at all.

The house we live in is enough for us. Larger than some, smaller than a lot. The living room, dining room, and kitchen are all connected with the stairs to the basement breaking it up. My mom recently painted the walls this cool gray color with a tint of green to them. I think she said it had "elephant" in the name when she was prattling on about it. The dark brown of the wall trim and railings that you can grasp while going downstairs look nice with the color. Pictures of me and Mikey are on the walls—mine is my school picture from my sophomore year. I had just found black eyeliner and to my mother's absolute chagrin, wore it in amounts that were beyond unnecessary. Mike's is one that the ladies at his preschool took before school ended earlier this year. Craig's computer desk in the corner near the garage door, behind him are the stairs to the basement.

I look down at Bear where he lays on the sandy brown carpet snuggled up to my feet. He hasn't left my side all afternoon.

Can Bear sense that I am freaking out? Because I totally am.

We all hear what we believe to be Jared's car pull into the neighborhood and collectively turn our attention to the large window across from where the couch sits. His arrival would be hard to miss even if we weren't sitting here waiting like creeps. Jared loves music and loves the added base and bounce he's adorned his little white Neon with. I don't hate it, as I too love music and love it loud.

Luckily, my protective parents don't base their opinions of Jared on the noise. They would probably judge him a little bit on song choice, but it's too muffled to tell what is playing.

We hear the engine die and I think my mom is already impressed because she didn't have to make me stay inside and wait for him to come to the door and knock. I realize then that we are all standing or sitting here looking like absolute weirdos, essentially with our ears on the door listening for him to come up the drive. Mike goes so far as to peek his head through the brown curtains to look outside.

"Mike!" I hiss, getting up and batting at his little head. "Move away from the window!"

I give my mom a pleading look as she walks over to grab him. All the while she laughs, amused by the lack of calm I am rocking.

Jared knocks after what feels like years and I make the introductions once he steps inside the front door. The small patch of linoleum puts us in a corner, the TV to our left and the window to our right, us facing the everything and everyone else like we are some tiny plastic stage.

"Mom," I start, trying to be chill. "This is Jared."

I internally wince a little as she steps into the already crowded space we're already occupying.

Subtlety is not her strong suit.

"Jared," she says a little too sternly for my liking. "It's nice to meet you. I hope you're respectful and nice to my daughter." She glances my way in time for her eyes full of blatant teasing to meet my glare.

She is doing this on purpose, trying to embarrass me or insert her already clear dominance by acting extra mom-ish.

I don't hide my eye roll.

But neither does she.

The apple doesn't fall far.

"Yes, ma'am. Absolutely, it's nice to meet you," Jared says steadily as he shakes her hand. Looking my way, he then says, "Trystan, you look beautiful." His eyes seem to sparkle with light.

He said that in front of my mother without even flinching. Excuse me while I simply pass away.

"You look really good too," I say, slightly quieter than he was.

And he does. He looks so good. A black T-shirt under a dark blue zip-up hoodie with light jeans and his boots.

So good.

"Call me Tracy. 'Ma'am' makes me feel ancient," my mom says with a little more brightness in her tone.

Awkward laughs are exchanged as I introduce Jared to Craig and Michael. Both of them being less intimidating and far quicker of a hello/goodbye process. After those are finished, I not so discreetly shove Jared out the front door and down the three red steps of our small front porch to the sidewalk that leads over to the driveway where Jared parked.

"Bye!" I yell over my shoulder to my parents as they stand at the door. We're halfway to his car, me still lightly pushing Jared down the concrete.

He opens my door for me and smiles his big, beautiful smile. It always reaches his eyes and I wonder if he ever smiles inauthentically. Does he ever have to force the 'happy' into his face?

I hope not when he's around me.

"How's your week been?"

His question is so casual, calming my anxiety.

"My week was good. I'm glad it's Friday. What about you?"

His smile is sweet as he drives, his gaze meeting mine.

"Mine was great. Long since I've been looking forward to tonight so much. But still good."

I remind myself to find my calm. To be steady and to not scare this really amazing guy away before he's even mine, or I his.

I don't ask where we're going, wanting to just let the date happen. Before I know it, we pull into the Applebee's parking lot. At our age, and location, the options for a date night are slightly limited. A bougie restaurant downtime is nowhere near the vibe we are going for. So, it's either Applebee's or Chili's.

You won't hear me complain about either.

Jared meets me at my side of the car, smiling as I close the door. "I was going to open that for you," he says, his tone light.

I laugh at him as places his hand on the small of my back, leading us to the restaurant. He asks for a booth and the host leads us to one in the smaller, quieter section. The pretty, blond waitress excitedly takes our drink and food orders, us having had plenty of time to decide on both, and buzzes away with a smile and a waft of some floral perfume that makes my nose itch.

"You're cute when you do that."

My cheeks warm and I smile at the table. "Do what?"

"Scrunch your nose like you just did. You're cute all the time but you do that at work too sometimes and I love it."

I say nothing back, not wanting to ruin the sweetness. We talk idly while we wait for our food. Jared and I share some mozzarella sticks, he introduces me to eating them with ranch dressing and even if we never go further than tonight, I will forever be grateful for that combination. We both laugh and talk and lightly gossip about our coworkers while we eat our meals. His is a chicken and pasta dish, mine is a chicken and rice one. He tells me all about how nice post-high school life has been and I complain about how busy Beth is lately with her new job at the local farm supply store. I don't think an uncomfortably silent moment is shared throughout the entirety of our time there.

Jared takes care of the bill and holds the door for me as we leave, placing a hand on the small of my back as we walk to the car. That spot where his hand was doesn't stop almost vibrating with energy. Not as he walks around the front of his car. Not as he gets in and buckles. Definitely not as he looks over at me and smiles, placing his right hand on the keys he left in the ignition to turn the car on.

Country boy things, I think.

It's a lovely night out tonight. The end of September, albeit unpredictable, is maybe one of my favorite times of the year. It's a bit chilly this evening, but I love these kinds of nights. Cool air, very little breeze, the sun is almost down so the sky is beautiful hues of purples and pinks. After a few minutes of music and driving, me having zero clue of the destination in mind, Jared pulls into the parking lot of a park.

"Do you want to go for a walk?" he asks as he puts his car in park and turns the music down, turning his head to look at me.

I've made a million and one memories at this park in my small bit of lifetime. Birthday parties for myself and my friends growing up have taken place at the little huts scattered around the small man-made lake. I have fished with Craig here before. Rolled down the very hills we are currently parked in front of as a kid, having the grass get stuck in my corse hair in the process. All of those suddenly pale in comparison to the memory I'm about to make now with Jared.

I nod and he tells me to let him get my door for me. I listen and take his hand after he closes the door. We walk like that, hand in hand, and I can't help but hope he will be holding my hand for a very long time to come. My heart feels excited and calm. My head—hopeful and content.

At this point I have decided I am just going to embrace my overactive, too-far-ahead brain.

We don't talk much during our walk. It isn't a forced silence, though. It's comfortable—companionable.

We walk at a slow and steady pace around the path. The lights from the lamps around the park reflect off the dark water. The sounds of passing cars from the nearby streets mix with the noise of the ducks and geese squabbling loudly from where they swim or perch. Fish breach the water's surface to have a late-night snack of bugs, making a splash as they fall back to where they once came.

When we arrive at the large, wooden bridge that crosses the pond and leads to a little island sitting in the middle of the water, we turn on to it, making our way to the small, old gazebo on the center of the land there. It's white and cracking now, with green and red stained glass in the top windows. Open sides all around give you a three-hundred-sixty-degree view of the surrounding area. The hillside on one side, away from the road, covered in dark green pine trees and large brown boulders. Another area beyond that is where the colorful swing sets and dark brown huts reside. Then there are the parking lots and the streets and houses that take up the remaining area.

The two of us have posted up on one of the white benches that line the inner wall of the gazebo, the wood cool to the touch through my jeans. Jared's left knee knocks against my right one, his hands are in his hooded sweatshirt's pocket. My hands rest in my lap, clasped together in an attempt to warm them up.

He must notice my slight shiver from the cooling night temperature because he says, "It's getting cold. What do you say we head back to the car? We can get some ice cream before I take you home?"

I don't dare mention to him that ice cream is absolutely going to wreck my stomach later because *hello, yes, I want to continue spending time with you.*

I look up at him to where he's now standing directly in front of me, his hand outstretched waiting for me to place mine in it.

"Can I drive your car?"

It's such a weird request, I know. But a boy who trusts you to drive his car is a major green flag in my unexperienced brain.

He laughs off the surprise of my question. "Sure," he says with the smallest lift of a shoulder. "The keys are in the ignition."

I put my hand in his, my far paler skin contrasting brightly against his that is sun-kissed. He barely moves an inch as he pulls me to my feet, his eyes never leaving mine. The cool air around us turns into something thicker—warmer. There is very little distance between us all of a sudden. I'm not the only one that seems to notice the shift in the air. We both flick our attention from each other's eyes to each other's mouths. I know I want him to kiss me, but I also know that I don't want to know if he doesn't want to kiss me, so while I am all for a woman doing her thing and making the first move—I refuse to potentially feel that sting of rejection in such a profound way. Not now, after such a wonderful night.

"Trystan," he says, my name landing somewhere between and a question and an answer.

"Yes?" I say almost breathlessly.

Why can I never breathe when he is near me?

"Can I," I see his throat bob, the nerves I didn't notice before coming out as he pauses. "Can I kiss you?"

I don't even answer him. I simply close my eyes and lean in ever so slightly, praying to God that I am not met with incredible disappointment.

And I am most certainly not.

He must apply chapstick religiously because his lips are the smoothest things mine have ever touched. The kiss was so light and simple and wonderfully momentous. It was as if the air just ceased to be, pulling away entirely. The rowdy birds all paused their chatter. The fish mid-jump froze in time, giving the bugs hovering near their open mouths another two seconds of life. Time seemed to just halt when Jared put his lips to mine. Every Princess Diaries-esque foot-popping moment that I have dreamed about came to fruition with this single kiss.

It's quite possible none of that actually happened but—holy shit.

"That," he says after what felt like the most explosive thirty seconds of my life, "was the best first kiss."

His eyes lock onto mine, the blue somehow brighter even in the dim light of the evening. Our breaths mingle with each other's, both smelling of the mint gum we chewed on in the car after supper. I can't help the small giggle that escapes me at his declaration. Or the full-fledged embarrassment that follows the annoyingly timed laugh. But he doesn't care about the laugh—maybe even enjoyed that I did it.

Before I can confirm verbally that I too am blown away complete-ly, Jared leans down and his lips meet mine again.

I feel his smile against my own as we slowly break apart, this kiss having been a little more... *more.*

I am no longer cold.

Companionable silence eases us back into the moment as we just look at each other for a long while.

This is it; I think to myself. This is what I have been yearning for, looking but not searching for. To be looked at with such desire and admiration. Like he really *sees* me and so far, likes what is there.

With his hand in mine, we walk out of the gazebo and across the bridge back to his car. He places one more chaste, smiling kiss on my lips before closing the door and walking to his side. As he puts it in reverse Jared looks over at me, his smile wide and his eyes alight, before taking my hand in his. He doesn't let go while he shifts into drive. Or while he parks at the ice cream shop.

Coldstone Creamery sits near a grocery store and a coffee shop. It's as cold inside as you might assume—very. We each get little bowls of ice cream before sitting down at a black two-person table. Mine has brownies and cookie dough chunks while Jared opted for a berry flavor.

He then proceeded to make a "it's berry good" joke. I didn't even have to force my laugh. He could recite the alphabet and I would find it just absolutely enthralling.

After ice cream, Jared obliges me and lets me drive his little car around town for a bit. We sing and talk. By the end of it, stomachs filled with ice cream and hearts with joy, I have decided that I really, really like Jared. The simple crush I had has grown into much more in the small amount of hours spent together. He's fantastic.

Once we are back to my parents' house and Jared and I get out of his car, I don't rush to enter the house. He doesn't rush me up the driveway either.

"I had a lot of fun tonight," I say.

I am standing with my left hip leaning on the passenger door, my thumbs hooked on to the pockets of my vest, my legs crossed at my ankles. Jared mirrors my stance, but instead of his hands going to his own pockets—he loops them under mine, grabbing a hold of me and pulling me forward lightly. We both laugh at my surprise.

"A lot of fun," Jared says.

Is he ever not smiling?! And will I ever find a limit to the things I would do for that smile?!

"Let me know when you get home tonight. So I know you're safe and stuff. Deer and whatever are probably out and about." I shuffle my feet back and forth, feeling excited and nervous.

Jared says nothing before putting his lips to mine, drawing me even closer to him. We kiss until the porch light starts to flicker on and off.

"I'll text ya," he says through a laugh, letting go enough for me to back up a foot and roll my eyes at my mom who has her head exactly where Mike's was a few hours ago—looking around the brown curtain in the front window and watching us.

"Creep," I whisper.

"They seem great."

And I think he means that. Which isn't surprising—my family is great.

"They are," I say before taking the initiative and kissing Jared one more time. "Drive safe."

I walk backwards towards the house. Jared is standing by his open driver's side door with one hand on the top of it and his other in a pocket of his jeans.

"Goodnight, Trystan Harper." It's the last thing I hear and his joy is the last thing I see before stepping inside my house.

I duck inside, shutting the door quietly, trying to keep my excitement contained. Outside I probably seem cool, calm, and collected. Normal. Not forever changed and thrilled and terrified. Inside... Inside I am screaming. I am kicking down doors and throwing plates on the ground while singing Whitney Houston's 'How Will I Know' at the top of my lungs.

I am less adept at hiding the inner workings of my brain that I had assumed so upon turning around from the door and walking a step towards the stairs to my room, my mom chuckles from where she is perched. She is sitting on the couch in a spot that makes it clear she knew she would be getting a show when I arrived. She's wearing a pair of gray sweats and loose red T-shirt, her long hair is up in a small ponytail. Her smile is as mischievous as it is warm.

"So," she begins, "how did it go, little one?"

I plop down next to her, curling my feet under me and sitting with my legs crossed. I grab a blue pillow from the other side of her and clutch it to my front. And then I dish it all. By the end of giving my mom the details of tonight's date, I am still beaming with a thrilling light.

"I think I am going to marry him and have his babies, mom."

She laughs at me, of course. I would laugh at me too.

I know I sound clinically insane but hear me out... *I can feel it.*

We are going to be forever and always.

CHAPTER FOUR.

FALL 2009.

I see Jared at McDonald's almost every shift that I work. Even the ones he's not scheduled, he drives to town to see me. Oftentimes it's a quick visit and I try to time my breaks in turn with it so we can sit in his car or out back at the small bench by the dumpsters. School takes up the majority of my days during the week, but evenings and weekends are *ours*.

It's only been a few weeks, almost a month, since the first date, but we have now been on several of them and each one has been equally as wonderful. At some point he called me his girlfriend and from then on, the titles just stuck.

Jared Dennis Barns is my boyfriend.

Squeals internally any time that fact crosses my mind

The rhythm we are finding with each other has been such a cool thing to experience. It's been so easy to find a flow. Our hands naturally rest together when in close proximity. Our eyes find each other frequently and always at the same time, a laugh usually follows the contact. We fit seamlessly. Even the kissing feels like something we have been perfecting together for eons, in the very best kind of way.

Our coworkers hate us. Only mildly and laced with amusement—but the fake gagging noises and the "get a room" comments are plentiful. We laugh them off and make jokes at our own expense, I'm not delusional enough to think we aren't slightly annoying. We keep our PDA confined to the break room or outside, sneaking a kiss or hug during a small break in customers, or before one of us leaves for home. Every now and then we'll get caught eyeing each other from across the assembly line or brushing a hand across the others as one of us walks by the fry station. We clearly aren't as stealthy with the flirting as we think we are.

I love it.

I love Jared.

I know, I know. I'm not even seventeen yet. Love is a big deal. And I agree wholeheartedly—it *is* a big deal. I'm not someone who shies away from love, though.

I have a philosophy—fall in love whenever you can.

Okay, so I got that specific mantra from Practical Magic. But it has honed and shaped how my heart operates. I firmly believe that love happens.

Whether it's a book that is so good it sticks with you for the rest of your life. An iced coffee that was made perfectly by Baylee the barista. A favorite time of the year like spring where the air smells cleaner and the flowers start to bloom. Or maybe it's a pizza place that has the best cheese sticks with that perfect kind of crispy browned cheese on the outsides of each piece.

Perhaps it's a handsome six-foot-two boy with eyes that shine like stars.

Fall in love. If you find it—hold on to it. And if you lose it—don't give up on it.

Now, while I enjoy seeing Jared at work and thoroughly love the fact that he doesn't stop his flirting in front of other people, I live for the nights we both have off.

Like tonight. Jared just dropped me off at home a bit ago after a little cruise-date. He recently got a new car, trading in his little Neon for this one. It's also white. A Lincoln Continental, I think. Grandma-car, that's what I called it. I'm sure he will have it looking like it was meant for him in no time, though.

I'm lying in my bed now, staring at my open ceiling, going through tonight's fun.

My room is... well for lack of better term—unfinished. Literally. It's in the basement of our home. It's a giant square down here, all open and spacious. The washer and dryer take up one corner, storage in another, and a "living room" in the third. My quarter consists of two concrete walls and two "walls" made of white bed sheets nailed to the wood beams in the ceiling. My door, if you could call it that, is the meeting point of two sheets held closed by wooden clothespins. I genuinely love my room, though. It's unlike anyone else's that I know, and I find that to be fun. My mom feels guilty about it being so undone, but I think it's cool and unusual.

Thus, making me cool and unusual, right?

The floor down here is also concrete with multiple rugs spread about creating a mosaic of colors and lines and splotches. None match or even really mesh with anything else—everything looks random but still somehow intentional. The ceiling is bare, it's got wood beams and ductwork, cobwebs, and dust. I've got posters on my solid walls and even some pinned to my fabric walls. The John Michael Montgomery one that my mom got me when I was a wee babe to "scare away the monsters" is my favorite. However, Orlando Bloom as Legolas is a real close second. I recently traded in my twin day bed for a queen size one, pushed up into the corner where the gray walls meet. I've got the softest, fluffiest white, puffy comforter atop it. A television sits in a large, bright blue stand across from my bed, housing VHS's from when I was small. Since the basement hasn't been finished, there's no closet—my clothes hang on an open, movable rack next to my dresser. On top of the dark brown dresser is a solid collection of dust, my purple cd player that currently holds the Breaking Benjamin's Phobia album, and some mismatched jewelry that I don't actually ever wear.

I aggressively yank my phone from its charging cord and flip it open to text Jared. I've about said those three little words to him every time we say goodbye, in person or over the phone. The anxiety of holding them in is overwhelming.

That single text message took three minutes to type correctly, my fingers moving so quickly that I had a million typos. After what felt like an hour of my thumb hovering over "send", I finally hit it. I think I'm sweating now.

Oh my gosh, your favorite singer is Taylor Swift, isn't it? :(

I laugh out loud, covering my mouth with my blanket to stifle the noise so my mom doesn't ask me who I am talking to. Nosy Nelly.

Well... yes but that's not the point.

Wait a minute, what's wrong with TSwift? Her lyricism is top notch.

Nothing, nothing. I was joking. What's up?

Well now I don't want to tell you.

Come on... I'm sorry. I want to know the secret.

Am I really going to do this? This feels so much bigger than when I told Shane I loved him in the eighth grade. This feels... like it might affect the rest of my life somehow. Monumental. And I'm completely excusing the fact that I am doing this via text. I think I would throw up if I was looking him in his perfect eyes.

Just do it. Don't be a baby. You're almost seventeen. You're practically grown.

I think...

My fingers hover over the lit-up keypad.

> I might love you.

Silence...

Maybe his phone died?

Do I have a signal down here in my room?

Does he have a signal wherever he is?

I'm off my bed now and pacing my room.

The walls in here start squeezing in on me with every breath I try to get down. I might wear holes into the mismatched pink and yellow socks I've got on.

Oh my gosh, I messed up. This is not good. Is there an unsend button?

Panicking. Panicking big time.

Panicking and... vibrating?

I snatch my phone from off my bed and stare at the screen.

Jared is calling me. He probably isn't the kind of guy to dump a gal over text so now he's calling to tell me I am certifiably insane and he'll see me around. I don't even blame him.

With shaky hands and a deep breath, I flip open my phone, bring it to my ear, and try to keep it together.

"He-hello?" I stutter, barely above a whisper.

"I felt like this would be better heard rather than read," he says with absolute calm.

A big pause from both of us before I slowly say, "Go on."

"I might love you too, Trystan," he says. The conviction in his words is nearly overwhelming.

I can't feel my toes. Or my nose. I think I've melted into a big puddle of smiles and love and goo. Because he loves me.

He loves *me*.

Realizing I have now gone radio silent after his confession I shake it off and finally say, "Oh, okay... well thanks for the call then."

Keep it cool Tryst. Don't scare him away now.

I stop my pacing to reach for the small Lego figurine of Darth Vader that Mikey gave me a few weeks ago when he put together some sort of spaceship thing with Craig.

"Let's talk tomorrow," he says as he lightly chuckles. "Goodnight, Tryst."

"Goodnight," I squeak.

I squeaked?! Oh my gosh.

I rub my palms down my face trying to shove my embarrassment back down. I told him I love him and then I squeaked. But he said it back...

He said it back.

I fall back on my bed, clutching my tiny phone to my chest, trying to commit the way he said, *"I might love you too, Trystan"* to memory.

Holy shit. He said it back.

We've been dating for a month now and steadily telling each other I love you for a few days. Today when he came to the door to pick me up for our date, he had flowers in hand.

White daisies in a tall, slim, clear vase.

Flowers for me, the girl he loves.

With a card that said—

HUNNY,

I LOVE YOU.

LOVE, J.

FOREVER AND ALWAYS

Head meet heels.

Another month flies by, everything continues to flow seamlessly between Jared and me. We go on lots of dates to Applebee's—that's our favorite spot now. We take a lot of aimless drives around town, listening to music and laughing and holding hands, kissing in between it all.

November in South Dakota is cold and sickly and when you go to school with 1,500 kids, the likelihood of you getting sick with eighty-six different things from August to May is high. Astronomical, really.

This bout of the flu came for me like it was something personal. And it isn't just any ol' flu. This one is a big-time flu with a fancy name about some pig or something, and no treatment options.

"Rest and hydrate" the doctor said after swabbing my nose three separate times. I almost swung at him that last time.

I'm miserable and dying and to make matters worse—I haven't seen Jared in days. It feels like my soul is itching to be next to his again. Maybe it's just my skin from the fevers and lack of proper hygiene due to being too exhausted to properly bathe, sure. But regardless, I am seriously missing him.

My mom is letting Jared come over today while my parents are at work, Mikey is at preschool. Jared offered to bring me soup and my mom said as long as there isn't any kissing then he can briefly stop by.

To my absolute chagrin, but understanding, I took that deal.

I was waiting, rather impatiently, by the front door when Jared pulled up. I open the front door and stand in the frame of it in my dingy grey sweatpants and even dingier once-was-white T-shirt, watching him as he gets out of his car. I give him a wave and a smile while he does the same, walking around the hood to the passenger door. My brows bunch, unsure of what he is doing. Understanding and joy replace my confusion when I see him stand up holding a bouquet of fuchsia gerbera daisies in one hand, the stems wrapped in white paper. In the other hand is a brown bag that I assume holds a very anticipated bowl of soup.

He smiles at me the entire way up the driveway to the door. Once he reaches me, he closes the space between us and leans in to kiss my cheek as he hands me the flowers. I lean into his touch, having missed it desperately, and take the bouquet.

"I missed you," I say as I press my nose to the daisies and give them a sniff. "I love that you know how much I love flowers."

He smiles as he walks by me towards the kitchen. I shut the door and turn to follow. He sets the bag he brought in with him on the counter next to the stove and takes the soup out.

"It's chicken tortilla, I hope that's okay. It's all Applebee's had today." He looks over his shoulder at me, him at the stove and me behind him by the opposite counter.

"That's perfect, thank you," I say.

I walk around the counter and go to sit on the stool. Setting the flowers in front of me I rest my chin on my palms and just watch. We have only been together for two months, but he already knows where to find almost everything here, having spent some time at my house lately. He grabs a silver pot and pours in the soup, turning the stove on to reheat it. He walks to the corner behind him near the sink to get a bowl and then a spoon from the drawer under that cabinet. All the while I stay put. Neither of us speak, we don't need to. The quiet with us is never loud enough to try and fill. After he heats the soup up, he ladles some into the bowl before placing a spoon inside. He turns around from the stove and walks the few paces to the counter I am sitting at, setting it down in front of me from the other side. There is no be-shy-don't-eat-in-front-of-boys-be-a-little-mouse feeling when I am with him. I dig in and internally moan at the warmth I feel in my chest. He doesn't bat an eye as I eat for what feels like the first time in days—probably because it actually has been days since I have had more than Gatorade and crackers.

Jared pulls out a little package of something that was still in the bag that once held the soup. He passes it to me, and I laugh a little. I look up at him, his eyes full of amusement and happiness. I can imagine mine mirror that.

The tiny plastic baggy with a cardboard label stapled to the top holds thirty-six little plastic glow-in-the-dark stars and planets. Green, pink, blue—all that really light pastel color. I pick out Saturn amongst them all right away. I couldn't wipe the smile off my face if I tried.

"I'll help you stick them up on your ceiling," he says.

I bring my gaze from his gift to his eyes again, almost the same blue as the little stars I hold.

Jared goes on, "When you came to my house last month you commented on how much you liked the ones in my room, so I wanted you to have your own." He throws in a small shoulder shrug as if to pretend this is not the cutest thing quite possibly ever.

Last month I drove out to his parents' house for supper. Jared and I were in his room while his mom finished cooking, innocently lying on our backs next to each other just talking. His shoulder touching mine, our heads on separate navy-blue pillows. At some point our hands found each other and our fingers intertwined.

He has had the same room since he was little, he had said. So, the now-faded glow in the dark stars and planets on his ceiling didn't surprise me. They charmed me, actually. They made me smile and when I brought them up, I let him know how cute I thought they were.

And he clearly remembered.

He remembered and he got me my own pack of them.

How is he even real?

I finish my soup while he puts the leftovers into some Tupperware. It's like he has been here all along, knowing where everything is and where everything goes.

"Come downstairs and help me with these?" I ask while shaking the little baggy at him.

I feel better than I have in days. More energetic. This morning I was sure I wouldn't even make it out of bed for anything. But right now, with the stars and the soup and the flowers and this kind boy—I could very well run a marathon.

Well, maybe a few feet of one at least.

With a smile and a nod Jared walks around the counter and grabs my free hand. He leans in and plants a gentle kiss on my forehead before leading the way downstairs. My heart flutters and my head rushes, his kisses having that effect on me every time.

Jared hasn't been in my room before. We usually hang out outside of the house or upstairs, never having had a reason for us both to go down here.

But now—here he stands. He starts looking through the movies in my television stand. The Princess Diaries, A Goofy Movie, Little Rascals, and many more classics, all making him smile.

I take a seat in my neon green folding papasan chair and just watch him as he looks around—taking him in as he takes my sanctuary in.

Jared is in jeans and a gray zip-up Carhartt jacket today, a yellow shirt underneath. He's got one hand in his pocket while he scopes out my posters. I internally sigh at how good he always looks. I also avoid looking down at the state I am currently in, avoiding mirrors until he leaves.

"Legolas, huh?" he says to me with a smirk.

"Can you blame me?" I say with a wink. "Something about that long hair."

He shakes his head and laughs, continuing his walkthrough.

I've had boys in my room before. Always while an adult was inside the house and the door to the basement was wide open, of course. Generally, nothing cool ever happened. Some kissing here and there but nothing wild. More than that has never really crossed my mind as a priority or desire, really. My mom has always been utterly honest and open and up front about how sex is something that is absolutely okay but not something that needs to be done until you're ready. *Really and truly ready.* And I comfortably and confidently have not been. Totally fine with the lack of experience far.

However, the more dates I go on with Jared...

The more he holds my hand or kisses my forehead after a hug...

The more flowers he brings...

The glow in the dark stars he remembered me loving so much...

The soup he shows up with when I'm sick...

All of what he does, who he is, without being asked...

I am starting to wonder if maybe that milestone is something that I might be ready for now. The two of us have only briefly discussed it once, just as a general knowledge kind of conversation, and left it there. Neither of us have seized that specific opportunity. It wasn't an uncomfortable conversation—it was actually quite easy to have with him. While I tell my mom next to everything, I have kept the specifics of my "sex life" on the down low. She's one smart cookie though, so I'm sure the only reason Jared is in here at the moment and my parents are fine with it is due to the fact that they trust me and know that even though details won't be up for discussion, I will be safe when it comes time for that all to take place. And being safe will involve a conversation with my mom, and a doctor. So, with all of that, and the other fact that I truly do feel like Death himself is knocking on my door, I've been given a momentary green light to have a boy in the house. Alone.

I am under no illusion that this is all completely based upon circumstance.

I move to stand and walk towards Jared, handing him the bag of what I call "ceiling confetti". The fact that he can look at me with so much kindness and desire while I stand here in my ugly sweatpants that are covered in random nail polish stains, a ratty T-shirt, and a dark pile of very unwashed hair twisted into a bun on top of my head—it is beyond me.

Once the sticky stars and planets are stuck on the rafters and beams, the process not taking nearly long enough, I am even more exhausted. And I didn't even do any of the work. Though I did thoroughly enjoy the show of Jared reaching up so high, his shirt rising with him ever so slightly, giving me a view worth looking at.

Jared notices the sleepiness that has crept into my face.

Of course he does, he notices everything.

"I'm going to head out, you get some more rest."

I am settled on to my bed already on my side, lying on top of my blankets with a pillow under my head and another clutched to my chest. I smile up at him and move to get up.

Jared places a hand on my shoulder and says, "No, it's okay. I know my way out."

He then leans down, kissing my forehead, and brushes stray hairs that have escaped my black hair tie out of my face.

"I love you," I mumble, sleep pulling me under.

"I love you too, babe."

That's the last thing I hear before I slumber deeply for the next ten hours straight. All the while I hear Jared's voice in my head whispering "I love you" and feel the phantom feeling of his lips on my forehead.

CHAPTER FIVE.

SPRING 2010.

The next several months went as well, and as quickly, as the first few.

My birthday came and went, hello seventeen. I got my braces off a few days prior to that—what a sweet gift. Thanksgiving with my family is always small, just the four of us—Christmas is the same. Two Thousand and Nine came and went, ushered out by Two Thousand and Ten.

Even though Jared and I didn't spend Thanksgiving or Christmas together we managed to find time to see each other the days before and after, exchanging gifts. I got him a bottle of American Eagle cologne, though sometimes I wonder if that is more of a gift for me than it is for him because wow—he smells divine. I also got him a pair of pink and blue "i heart-sign boobies!" bracelets. He laughed and put both the bracelets and the cologne on immediately. Jared got me a white hoodie from American Eagle and, per his usual, *flowers*. White lilies this time.

The card on this one read—

HUNNY,

ONE CHRISTMAS DOWN, A

LIFETIME OF THEM TO GO.

I LOVE YOU.

FOREVER AND ALWAYS.

We're almost halfway through our first year together and I don't remember what life was like before Jared.

B.J.—Before Jared, if you will, was dull and drab. I wasn't lonely, I had and still have my best friend, Beth. But I look back and can't believe how... *muted* my life was before Jare. It isn't that he takes away from who I was before having him in my life. He simply and wonderfully adds to it. It's like whoever invented chocolate chip cookies. They had a bomb cookie to begin with, all sugary and soft. But then... then they added some magic. And what once was great, was still great with a little extra *something*. That's what being with

Jared feels like. The laughter and the memories and the love—my soul feels brighter because of him.

Perhaps that sounds unhealthy, I don't know. But really—the comfortability and just general ease that we have fallen into is so serene. I don't feel as though I have settled— I simply *feel* settled. As though *he* is my peace.

He's wonderful.

So wonderful, in fact, that things are progressing with us in more... physical ways. It feels so natural and, as cheesy as it sounds, meant to be. Which is what has led me to this very moment.

I just got back from hanging out with Jared. We went to a movie, *Dear John*. It was so sad, and then so happy. Jared kept his arm around my shoulders the entire time, the popcorn bucket in his lap and the box of Buncha Crunch in my hand, a shared Sprite in between us in the cup holder.

Now, here I stand in my jeans and black V-neck T-shirt. Hanging up the white zip-up sweatshirt I got from Jared for Christmas. I work up the courage I need for this conversation.

"You can do this. It's just your mom. You're seventeen. It's fine." I mumble to myself.

"Mom," I half-yell from my room. "I need to talk to you,"

She's across the way from where my room is, switching laundry over from the washer to the dryer.

"Daughter," she replies back like always. "What is it?" she asks as she parts my sheet-door and sits next to me on my bed, blissfully unaware of what sort of conversation is about to take place.

Her dark hair is up in a brown claw clip. She's got on my least favorite pair of pants she owns—dark green slick pants. I not-jokingly tell her I will throw them away every time I see her wearing them. She jokingly threatens my life immediately after. A red hoodie she purchased from Michael's school really brings it all together, providing the most Midwest-comfy-mom outfit. I suppress an eye roll at the pants. Barely.

I really hate them.

I clear my throat and get up, walking across my room to mess with the dust on my dresser.

"I'm seventeen now… So don't freak out but I think Jared and I are going to have sex soon." I say the second part much more quickly than the first.

There is a marginal amount of silence that passes through us. The air all of a sudden feels just a little bit heavier, and I don't know who is more anxious now—me, the teenager who just told her mother she needs birth control because she's planning to lose her virginity in the near future. Or my mom, who just got told that her teenage daughter is planning on losing her virginity in the near future. My back is still to her, and she hasn't moved. I don't even know if she's taken a breath.

Finally, on a long-held exhale, she says, "Oh. Okay. Right." Every word is clipped, a brief pause after each.

Thinking she is about to have a stroke I quickly throw out, "You wanted to kno-"

"Yes! Yes." she interrupts. "Right. Give me just a moment."

She rubs her hands on her thighs, the stupid 'whooshing' sound from her pants grates on my eardrums, before standing up and walking right on by me towards the door. I turn to face her and we both smile slightly. Uncomfortably but also not.

"This is fine. I love that you're telling me. It's not embarrassing. It is all natural and fine and you're a smart, young," she gives me a pointed look and puts emphasis on 'young', "woman. Just..." she takes the biggest breath I think her lungs could possibly handle.

"That was a pretty big inhale for something that you're saying is fine, mom," I say, now questioning if I should have told her or not.

But of course I should have told her. It isn't like she is shaming me for my decision or asking a million unnecessary and boundary-crossing questions. I feel like, all in all, this exchange is going as it should. My stomach won't cease the churning feeling, but it's all fine.

It's fine.

After a moment of contemplation, she continues. "Okay. I'm fine. You're fine." She looks at me and her shoulders visibly relax a little and a small smile crosses her face. "I'll make you an appointment and get you set up on birth control. I am going to have to tell Craig. Just so he knows. It doesn't need to be some big secret."

She must have seen the silent plea in my eyes to not tell him. For no reason other than how weird that will be for everyone involved.

"Well, that's fine but you've lectured me and stuff, for like, years, so can he just, like, not?"

I do *not* want to discuss sex with Craig. I barely want to discuss it with my mother.

"Yeah, I think he'll want to skip out on that topic with you, or anyone else."

With a wink and a small nod followed by a strange moment of eye contact, she whisks her basket of laundry upstairs and, I assume, resumes her inner panic.

Aside from the conversations I had with my mom and the doctor the following week, it wasn't really discussed again. "It" being sex. I'd never really felt like my parents didn't trust or respect me as a human being, but the fact that they do has never been so clear. I've never felt so respected and trusted by them. Turns out, communication and honesty go a long way. On both sides of the parent-child relationship.

That all brings us here. Jared and I's six-month anniversary. The weather in the spring here is just as dicey as the fall is but today is beautiful. It's a nice sixty-four degrees and the sky is open and blue. The sun is warm. The air smells clean and fresh. Much like September in South Dakota—I love March.

Jared and I have experienced a lot of firsts with each other. Obviously, this milestone being one of the more major ones. We know the importance of it, having discussed it thoroughly with each other. Both of us want this to be something neither is uncomfortable with in any way. Jared got a hotel room for the occasion, which screams "this is so weird" but we did it to prevent the cliche backseat of a car kind of moment. We won't be staying the night here—we're not thirty for crying out loud. We just wanted to both feel safe and in the moment. Not rushed or preoccupied with feeling like we had to sneak around in one of our rooms.

All of our planning led to an incredibly right experience. He was kind, and it was beautiful.

I'm lying in his arms, both of us now clothed again, on the king size bed. Jared had opened the curtains after we got dressed, letting the sunlight in. I tug at the hem of his brown T-shirt, rolling it between my fingers. Jared brushes his fingers through my hair, not having thrown it back up into a bun.

"I love you," he says quietly, placing a kiss to where his fingers just passed.

I smile and look up at him. I take him in like I usually do. From the way his hair falls just a little bit onto his forehead, how his blue eyes look nearly illuminated against the tan of his skin. I trace the lines of his smile with my finger, my light blue nail polish looking stark by his face. My mind takes me to fifteen minutes ago before we put our clothes back on and my smile grows. There was fumbling and giggling and a lot of silent "are you okay" looks. Beyond all of that there was so much affection and respect. Through every moment of eye contact and shared breath, the unwavering love was there.

"I love you too."

After everything was all said and done, the moment turning a bit awkward in the most normal sense, we decided to go to my house to just hang out and finish spending the day together. We are walking hand in hand out of the hotel to Jared's car. In the last couple of months that he has had it, he's adorned her with blue LED lights in the doors and on the dash, loud speakers behind the backseat, and tinted anything he could legally darken. It went from "Grandma Car" to "Jared's Grandma Car."

He opens my door for me but as I go to slide in, he gently grabs the back of my neck, his fingers lightly tangling in my dark hair. I pause and look up to find him staring at me intently. It's such a piercing gaze. As though he is letting me know that I'm not the only one changed, and for the better, from today's events. I straighten back up, standing between him and the open car. I look back at him, showing him what he's showing me.

His stare and smile are making me think we both need to just turn right back around and go into the room we technically still have for another sixteen hours.

"I love you," he says.

It's the way he says it that almost undoes me entirely. It's with such conviction—like it's absolute, never changing. It's as if someone were to tell you it's raining as you stand there, under a dark sky, while it is in fact pouring. Like an obvious fact.

I love how sure he is about us. About me.

I smile back. "I love you too Jared. *Forever.*"

"And *always,*" he says, like he does every time.

He bends down and his soft lips meet mine. I don't know how long we stand here, in the parking lot of a hotel next to the open door of his car, but I think to myself "*I don't ever want to stop kissing this boy.*"

My heart stays a flutter as Jared shuts my door after I get in. The instant Jared is seated and buckled he reaches over and takes my hand in his, setting them both on the gear shift. Before putting the car in reverse, he looks over at me, his eyes wholly focused on mine. Bringing the back of my hand to his mouth he says, "thank you." His lips never leave my skin.

Such a simple phrase, "thank you". One you hear every day and for a multitude of reasons.

You thank the old man at McDonald's for holding the door open for you. You thank your mom for the little bit of cash she gives you for no reason other than the fact that she can. You thank the janitor at school when you walk up to the trashcan he's standing at to put an empty bottle of XXX Vitamin Water in the bag he's holding open for you.

I hear the unspoken words though.

Thank you for loving me and allowing me the opportunity to love you back.

I feel that thank you in my bones. In the very atoms that make up my being. I don't know that I will ever be as blissfully and irrevocably happy as I am right here. And in this moment, if this is the peak of happiness for me in this lifetime, I'm pretty sure I'm okay with that. To be seventeen and feel a love this big—to to *be* loved in such a large, life changing, soul altering way...

How lucky I am.

By now my family has acclimated quite well to the newest addition. Jared fits in so nicely here. My mom isn't a very affectionate person to anyone outside of her children or husband, and even she has hugged Jared a handful of times. My stepdad, being in the military, usually gives a curt, but pleasant nod and "how are you Jared" with every greeting. But Michael is *obsessed* with him. Sometimes, when the three of us go out to the store or if we take him to the park, people will assume Mikey belongs to the both of us. With blue eyes like Jared and the small features we share. I relish in that—the possibility of that becoming a reality some day. Jared never corrects the strangers that assume.

We don't even make it halfway inside the door before Mike is all over Jare.

"JAREDDDDDDD!" Mikey bellows as he flings himself into Jared's open and waiting arms.

Jared doesn't even blink as he scoops Michael up into his arms and swings him around our living room. Before setting him down he flies him around the house like he's an airplane—swerving around Bear and towards my mom making her laugh, over to Craig sitting at his desk. Jared finally lands Mikey with a small thud on the couch, startling Bear and making everyone giggle.

If I wasn't already in love with Jared, I'd have fallen right off that cliff with the way he treats my baby brother.

Michael immerses himself into his toys after the giggling ends, a bright orange and blue racetrack for his Hot Wheels now taking his attention. Jared's is back to me as we mosey our way to the dining room that's connected to the kitchen. A six-person brown, oval table sits in the center parallel to the sliding glass doors that lead to the backyard. A China hutch on the wall furthest from the kitchen has our unused "good plates" sitting on the shelves with piles of mail and random junk littering the main shelf. Jared and I each take up a spot at the table and watch my mom in the kitchen.

Tracy is putting together homemade personal pizzas for everyone for supper tonight. The dough is the kind that comes out of a red tube. She's got a pan with ground hamburger on the stove. An opened can of black olives, a bowl of sliced mushrooms, a cut up onion on a green cutting board all sit next to the stove. A little baggy of pepperonis and one of diced ham sit on the other side close to the fridge. As I get older and am introduced to other people's mom's and the operations of their lives in their home's, I am being constantly reminded that I am beyond lucky to have the mom I do.

"Come put the toppings you want on these, kids. They can go in after these ones," she says over her shoulder with her back to us while she places a pan in the oven.

Jared's in the kitchen before me, no hesitation, and we decide to test our knowledge and make a pizza for the other person. He's a pretty simple guy so I stack on the pepperonis, ground beef, and diced ham. I shape his pizza into a heart for extra pizzazz—it being our six-month anniversary and all, and me being the *extra* kind of person that I am. He's got onion, pepperoni, and ham on mine. Both of us end up very happy with the results.

We fill the time we have while waiting on the food with a few games of rock paper scissors. Mikey notices what we are doing at the table and joins us. We let him win every round. By game twenty-seven everyone is laughing at how intense Mike is while playing a game. When the microwave timer dings signaling that our pizzas are ready, Mikey is pouting while Jared and I walk to the kitchen. Jared musses his hair as he passes and tells him that he will play with him again later. While Jared walks towards the stairs to the basement with plates of pizza in both hands, I grab two glasses of water and follow him.

"Thanks for the pizza, Tracy!" he hollers, pausing and peering over the wooden railing.

"Any time Jare. You're always welcome here," my mom says. Meaning it a thousand percent.

Her and I smile at each other as I round the corner to go down the steps.

"Thanks, ma."

"You're welcome, sweet pea."

Jared and I have both finished eating, leaving nothing but crumbs left on our plates, and are now halfway through the Sixth Sense.

We are posted up in the living room part of the basement. No sheets, aside from the one that separates this room from my bedroom, hanging here, just concrete walls and open space. My parents put their old, smaller flat screen television down here when they upgraded to a larger one upstairs. It sits on a black and glass T.V. stand with a GameCube and DVD player below it. Next to it on both sides are brown bookshelves filled with random books and board games that haven't been touched in years. Across from the television sits the small blue loveseat we are occupying, pressed against one of the "walls" to my room, complete with a matching footrest that our legs rest on.

It's getting a little late and I know Jared is tired. I'm sitting up with my feet out on the ottoman and he's got his feet up as well with his body bent at what has to be an uncomfortable angle, laying almost on his side. His head is in my lap with one arm curled up under my leg that is closest to him, and his other arm is draped across—he is essentially hugging my thighs to his chest. He's rubbing lazy circles with the hand that rests on top of my legs and they're starting to get slower and slower, as is his breathing. I'm running my fingers through his thick hair, and I can't help but to imagine what life will look like when we're doing this in five, ten, thirty years.

Our own house with our own dog and our own television. Him working until six every evening at some blue-collar job that he loves but hates all at once. Me being home by five from whatever career I eventually have to decide on. Supper waiting and ready for him—pot roasts and tacos and homemade pizzas. A life with him that is full of laughter and falling asleep with his head in my lap on our couch.

What a beautiful life that will be.

I don't want him to drive home after having fallen asleep here so with reluctance I lean down to his ear and brush my lips there.

"Jare," I whisper.

I feel him shake like he had a shiver, and I can't help but feel proud that I can cause that kind of reaction.

Still by his ear I say, "I would love nothing more than for you to fall asleep right here and stay all night. However," I say slowly, "we don't have that kind of parents. So let's get you up and I'll walk you outside before you're too tired to drive home."

He tightens his arms around my leg and gives a good squeeze before kissing my thigh where his cheek has just left and sits up. Sighing the whole way—the man is practically pouting.

I shake my head at his demeanor and grab the hand he now holds out to me, pulling me from the couch and into his strong arms. He kisses me softly, his lips fitting perfectly with mine, before we make our way upstairs.

He says goodbye to my parents, both of them sitting on the couch together watching some hunting show. My brother is asleep already so Jared tells me to give Michael a high five in the morning before he goes to daycare. I roll my eyes playfully and continue walking outside to his car. When I reach to open his door for him, he grabs my wrist and spins me around, leaning my back against his car. With his hands boxing me in as they lay flat against the top of Stella, he leans his entire body into mine.

Stella is the name I gave his granny car, much to his displeasure. But a car needs a name and he refused to figure one out. I did what I had to do for sweet Stella.

I am trapped by tanned muscles and blue eyes. He brings his forehead down to mine. The night is lovely—cool but no wind. The stars above are dimmed due to the lights of the city but out here on the outskirts you can still see them a little bit more than in town. This late at night the neighborhood is quiet, peaceful.

"I love you. Thank you for today. Not even just the beginning of the day," he pulls back slightly, giving me a wink, "Although thank you very much for that."

I swat at his chest and grab his shirt, bringing him back to me—missing the contact already.

He continues, "But all of the day. The pizzas. Your family. The laughs. The hair twirling. You." He takes a deep, settling breath and rests his forehead on mine again.

Sometimes my heart gets sad for Jared. He has a brother and lives with his mom and stepdad, while his dad lives out of state. So, he isn't a stranger to a family dynamic. By a very basic sense, he isn't alone. But his family doesn't seem to function like mine. Not that every family does, I know. I'm not around his enough to know exactly how they do operate,. But I do know that Jared enjoys the time he spends with my family almost as much as the time he spends with me. And I also know that he doesn't feel that way about his own. It makes me a little angry too, in a way. To know that he doesn't get the same sort of love and affection from them even though he is beyond deserving of the very best kind of love. I am not naive enough to not understand that each family is different—I get that. I know everyone is different, and live their own way, and neither his mom nor mine are "right" in that sense. I just get the feeling that if I did get a closer look, if I were a fly on the wall—I would learn that maybe my mom is... well, *right*.

"Not to be too presumptuous or too forward but they'll probably be your family someday too so... You're welcome," I say with a wink and small grin.

He doesn't do deep conversations often, so I like to try and keep it light for him when I think he needs it. And right now, with the way his brows are pushed down, his eyes just a shade darker than normal—I know he needs bright and airy, love. And I enjoy being those things for him.

"I love you. Forever." I say in a more serious tone. I lean up to kiss him.

"And always," he says, kissing me back.

With a few more drawn-out kisses and some flashing of the porch light, courtesy of Craig this time, Jared is in his car and backing out of the driveway. He waves goodbye and I'm left feeling so full and at peace.

I can't believe I get to feel all of these things at a sweet seventeen.

CHAPTER SIX.

Texting in school is frowned upon. Well, technically it is forbidden but no one really adheres to that. So, here I sit with my iPhone in my lap and my head tilted down, one arm bent on my desk and the other by my legs, with my finger scrolling through a text message thread.

The small, sleek, white cell phone feels a little heavier in my hand right now than it normally does. The argument currently being had within—weighing it down.

"Harper!" I hear from across the classroom. I whip my head up to the area from which the holler came from, almost throwing my phone to the floor.

I really need to get a case like my mom told me to.

I attend a high school on the larger side, I think. I am sure compared to bigger cities it is probably quite small, but for here—it houses a lot. I think the average number of students is around 1,500. My junior year class alone has about 400 kids. The gray-stoned main building is a giant square, housing the lunchroom, auditorium, and the classrooms. There isn't any sort of vocational buildings at this school, things like drama and choir all take place within the main structure. There is a massive brighter gray colored gymnasium on one side of the lot, named after someone who paid a lot of money for that bad boy however long ago. A practice field for all the sports teams sits adjacent and across the street from the gymnasium. Several parking lots surround both buildings, one for staff and then others for each class level with access to drivers licenses. Though some brave few from the freshman or sophomore classes will dare to park where the seniors have taken root, thus causing minor scuffles. One day a sophomore parked their little Geo in the wrong spot and a whole slew of muscled senior boys carried—picked the entire car up and *toted* it—to a whole other parking lot. The whole school, the car's owner included, got a good laugh out of it for a few weeks. In Rapid City you can drive, very limited, at fourteen, pending your parents and passing a test. The seniors and juniors typically use the same, larger lot—that's where I park. Every day in the same spot; front row, four spots in from the right. It's a good school, the wealthiest of the few in town as far as public schools go.

The classroom I'm in now is one of the larger ones. It has two rows of six tables, each fitting three students. The classic blue chairs to sit in that are great for popping backs if you are limber enough. Huge windows line the back wall of the classroom giving you a lovely view of the parking lot I use. White, large bricks are covered by posters. The typical ones—"Dare to Soar" with a flying eagle, something about changing the world with a globe, and a bunch of science related ones depicting bones and vascular systems. This *is* anatomy and physiology after all. My favorite class with my favorite teacher.

My favorite teacher who is glaring daggers at me from his desk at the moment. Mr. Banks is looking directly at me, narrow dark eyes and zero amusement on his pleasant and round face. As far as high school teachers go, in my small experience, Banks is largely lenient and relaxed. In the same breath though, he isn't a pushover. I know he's serious purely by the tone in which he used to shout my name. Standing at five feet eight with the stature of a wrestler-turned-dad, he is the non-scariest teacher here. That doesn't mean he isn't well respected though. His dark hazel eyes are kind, and his smile always seems genuine. His brown hair is always just a little messy, like he's constantly running his hands through it from stress or something. Probably stress due to me at the moment, I suppose. Sometimes you can catch him in the hall talking to his wife who teaches English. They are the ultimate old, married couple goals.

I try to play it off like I wasn't doing anything, but the man is anything but stupid. I slide my phone between my thighs, smiling tightly and looking him in the eyes.

"What's up Banksy?" I offer the nickname as an attempt to calm the annoyance creasing his forhead.

"Do you think I'm dumb?" Banks asks me. "Do you think that I think you're just staring at your crotch for fun?" I say nothing, shrugging my shoulders. He points his short finger at me. "Put it away or at least be brave enough to have it out on your desk, Harper. Come on."

Absolutely exasperated by me already and class has barely begun.

He only ever calls me by my last name. I like to think it's because I'm one of Mr. Banks' favorites.

"Yes, sir. Sorry." I half-whisper as I set my phone on my desk, looking down. I quickly raise my gaze back to where Mr. Banks sits at his always-messy desk. "My boyfriend is being such a jerk though right now Banks and like, he's not even mad AT me!" I less than whisper as I angrily flip my phone over just so I have something to do with my hands.

No one in class pays me any mind. This period is so relaxed, everyone minds their own business. Mr. Banks rolls his eyes, pushes out from his desk, walks to mine and crouches down.

"Listen kiddo, us men, we're jerks. Don't let him be mean to you. You can be there for someone without being used as a punching bag for them." He smiles softly.

Before walking away Mr. Banks grabs my phone, and gently puts it in my gray and black backpack before knocking his fist on my desk twice and walking away.

I'm almost certain that he did it just so I would have to take a break from the argument going on in there.

Example eight-hundred-four of how Banks is the best.

A couple class periods later, instead of doing my math homework during my free period, and in an effort to ignore my phone, I choose to write Jared a little letter. Sometimes my feelings come out better when it's pen to paper. I started writing little notes and letters for him during school pretty much right when we started dating. Just for fun, something cute to do. Over the last almost seven months I've written him probably a dozen notes.

I don't love being at school—I find it quite boring to be honest. I don't have many friends here that I talk with constantly or fill my time with. I sit with a small group of great people, but I definitely always feel like I'm just kind of... *there*. I don't contribute much to conversations, not in a rude way but more of a quiet way. I laugh at jokes genuinely and I don't sulk by any means, but I just kind of exist with the group that has adopted me. I think that's probably more of a me problem than it is a them problem but I've got Jared, and Beth, and right now I'm content with that. My letters to him are usually ones detailing an extra boring day or talking about the future. I'll add little colored flourishes and scribbles. I always put the date in the top right corner and start each one off with "My dearest Jare,". Every single letter ends with "xoxo love, forever and always, Tryst". *I love consistency.* Then I fold each one into a tiny little square that can strategically be closed and opened with a triangular flap, almost origami-esque.

This one, though, isn't my typical happy or written-out-of-boredom letter.

I don't understand why he gets so worked up about his family and instead of talking to them about it he takes it out on me. I mean, I get why but I don't get *why*.

My dearest Jare,   04.13.2010

First, I love you. Forever and always.

I'm sorry you're having such a bad day. But you've kind of
made my day a bad day too and now I'm ignoring your texts
and upset about how mean you were this morning. So instead
of continuing to fight with you I'm going to write you this
letter. Set it down in front of wherever you are at work tonight
when I get there. Smile at you so you know I'm not mad. And
then walk away because work is for work, and we can talk after.

When we first started dating you wrote me a note one day that was a list of reasons you love me. I look at that note sometimes just to make myself smile and look at your nice handwriting. You had listed things like my smile and my laugh, the way I interact with my baby brother, my butt (thank you very much), and that your mom will love me. I think you got that last one wrong though from the sounds of it... And I won't lie, my feelings are pretty hurt. Not by you, but by your mom. I like to think I'm a fairly likable person. I smile and shake hands. I listen attentively in conversations. I don't make out with you in front of her. I always take my shoes off by the door if we go there instead of my house. So, why she doesn't like me, I'm not sure. And the way she is giving you a hard time about it, that makes me really sad for you. I'm sorry if I am causing any strain between her and you. I'm sorry she doesn't like me. I'll try to figure out why, maybe? And then fix it? But for now, just know that I hope that it changes, and I hope that if it doesn't then you know that I still love you.

Okay, that's all.

love,

I'LL NEVER BE.

forever and always,

Tryst.

xoxo

I fold up my letter like I always do and ignore the urge to check my phone. He wasn't super mean today necessarily, but he did kind of insinuate that it is something I *did*. But couldn't, or rather wouldn't, tell me what. The whole thing left me feeling totally let down but I don't know by whom—Jared, Darla, or myself. Jared because I find honesty to be something I don't take lightly. Even if it might hurt my feelings, I thrive on the truth. Darla becasue what the fuck could I have possibly done to the woman? I hardly see her and I'm incredibly respectful around her, really good to her son. I have my flaws, definitely. But nothing that I have heard is worthy of total dislike. And then myself...

Have I changed in a negative way that I'm not seeing? Did I do something wrong to hurt her feelings or cause some sort of disconnect between us? Did I do something to Jared and maybe he confided in her and I don't know about it?

He did give me some minor details about what had his mood all sour.

Last night, when he got home from having supper at my house, his mom was waiting for him at the kitchen table, I guess. From the sounds of it she was mad about how late he's been getting home lately.

But that doesn't make sense to me because he's been way later, even before we started dating and we were just hanging out as friends. At that point I wasn't the cause of it, and it didn't seem to be an issue then. So, I don't think that's it. There's got to be more to it.

When they started discussing the reason for her being bothered, she had called me "that girl" to him I guess. When Jared told me that detail, or rather let that part slip—it getting lost in one of his longer text messages that he must have just been flying through, my chest felt like it might have cracked just the slightest.

"That girl".

What a weird way to talk about the person your son loves, right? I'm only seventeen—a "mature" seventeen but still, I am a *kid* by all accounts. I'm not naive or proud enough to not acknowledge that fact. What could I have possibly done to this grown woman to make her so hostile about me if the small amount of information I got from Jared today is to be true? Maybe she found out Jared and I are having sex and that upsets her? But he's almost nineteen. They aren't catholic, or even religious in any form from what it seems, and we don't do anything of that nature in her home or take it upon ourselves to act out any sort of PDA in front of her.

I'm telling you—respectful.

What could I have done to cause such discord between myself and this adult woman I have only been around a handful of times?

I'm not sure. But what I do know is that I have got to stop stressing about what *could* be going wrong when I don't even know for sure that I am the problem. Or what the general problem is.

Okay. Breathe Trystan. It's going to be fine.

It *will* be fine.

I go about the rest of my day at school on autopilot.

The entire twenty-minute drive across town and to McDonald's for my six-hour shift is filled with a million and one thoughts.

What will Jared's mood be like?

Has his mom voiced her issues prior to now?

Clearly there is more to this story but will Jared share that all with me?

Why does this woman dislike me?

I get to work early enough to change into my uniform in the bathroom and add an extra layer of mascara before walking out the door. I leave my hair down so when I walk through the work area and Jared sees me, he remembers how pretty he thinks I am. You know just in case he forgot or is blinded by anger or something. I put the note I wrote him in the pocket of my red shirt and make my way towards the break room where I will sit and wait for my shift to begin.

We still haven't talked since this morning. I think it's the longest we've gone without even a quick "Hi. I love you" text. As I walk through the assembly area, I realize I'm a bit on edge. Slightly anxious, maybe.

Okay, more than slightly and definitely not maybe.

He can't be mad at *me*, right? I mean, of course he *could* be...
But, I didn't *do* anything—I know that much. Not today at least.
I didn't even lose my cool while he was being short and snippy with
me about his mom. And I am sensitive as heck to other people's
attitudes towards me.

I walk to the back of the store, raising my chin, and squaring my
shoulders. I focus on keeping my stride even and straight, all the
while I feel as though I might trip over my mixed-up emotions at
any moment.

I'm not in the wrong here, I remind myself. And I won't act like I
am.

I see Jared standing in front of the order screens and food catch,
the area occupying the almost exact center of the building. Zero
chance of avoiding him from where he's at.

Not that I want to, or whatever. I'm fine.

He looks so handsome today—everyday. The bright fuchsia button up shirt he has on today is my favorite of his work shirts. He has
the long sleeves rolled up on his golden forearms, showing off the
cords of muscle there—also a favorite of mine. I avoid looking him
in the eyes, knowing that my resolve will melt with the contact, my
chin will sink along with my shoulders and all of the crazy emotions
I have felt all day will just pour out of my body.

I pick the note out of my breast pocket and set it down in front
of Jared, giving a quick glance at his face and smiling softly so he
knows that even though I'm upset, I love him. That that fact doesn't
waver. I would hope that he wouldn't question that, but reassurance
is never something to be complained over, I suppose. He meets my

gaze with a look that I know means he is sorry. His blue eyes say everything. We don't need to have some big dramatic conversation in front of everyone, so with another smile and a squeeze of his hand in mine, I finish my walk to wait in the break room before I clock in.

The break room has one small television that gets used for orientation videos hanging in a corner. The walls are all white with a few laminated pieces of paper with random bits of news or the standard hand washing instructions hanging around. A white table with four chairs sits against one of the walls. The same brown tile that runs throughout the rest of the store is also in here. Quite plain, but does the job of a break room I suppose.

It's Tuesday so I hadn't anticipated tonight to be very busy. It's not until I look at the time my phone that I am shocked. It's been five hours since I walked in the front door and neither Jared nor myself have had time to do more than smile at each other. Each smile gets more relaxed, setting my pulse in the same direction.

I'm in the walk-in cooler grabbing what I need in order to prep some salads before clocking out and heading home. I'm on my toes reaching for a box of lettuce when I hear the door open and close behind me. I know the goosebumps on my neck aren't from the cold. I smile as I turn around—there *he* is. Looking at me with the most apologetic and sincere eyes. I don't make the first move though. The ball was left in Jared's court, and there it remains until he does something about it.

My mom taught me my worth early on in life and right now I know that he owes me a real, honest apology for being so rude today and not giving me a solid reason as to why. And an explanation is owed, I think. I won't waver until I get those things.

But damn it if I don't want to just give him a hug and a kiss and be done with this whole thing.

Jared walks up to where I'm at and grabs the box of salad mix out of my hands and proceeds to leave with it—not a word exchanged between us. A little taken aback, I try to shake it off and grab the rest of the things I need that I've already put into a box to carry easily and make to follow him.

My gut churns and my brain starts to work in overdrive, throwing my pulse at least forty beats a minute too high again.

What is he thinking?

Does he want to know what I'm thinking?

Even with the cool temperature of the walk-in fridge, I feel my skin heat and a sweat break out.

At the prep table we stand side by side for a few minutes, still silent, while we open packages of lettuce and cheese and whatever else. We work in tandem as we label bowls with white stickers. My anxiety is still present, steady and firm, but I also can't help but be totally fine with the way we're both just... working together. Like a true team.

Jared sighs and sets his hands flat on the prep table. His strong fingers flex once, twice, before settling flat—the bronze coloring returning from the white of the strain. I continue filling bowls with lettuce, knowing by now that he just needs quiet sometimes when he's in his head. I think it's often loud enough in there without me pushing to get his thoughts out. Even though I desperately want to know what is going on inside that pretty head of his before I just combust and the flood of emotions I have going on drowns us both.

"I'm sorry," Jared starts after a long moment. "Trystan, I'm so sorry." He turns towards me, leaning his hip on the table with one hand in his pocket and the other extended towards me and resting on my shoulder gripping lightly.

Like he's steadying me—or maybe himself.

I finally stop what I'm doing and turn to him, resting my own hip on the table and grabbing his hand from my shoulder to hold it between both of mine. We're rubbing idle circles with our thumbs on each other's hands, and I give him a soft smile. He brushes a stray piece of hair away from my forehead, placing it behind my ear before going on with what he needs to say.

"She's mad because of shit that has nothing to do with you, or even me for that matter, and she needs to get over it. It's not your fault. I'm sorry I took it out on you."

He pulls my hand to his mouth and closes his eyes while he rests his lips on my knuckles.

I take a steadying breath before asking, "What is she mad about then?"

Before he tells me not to worry about it like I know he was about to, I add. "I clearly have the right to know Jared. It can't simply not be about us or me when you told me earlier that she's mad about the time away from home or whatever it was."

I'm trying to keep sympathy in my tone, but I don't like secrets and I really don't like other people choosing for me what they think I do or don't need to know.

"It's about Kerry." He must have seen the surprise on my face because he only pauses briefly before he continues. "I guess he's pissed that we're dating."

I drop his hand, mostly from shock but also annoyance that he just told me this isn't about me.

Jared mirrors my now-standoffish position. Both of us have our arms crossed over our chests, our shoulders squared, our facial features a bit more hardened than they were a moment ago.

"The first time you came to my parents for that lunch," he says as though it's a question. I give a nod. "Kerry invited you?" I nod again, this time slower and raising my brows, still not understanding where he's going with this. "Kerry invited you and you ended up calling me for help when you got lost and then we spent the whole day together." He says it so fast I almost don't understand him.

But then it all connects in my brain.

Kerry.

Kerry has been upset that Jared asked me out. And that I said yes. That, even though I never gave a single hint or touch or inkling that I might have been into Kerry, I chose Jared and somehow that slighted him. And Kerry has been talking to Darla about it. I knew things had been different between the three of us since Jared and I went official. But I had just assumed it was because we were a couple now and Kerry didn't want to third-wheel.

"Kerry ditched us the second we got back!" I practically yell, getting immediately defensive. "And also, I was friends with BOTH of you all summer!" I throw my hands up in front of me before dropping them to rest on my hips.

"I know," Jared says without making eye contact.

If Jared is uncomfortable then I hope he realizes how awful I must be feeling because this seems to be going in an absurd direction. I have never once given Kerry any indication that I liked him as anything more than a friend. And thinking back on it, I was very open about the flirting I did with Jared the entire summer before we started dating.

I say as much to Jared, and he gives me a soft look like he knows all of this and has relayed this information to his mother. And maybe even his brother.

Like he read my mind he says, "I told them both this. But Kerry went to my mom and told her all of this bull shit about how we're having sex and your mom got you on birth control and lets us hang out in their basement, assuming that we're, I don't know, using her house as a-"

"As a sex house?!" I whisper aggressively. "My mother would NEVER let us hang out down there if we were doing that! And she would know! I can't keep anything from that woman even when I try!"

He reaches out and grabs my arm, pulling me closer to him so that now he has one knee resting between mine. Our hips still lean on to the table's edge, steadying us.

"I know." His pleading eyes settle my panic a little. "Honey, I know. It's not us. It's Kerry being a whiny, sore loser." His face morphs from understanding to irritation as he looks away.

At least I'm not the only one offended about this whole thing. Or the only one beyond pissed off at Kerry.

"So, what now? Your mom thinks I'm some brother switching tramp? And your brother is basically feeding her that information? What do we do?"

Darla isn't physically threatening by any stretch. She's maybe three inches over five feet tall, and as big around as my right thigh is. She's tiny. Turns out I don't need to be concerned about her trying to physically attack me though—just verbally behind my back. Her cropped, pixy styled hair is brown with the kind of highlights you get from the cap with the holes in it and a box of bleach. Up until today I didn't mind any of what she is. Abrasive and a little rough, but it all seemed doable.

Now though... *I kind of hate her highlights.*

"Well," Jared's voice is getting a little lighter. "Now I just stop telling Kerry anything at all. And I ignore my mother's irritation like I usually do. I'm hoping you can do the same because this," he gestures between him and I, "has nothing to do with her. Or him."

I take a deep breath and move the little bit closer that was available. There is no space between us now. I wrap my arms around his waist, and he grips me behind my elbows. I can't seem to bring my eyes to his, though. I feel embarrassed. Not embarrassed of us but of what we—of what *I*, seem to be doing to his family all of a sudden. Embarrassed that this is even a conversation we are having to have. I hate that his relationship with his mom and brother is getting even slightly strained and I seem to be the root cause.

With his forehead touching mine now, I swallow my nerves and look up to meet his gaze. He's smiling at me like he's still sorry, though not about us. I realize then that I was nervous he was sorry *about* me, not *for* me. I touch my nose to his and shake my head, as though I can shake the frustration away, before kissing him softly. He tightens his hold and kisses me back firmly, taking my breath, and some of my anger away.

This was our first fight and it hardly had anything to do with us or our actions in a real way.

How dare his family try to suck away our happiness.

Later that night when I get home my mom is still up. I settle next to her on the couch, laying my head in her lap.

"How was your day, little one?" she asks while running a hand through my hair and muting the TV. Gordon Ramsay was just yelling about someone's Alfredo or something before he was silenced.

I take some moments to gather my thoughts while watching the terrified cooks flounder around a massive, steamy kitchen. I keep my hands busy by scratching at the slick material of my mom's maroon-colored pants, unable to bring myself to harass her about them at the moment. I release a sigh that I think I must have been holding in since the start of today's fight.

Finally, after working up the nerve, I tell my mom about today's argument with Jared.

"Jared's mom was being kind of mean about me, to him." I say it all slowly and calmly, knowing full well my mom is not a meek mama, but a definite bear.

I feel her entire body tense. If there's one thing about my mom, my whole family really, it's loyalty. To a fault. We got to bat for each other hard. We don't take kindly to people making the ones we call *ours* feel like shit.

"What do you mean about you? What's there to be mean about?"

I can tell she's trying to rein in her automatic irritation. So, still slowly, I explain to her what Jared shared with me.

At this moment I feel so... *young*.

I don't understand. I don't even know if I *want* to understand. A grown woman should not be acting like this towards anyone, right? Let alone their son and his teenage girlfriend?

Right?

My mom and I decide together, after discussing a my thoughts on the matter a bit more, that it's best if I probably steer clear of Darla's for a while.

Which shouldn't be an issue in a week or so because Jared and Kerry just signed for their own apartment together in town.

Shit. Jared *and* Kerry just signed for an apartment. Together.

CHAPTER SEVEN.

The next week and a half after Jared and I's argument goes by quickly. School and work continue on as usual. There are no more conversations or bad days surrounding Darla or Kerry. I rejoice in that fact with each passing night.

"Thank you, Lord, for not allowing Darla to overstep her son's boundaries—thus not making either of our lives Hell today. Amen."

Prom for my school is quickly approaching, the halls are bedecked with dark blue posters displaying the theme—*Starry Night to Remember*. Conversations about dresses and suit colors, transportation, and flowers—it's all a buzz.

Most girls dream of their wedding day—the dress, the people, the colors, the flowers.

Me?

I've been dreaming of prom for as long as I can remember. Since the first time I recall watching Beauty and the Beast and thinking *"that* is the dress I will wear someday."

Over the last weekend I baked a dozen funfetti cupcakes and topped them with vanilla frosting before decorating five of them with "PROM?" in bright red gel frosting. I was pleasantly surprised by how enthusiastic my out-of-high-school-boyfriend was when saying yes.

I'm currently standing by my dark blue locker, in between classes, when my phone vibrates in my back pocket. Upon opening the text from Jared, I immediately blush and think about how blessed I am to call this boy mine.

Boyfriend<3

What do you think?

Wow! You clean up nice!

And oh boy, does he. Jared with his perfectly tanned, toned, thin frame, his slightly messy brown hair. On a normal day in his jeans and a T-shirt—he is handsome. In a bright white tuxedo with shiny white shoes and a buttercup yellow vest and bowtie combo? I am a lucky, lucky girl.

Easy, I've got a girlfriend already. She's kind of the jealous type.

She sounds awful… give me a chance? ;)

haha! Did you know I've been wearing my jeans too low my whole life?

> The lady fitting these told me that pants are supposed to go way above where I usually wear them. Who wears them like that?!

> Clearly not you…

I slide my phone into my backpack as I take a seat in my last class of the day, having finished the conversation with Jared while walking from there to here.

I don't think I've absorbed a single sentence this whole year about the world or its geography in this classroom. I look up at the clock above the whiteboard, impatient and ready to leave for the weekend. The black hand is ticking around the white face, slowly. Ever so slowly. Twenty-eight minutes until it's the weekend.

Twenty-seven.

Twenty-six.

The ringing of the bell pulls me from the incredibly deep fog I was in. My brain stopped counting down twenty minutes ago. It wasn't radio silent up there. The daydreaming provided a solid distraction. I thought about Jared's new apartment. How he'll decorate his room—how he might ask me to help. The cute little porch he said they have on the back of the place. Then my brain went ahead in time, to the apartment Jared and I might share someday. All the things *that* would entail. I caught nothing that was said in class.

I get to finally see Jared's new place tonight. Due to my excitement I'm one of the first ones out of the doors and in the parking lot. Once in my little red car I shoot Jared a text, letting him know I'm headed over. I am stopped in my tracks, hand on the gear shift and foot on the brake, when he texts me back right away.

> Give me 30 minutes. My mom is here and she's in one of her moods.

I don't want him to feel worse than I'm sure he does for even having a reason to tell me to hold on, but wow. So, it's still bad then. I guess I haven't asked, though now I think that maybe I should start.

> Tryst... I'm so sorry. 30 minutes. I'll make it up to you. See you soon.

The excitement I had felt moments ago, pulsing through me like a flow of energy through my veins, dissipates immediately. I settle into my seat, not even bothering to turn the radio up, while I sulk in the quickly emptying parking lot. I try to not question everything. To not wonder what was said behind my back or what's been going on in the last almost two weeks.

Thirty minutes feels like forty-six years, but I finally get the go ahead and make my way towards Jared's new home.

It's a cute dark gray duplex, only a fifteen-minute drive from my school or my home, sitting almost right in the middle.

Convenient.

Jared is waiting on the little red, wooden steps at the front, next to the driveway. The bright, white front door behind him sets off a glare from the sun as I pull up to the curb and park.

"You've got quite the manicured lawn for being so new to the neighborhood," I say teasingly.

The building sits in the middle of a cul-de-sac with four identical homes on either side. The lawn does look nice but that's because Mr. Big Shot moved into an area that has people to manage everyone's lawns for them. Fancy Man. Jared actually hates it though—the area they moved to. He was fine with a less ostentatious neighborhood and complex while they were looking for a place to live. *Kerry* liked this place the best, and I'm starting to realize that what Kerry wants—he usually gets.

Because whatever he wants is usually conveniently backed up by Darla.

Insert eye roll.

Kerry has already locked himself in his room when we make our way up the stairs and inside.

The main floor has two bedrooms on opposite sides of the spacious shared dining room and kitchen. There's a master bathroom in Kerry's room and a full bathroom next to Jared's room. The walls are all a shiny, fresh white, and the carpet is this beautiful sandy color with specks of darker browns throughout. All very standard—very crisp. The kitchen is adorned with light brown cabinets and stainless-steel appliances. An island separates the kitchen from the living room with a pair of black stools nestled under the counter. There's a set of carpeted stairs that lead down to a small office and a living area that I'm sure Kerry will take over as a gaming room.

Quit being pessimistic.

As annoying as Kerry has been the last few months, and how not excited I am for Jared to be living with him in this close capacity, I'm beyond proud of my guy for getting a place that's half his own. Aside from all of the good it will do for him to be out of his parents' house and making his own way, I'm selfishly hoping it'll ease the tension going on between his mom and me.

And maybe even remedy things between Kerry and Jared in the process.

Jared has all of his things squared away in his room already. A big king size bed with a dark chestnut wood headboard, matching end tables and dresser, take up most of the space. The dresser has just enough room to open fully and his large flatscreen television sits atop it. All in all, he seems pleased with the arrangements.

"I brought you a housewarming gift," I say as I press a kiss to Jared's cheek.

I hand him a picture frame that has a collage of him and I over the last few months.

"This one is my personal favorite." I point to the picture my mom took of Jared and I getting ice cream with my family back in October.

He was wearing my favorite dark blue American eagle sweatshirt that he owns and had his black Oakley sunglasses on top of his head. I had my hair up in a horribly messy bun and I was wearing a terribly tattered light blue sweatshirt that had my high school mascot on it—a Viking rowing a boat in a very much cartoonish way. He always looks so put together and I seem to always be... *not* put together. I recall that his ice cream sundae that day was way better than mine, so I had convinced him to switch but as we made the swap the ice cream on top of my cone slipped and fell. In the rush to save either the ice cream or our clothes, Jared and I had ended up bumping heads and spilling his banana split all over ourselves. The picture is of him laughing with his whole face, eyes closed and mouth open, face turned up towards the overcast fall sky. I've got my hands up in the air while I give him a completely defeated look, taking in the mess on his shirt. It is one of my most favorite memories and photos.

"Tryst, I love this so much. I gotta grab a nail and the hammer."

I stand by his bed, looking around, as he rushes away. But he quickly turns around and sets the frame on the bed, grabs me by the waist and gives me one of his deep, lasting kisses.

"Thank you. I love it. I love you," he says, his face hovering just above mine.

Before he runs off for real this time to grab what he needs to hang his gift, he kisses me on the tip of my nose.

I think those are my favorite Jared-kisses. The quick, but intentional, tip of the nose ones.

We spend the next couple hours putting away dishes and breaking down his moving boxes. It's all feeling very domestic. I can't help but daydream some more about how this is going to be for *us* and *our* things someday.

We'll be breaking down boxes after starting a load of laundry and putting away half a dozen plates, cups, and bowls in our new apartment.

Floating back to reality, I ask Jared, "Do you think we'll have a dog?"

My back is to him while I rearrange the random containers on top of the counter. The flour, sugar, butter, coffee, and toaster are all just such difficult things to find *the* spot for.

Without missing a beat, he says, "Oh yeah definitely. A lab I bet. Named," he pauses what he is doing and leans his butt against the counter, crossing his arms and ankles and contemplating.

"Rosie?" I suggest, turning around to face him with my hands on my hips. "Pauly?"

"Charlie?" His eyebrows raise in excitement.

"Oh, I could do Charlie."

"And we'll have a big couch with big cushions that we can sit on, or both lay down together on, and comfortably fit while we snuggle up on Friday nights." He turns back around and continues to put utensils into the drawer in front of him.

"And a coffee table in front of the couch," I say, my tone stern and serious, with a nod of my head even though his back is to me.

"A coffee table?" He peers at me over his shoulder.

"Yeah, so on those Friday nights you can bring a pizza home after work, and we can sit in the living room on the floor at our coffee table and talk about our week while we eat. Charlie will be all snuggled up on the couch hoping we drop a pepperoni or two." My hands fly all around the space in front of me as if I am painting an image in the air.

We stand there, opposite sides of the kitchen, filing new ideas into wherever our brains might keep that information stored.

"And then when we have kids," Jared says with so much ease. "We can watch movies like *Finding Nemo*. Same couch. Maybe a house by then. Same Charlie. Same us." He throws me a wink and I answer with a happy giggle. "The five of us can lay on our big couch together, pizza and silly kid movies, every Friday night."

"I think that is the best idea you've ever had, Jare." I shake my head while saying it, the smile that has been plastered on my face since the beginning of this conversation going nowhere.

He closes the short distance between us and pulls me in by my waist with one hand while his other wraps around the back of my neck. His fingers tangle in my hair. I look up at him and he's got the most hopeful, dreamy look in his eyes.

"I can't wait to feed Charlie pepperonis behind your back while you tell me about your day."

He kisses me on the nose before moving to my lips.

Jared kisses me for the next hour before I have to leave and head home. I daydream about Charlie and Jared and the future with him that I am already so in love with.

CHAPTER EIGHT.

Prom is finally tonight. T-minus six hours until Jared picks me up from my home. Every time I start to think about the moment he sees me, my stomach flutters like it's the first time we've ever gone out. It's been over six months and it's still so fresh and fun.

I'm getting my nails done with Beth this morning. Because we don't go to the same school, and we don't work together anymore, I hardly see her now.

Beth and I met at work a few years ago when we both first started at McDonald's. Up until last year we were just friendly with each other. Now though? We are nearly inseparable—when we're not with our boyfriends that is. So really, we text a ton and see each other when we can. We third wheel it with each other's couplings if one of our boyfriends are unavailable to double date, though. We try.

She's the total opposite of me in every way. Tiny, height and width wise, beautifully straight golden blonde hair, though that changes with her mood sometimes. The greenest eyes with the most incredible ring of amber around the pupil. Fun and bubbly but serious and charming. She's incredible and kind and smart. We even dress differently most days. Today I have on plain black leggings to hide the legs I hate, with a plain baggy gray T-shirt and a messy bun. Beth, the cute little model she is, has on nice, weathered jean shorts and a hot pink ribbed tank top. Her hair is braided nicely down her tanned back.

Opposites attract.

This girl is my soulmate though, and I am so thankful for her every day.

Beth is getting just her toes done and I'm getting just my fingers done so we're not sitting next to each other. Instead of yelling across the salon like she tried to do when we sat down—we're texting.

> What are you getting done?

Beth is the Best

> I was thinking black with a silver glittery swoopy style on my big toe. What are you doing?

> A classic French tip. My dress is already bright, and I think that will look best with it.

> Are you excited!? When I went to prom 2 weekends ago it was so fun. There was so much yelling and singing and dancing. My throat was so sore the next morning.

Yeah, cause of the singing… ;)

I'm kind of nervous… I've never been "done up" so much before and what if Jared likes that version more than my average and slightly boring normal self?

Then he'd be an absolute tool and I would have to beat him up by the dumpsters at McDonald's.

Thank you for looking out haha

anytime.

But really, he loves you. He loves you probably more than any nineteen-year-old has ever loved a seventeen-year-old girl. It's not a secret. What's he wearing tonight?

I give Beth the details of Jared's tux while the nail technician finishes up my left hand.

I can't WAIT to see you in your dress again! I think I've forgotten what it looks like.

When we are all done and paid up, we leave the salon and head to my house. Beth is going to stay until I leave later for the dance. She'll keep me company while my mom's friend does my hair and I do my own make-up. I didn't want anything wild for my hair. I usually keep it in a bun or down straight. But for prom I made an exception. My mom's friend, Cara, put my thick, dark locks into a beautiful curled updo with some pieces framing my face. She added in a bunch of jeweled pins to bedazzle it, per my request, and I just know that I'm going to need Jared's help tonight to get those and the seven-hundred bobby pins holding all of this shit up, out of my head.

He'll enjoy it though. He loves helping me with weird little tasks like that.

I did my own make-up like I would on any date night but added some darker eye shadow and a really pretty mauve lipstick.

My dress... *Oh my dress.* It's one I've always dreamt about. I knew I wanted a bright, soft yellow ball gown to wear to prom someday. And here it is—a dream come true. It fits like a glove. Hugs every curve and dip perfectly. Maybe not the most comfortable thing to sit in, but I can push through supper to get to the good part. It is sleeveless and has a sweetheart neckline that has sequins sprinkled all across it. It's the prettiest shade of buttercup yellow and has little lace details spread throughout the bodice and down to the skirt. It's perfect and if I never wear another dress like this again in my life, I'll be okay with it. It's that good. How will I ever top it?

I'm anxiously waiting in the kitchen now for Jared to arrive. He's not late but I'm so ready to see him and have him see me. I feel my heartbeat kick up when I hear his music as he turns the corner to our house. My breath gets caught in my throat and I look at Beth who has her phone out with the camera on, ready to snap all of the pictures. She gives me a small, reassuring smile and I relax just a bit.

She's such a good friend, always the hype girl and getting the best shots of important moments.

A light knock grabs my attention and I quickly snap my gaze back to the front door.

Why am I so nervous?!

Jared loves me. He loves me in sweatpants. He loves me in baggy old T-shirts. He loves me in nothing. Of course, he's going to love me all done up to the nines.

Anxiety can be relentless.

My mom opens the door and I round the wall separating the kitchen from the living room and there he is... my guy. My Jared. My...

Gosh he is beautiful. Dashing. Handsome. Gorgeous. He put a little bit of gel in his freshly cut and styled brown hair. His eyes have that extra blue shine to them against his white suit. His soft, yellow vest and bow tie are lovely contrasts and I can't help but smile at his square toed, freshly cleaned, and polished cowboy boots. Absolutely stunning.

He sees me giving him a once over and decides to do a little turn for me, palms held upwards as he raises his hands.

"You look incredible," I say as I take a step forward. I halt, though, as he throws a hand out, stopping me.

"Let me look at you," he says as he twirls his finger in the air. Seemingly not at all embarrassed that my parents and Beth are still here.

Watching this, watching us.

But I spin for him anyways, huffing a small laugh out while I do so. Throwing my hands out to the sides and rolling my eyes while the bottom of my skirt lifts just enough to reveal my black flip-flops.

Comfort, you know? I'm a sandal girlie.

He lets out a long whistle as we bring our eyes back to each other.

"You look," he pauses and takes a step forward, "like the most stunning person that has ever walked the face of this earth. If I weren't already completely in love with you," he winks at me, sending a total shudder to my core, "then this right here would have done it. You're beautiful."

I feel color creep into my already blushed cheeks and pick my feet back up to finish closing the distance between us. He kisses me on the cheek before we return some of our attention to the other people in the room.

Jared claps his hands together while looking at the audience around us.

"Right. Well. Flowers!" He says excitedly, waggling his brows.

My mom and Beth snap photos while Craig takes a video as I pin Jared's boutonnière to his suit jacket. Mikey is at his friend's house—his hyper energy would have sent me over the edge today.

We went to the flower shop together last month and picked out the prettiest arrangements. I may be an odd one, but there is something about simplicity in things like flowers. Baby's Breath with yellow ribbon tied around the stems to match our yellow attire. That's it. I loved the idea of the contrast in colors against my now spray tanned skin.

He places the corsage on my wrist and swiftly brings me in with his hand on my lower back and the other still on my flowered wrist. We pause there—just looking into each other's eyes. I make a mental note to be sure to print one of the pictures from this very moment to frame for my room.

How lucky I am to be loved by this boy.

Quick hugs goodbye get doled out and then we're out the door after what feels like five-hundred pictures. My mom is letting me stay at Jared's apartment tonight for the first time which seems like such a huge accomplishment for me, so she gave me a brief lecture for the tenth time before we left. I feel like it says so much about how my parents trust me and also trust the boy I love.

We pause by Jared's car, freshly cleaned inside and out, and I kiss him before saying, "Thank you for being so incredible."

"You make me want to be." Jared kisses me again before I sit down in my seat. He pushes the bottom of my dress into the car, closing the door and getting in his own spot.

"I love you," we both say at the same time. The laughter fills the quiet as we head off down the road.

The night goes off without a hitch. Supper at Ruby Tuesday was lovely. I spilled nothing on my dress to my utter surprise and delight. We arrived at the venue in time for a picture together before going in and dancing the night away.

The photographer they hired had set up a backdrop that gave serious *The Starry Night* painting vibes.

Prom itself is in an event center. I have been to hockey games and a couple concerts here. Tonight, they have it decked out in different shades of blue's and yellow's and gold's. From balloons to streamers to the tiny star shaped confetti sprinkled on every table. It's spectacular.

The small group of friends I have at school, first-boyfriend-Shane being the ringleader, went together as many are dating another within the circle, and we sat with them. The few times we actually sat down, that is. We stayed far longer than I thought we would. I don't why I had such nerves about Jared being bored or acting as if he was bothered by being there, but I think he might have had more fun than me.

The image of him scream-singing *Get Low* by Lil Jon is something I will remember for the rest of my life.

He whisked me out the door, Irish goodbye-ing my friends, and to his car with giggles and promises of ice cream before going to his apartment.

As he opens the car door for me in the loaded parking lot of The Center, his white Continental sparkling in the streetlights, I place my hand on his chest and look up at him.

The night is cool, very little breeze. The stars are dim here as we are in the middle of the city, but it's surprisingly quiet out. The only real noise being heard is the mumbled bass and yelling coming from inside the building.

"Someday I'm going to make you replay your version of *Get Low* for our children while we sit on the couch and watch you. That was awesome."

"Will there at least be popcorn for the show?" he asks with a sly grin.

I love that ornery smile.

Jared places his hand over top of mine where it lays on his chest.

"Absolutely, there will be popcorn. I'm not a monster." I wink at him as he leans in for a kiss.

This moment, Jared and I making plans for a future we both want, in the middle of a packed parking lot with nothing but a dull roar of music and the night sky surrounding us—this is what I love most about *us*. That it can be just us—no matter where we are or what we are doing. It can be just Jared and Trystan, in love and happy.

I don't know if it was Jared's bed, that shit is *comfy*, or the soothing sound of the cool early May breeze outside the open window, but the peace in which my dreams sought out and found was unlike anything I have ever experienced before. Resulting in one of the best nights of sleep I have had in a while, possibly ever.

We weren't hardly through his front door last night before Jared had his white, long sleeve shirt unbuttoned and his belt undone, ready to change into sweatpants and a T-shirt. The second he was done getting changed, I was standing in front of him with my back to him in a silent request. He unzipped my dress and I quick-ly changed into the sweatpants and shirt I had brought with me. Even in our leisurewear we matched—unintentionally. Light gray pants, his blue t-shirt to my blue long sleeve shirt. He laughed at my make-shift dance moves a little while later while I sat in front of him at the kitchen table as he de-pinned my hair. Jared was fast asleep by the time I got done brushing my mess of hair and wiping the make-up from my face.

If you were taking Jared at face value, you wouldn't clock him as someone who is often stressed. He is light and airy, funny and sweet, the calm to any storm. Lately, though, it seems like these small moments of quiet and ease are becoming sparse in his life. His brows are a bit more bunched on a regular basis. His tone when talking about his family is a bit more strained. His fuse is anything but short, but it has lessened some in recent weeks.

So now, while I watch him in the early mornings of this Sunday, I revel in the calm he's feeling while he sleeps. His tousled hair, his full lips slightly open and carrying small snores. I can't help but think about the worries he's acquired lately. I know I'm only seventeen and he's not even nineteen, but it truly feels like we are in this life together. Like, *together-together.* In a lot of the same ways I see adult couple's are. I'm not naive enough to think that shit isn't far harder for actual adults, or that it won't get more difficult at times and while life goes on, but still... It doesn't feel like we are teenagers in some *small* sort of love. This love between us feels very... big.

Jared's mom has been giving him a really hard time still about the weirdest things. He hasn't been giving me a lot, if any, of the details, but it's starting to seem like I might be a problem for her *still.* But that can't be the case, right? I barely see the woman. And when I do, I'm perfectly respectful and act accordingly. I don't go out of my way to kiss her ass because I can't ignore how she has treated Jared, myself, and my mom in her snide comments and jabs. But I make a real effort to be cordial. We still don't make a scene in front of her as far as PDA goes. I watch my mouth even though she swears like a sailor. I get along with her husband wonderfully, Todd is beyond kind.

I like to think I am a likable person—I try to be at least. I definitely prefer to be liked, but who doesn't? With that being said, I make a conscious effort to move in life with genuine kindness and optimism. I try not to let other people's actions or opinions dictate how I operate. The thought that Jared's mom might *dis*like me is starting to really stress me out, though. It's something I find myself thinking about far more often than I should be.

It isn't even 9:30 in the morning and I'm spiraling.

I don't know if Jared can feel the stress radiating off me at this moment, but as I move my body slightly to go to lay on my back, I see him move his head. I pause and look back to him and am met with his sleepy, cerulean eyes.

"What's the matter?" His eyes narrow.

"Nothing," I say too quickly.

He sees right through that.

"It's your mom," I say with as much ease as I can muster.

As the words left my mouth, he tensed up under me. I shifted myself over so that I am now on my right side completely, laying my head on my pillow with one hand tucked under my cheek. Jared does the same, his eyes now more alert.

He's too quiet.

If there wasn't something to be worried about he would have easily told me—reassured me.

I force myself to ask, "What's going on Jared? Don't tell me nothing. There is clearly somethi-"

"She's just being a bitch. It's nothing you need to worry about," he says gruffly, his eyes now avoiding mine.

"If it has to do with me then I definitely deserve to know what's being said. I don't like feeling out of the loop."

I can feel my chest tightening and my breathing start to quicken.

Jared takes a deep breath before saying, "She knows you're here often and Kerry seems to have a problem with that, so she has to have a problem with it." He pauses like he is questioning if he should say the rest. "He complained to her about us having sex here and she thinks that is a problem."

"He told her what?!" I yell as I sit up abruptly. "Why would he tell her that?! How does he even know that?! We don't do any of that when he's here! Or at least when we think he isn't!"

Kerry doesn't have a super active social life, but he's gone frequently enough that we don't really push our luck with setting him off or giving him reasons to complain. We "time" things, if you will. There was a time last week though that Kerry got home while Jared and I were in the middle of some *quality time*, and Kerry had knocked needing to ask Jared a question. He must have heard something in Jared's voice to make him understand why the door was shut and locked this time. I don't know why that would be something he felt the need to relay to his *mommy* though.

"Relax Tryst. Breathe, babe. It's fine." He runs a hand down my arm. "This is my place too, just like it's his. We aren't being reckless or dumb."

"Okay." I say, unbelieving, as I lay back down, facing Jared again. "I don't understand what the issue is with all of this. If Kerry wanted to have anyone over, you wouldn't care. Why does he? And why does your mom think she gets any sort of say or that she gets to have feelings over it when you're both adults and she doesn't pay for anything here?"

"I don't know honey. I just know that she's been giving me a hard time the past couple weeks about you being here."

He quickly looks away from me and towards his ceiling, almost like he feels guilty or is holding something back.

I prop myself up on my elbow, still looking at Jared and narrowing my gaze.

"There's more." I declare. "What else is she saying?"

"She just... Please don't freak out." His eyes are pleading as they look into mine. "I told her she was being awful. Okay? Just... I have your back. Don't get upset with me, please."

I say nothing, swallowing down any sort of response.

He rubs his face with both hands before saying, "She asked if you were pregnant because apparently... She noticed you've..." he stops talking.

"I've what, Jared?" I sit up completely now, out of Jared's reach.

I'm feeling slightly betrayed right now and it's making my heart sink. Betrayed over the fact that he hasn't been openly honest with me. What all is he keeping from me and what kind of conversations is everyone having about me? And why am I just now finding out about this?

"She said she noticed you've gained weight, I guess. I haven't noticed," he says quickly.

Jared shakes his head with a disgusted look on his face. Still laying down, he reaches out a hand to me, trying to pull me to him. I pull further out of his reach by getting off the bed.

"I'm sorry," I say, absolutely stunned. "Are you telling me your mother is talking about my weight with you? Why would she think that is an okay thing to do, Jared?" I hear the accusatory tone I am now carrying, but the ache I feel in my heart is preventing me from fixing it.

He told me he wouldn't keep shit from me.

I start pacing his room. I'm in nothing but my shirt and black boy shorts now. My hair is an absolute mess from the copious amounts of hair spray I used last night, the braid I put it in before sleeping now a fallen-out disaster.

Last night.

How could one of the best nights of my life end and then quickly transition into one of the worst mornings of my life? Am I being slightly dramatic? Maybe. But what the hell is going on!?

Why is this grown woman out to get me?

What does my weight have to do with her?

And why does my boyfriend, who told me he would be honest about issues like this, feel like he is doing the right thing by NOT doing that?!

Jared is sitting up in bed now, in his gray sweatpants and nothing else, bracing his arms on his pulled-up knees.

"I obviously told her you're not pregnant and that your body is none of her business. And that she was way off base saying anything about you in any way. I told her you're on birth control and then she started talking about how irresponsible your mo-"

I hold up a hand, signaling Jared to stop speaking. I raise my eyes to look him dead in his.

"Don't. Do not finish that fucking sentence," I say through my clenched teeth.

He was talking so fast just now that I don't think he knew what he was about to say to me, like his brain couldn't catch up to his mouth.

I'm sure if it were quick enough the alert message would have read something like "ALERT, ALERT. DO NOT BRING UP YOUR MOM TALKING SHIT ABOUT TRYSTAN'S MOM. ALERT ALERT."

"Unless you want me to go full psycho and head straight to your mother right this very second," my voice getting louder with each word, "don't you dare tell me that she was talking shit about *my* mom."

My voice may be getting louder but the lethal calmness in it is steady. I'm fuming now. My hands are shaking. My brain is going a million miles a minute. I all of a sudden feel like my stomach is weighed down with lead. I start looking for my pants and a bra to throw on.

I have got to get out of here.

"I need a brush," I say quickly and breathlessly, the panic overriding the anger.

"What?"

I look around frantically, barely seeing anything, barely hearing anything. The hysteria in my body seems to be pouring out of every inch of me. And at this point there is no stopping it.

"I need a brush," I say again, more to myself than anyone else.

"Trystan, just hang o-"

"I NEED A BRUSH JARED!"

My whole body feels like it's going to shake out of itself, like my insides are being pulled by some sort of magnetic force and trying to exit through my skin.

Jared is out of bed now and walking towards me, cautiously and slowly.

Smart.

My brain is screaming so many thoughts all at once still.

How can she not like me?

Why is my weight something she feels like she can comfortably speak about?

Why is she conversing about me at all with Kerry?

Was Kerry or anyone else there for this conversation about my fucking body size?

Why was my mother's name in that horrible woman's mouth?

WHERE IS MY DAMN BRUSH?!

Jared's thick arms wrap around mine, his front to my back. I have my face in my hands now. I don't know when I started crying, but I can see Jared's forearms shaking with the movement coming from my own body.

"Tryst," he says from behind me, his face buried in my still unbrushed hair. "Baby. Breathe. I'm so sorry I didn't tell you this when she first said it. I wasn't trying to hide it." His voice is quiet but sure. "It's not that it's not important, I know it is. But I just didn't think it mattered at the end of the day. I love you. You love me. What anyone else thinks... It means next to nothing to me."

My voice breaks through my hands, "Not to me Jared... what your mom thinks doesn't mean nothing to me."

I wish it did.

He says nothing. I say nothing. We stand there, my arms now underneath Jared's and my hands holding his forearms, my fingers pressing hard into his arms like if I can just hold on a little more—I don't know. He has his head turned to the side and leaning against the back of my head. My chin rests where my fingers meet his arm.

The tears have ceased, the shaking has slowed. My brain is a little quieter and slightly less angry. It's more sad than anything now.

I pivot my body, never leaving his arms—he doesn't let me. I tilt my head up and look at Jared. He's chewing the inside of his bottom lip and his eyes have lost the usual spark they hold.

I know that face. It always says what his voice needs a few minutes to work out. I know he feels horrible. His mother's words are not his fault. But how could he not tell me this before today?

"You can't keep that stuff from me," I finally say, trying to rein in the anger and failing. "If there's a problem, I need to know about it. I can't fix something if I don't know it's broken." My voice breaks and the tears threaten to make their return.

His whole body relaxes with a breath.

"Tryst, there isn't anything that is broken. My mom sucks. It's not you. It's not even me. She's just... difficult," he says.

"She can't speak about my mom like that. She has no right."

That's where I am clearly hung up. Darla spoke poorly about my mother. And if she's comfortable enough to do that with Jared then who else could she possibly be conversing with about her? It is unacceptable and my mom doesn't deserve this.

"I know. And I told her as much before I hung up on her that day. Please don't worry. I like you as you are, in every way. I love your mom. I love you. She's my mother but she doesn't count as a voting member in my love life." The conviction he carries in those words calms my heart a bit.

He grabs my chin with one hand and uses his other to pull me closer to him as he plants a kiss laced with apologies on my lips. I can taste the saltiness of my tears still lingering behind.

"I really need to brush my hair," I say solemnly as I put my forehead to his chest, trying to cut the tension with a small bit of humor.

We both try to lighten the mood with a little laugh before we hunt for that damn brush of mine.

And while the room doesn't feel as heavy as it did ten minutes ago, it certainly doesn't feel as light as it did forty-five minutes ago.

CHAPTER NINE.

Jared's apartment is relatively close to my school and since spring has been, well, springy, my lunch period and following free period have been spent there when Jared isn't working—or out and about. Which is often considering he chooses to get scheduled in the evenings during the school week so we can spend aforementioned afternoons together.

Have I told you lately that I love him?

Kerry works from home now, so we have been enjoying most of our time together on these afternoons outside on their little porch so as to not disturb his workday with chatter.

And so I don't have to see his two-faced face.

The porch on the back side of this duplex is a cute, small area. The guys got some patio furniture recently. A loveseat and two matching chairs. They are the whicker kind, dark brown, with really pretty blue fabric cushions. Jared even sprung for the matching coffee table that has a built-in fire "pit" in the center of it. We've been lighting that bad boy up on the weekends while we relax to the 90's Country playlist on Pandora.

Currently, I've got my feet propped up on the unlit table while I sit on the loveseat. A can of peach sparkling water in one hand and a half eaten peanut butter and jelly sandwich on a paper plate sitting on the ground next to me.

"Remind me when you have to go back to school?" Jared asks as he exits the sliding glass door and kisses the top of my head, passing by to take a seat in one of the chairs.

I pick up my phone to check the time, silently hoping time hasn't moved at all.

"I've got," I do the math in my head, "thirty-eight minutes until I need to leave. I can leave before then though if you need to go somewhere. It's not like I can't work on my homework in the school."

Jared takes a seat on the chair across from me on the other side of the table, looking extra cute today. I don't think there is a single thing different about his appearance compared to any other day but man...

The usual light blue jeans from the Buckle. Same style of American Eagle T-shirt, todays is a soft yellow, and is accompanied by his standard light gray zip-up hoodie. Seeing him in no shoes and just socks always feels weirdly intimate, like I see him in a place no one else does. Which I do... Obviously.

Standard Jared. But still, *wow.*

"No, no. You don't need to go anywhere." He shakes his head before taking a sip of his own sparkling water.

I shake myself out of the daze I fell into while admiring Jared, blinking a few times before meeting his gaze.

"I just can't ever remember what time English starts for you."

"One-twenty," I say with a smile. "You look very handsome today, have I told you that yet?"

He looks down at himself and raises his shoulders a bit. "You haven't, but thank you," he says with a wink. "You always look beautiful, especially when you're being all studious and reading a book."

"I'm so over this one." I hold up Romeo and Juliet. "It's good—it's fine really. I've seen the movies though and have read this once already. and... I need some like, *stable* romance or something." I shake my book at Jared to add some drama.

Like that is something I lack.

"Well, you've got less than a month left of the school year and then you're done for a few months."

"And then a whole other school year before I'm done-done." I sink back on the couch a bit more, simply to pout, setting my book open pages down on the ground next to my lunch.

Jared laughs, not giving in to my antics before he gets up. He circles around the table to where I'm sitting and pulls my feet with him as he sits next to me, resting them on his lap. The sun shines off my bright pink toenail polish.

"Don't rush the easy part of life, babe."

"I know," I lay my head back, resting it on the arm of the couch. "But I just feel like I'm missing out on so much every day. I could be working full time, and we could be hanging out even more, and going out or on little trips, and seventeen has been cool, but I feel like I'm ready for, like, twenty-four."

"Slow down honey," he says with another laugh while he switches from the foot he was rubbing to the other. "We're young. We have plenty of time to make memories and do all the things we want to do before you're twenty-four."

I'm a dramatic human being by nature. I over think and over feel and overindulge. I'm just... *over*. Suddenly I'm struck by this overwhelming worry and sadness that by the time I'm twenty-four I won't be sitting next to this especially beautiful human being anymore. And then where will I be?

"I'm suddenly very content with seventeen," I say quickly, removing my feet from Jared's grasp.

I move over to sit next to him and lean into the crook of his shoulder, resting my head on his chest. I stay quiet, choosing to keep my previous melodramatic thoughts solely to myself. I'm crazy but sometimes I like to keep that shit to myself.

"I love you now and I'll love you then," he says with a long kiss to the top of my head.

"It's like you knew what I was spiraling about," I say with a half laugh, half pout as I turn my head up to look at him.

His eyes are so dang blue today.

"I know exactly what you're overthinking about." His look tells me he does and that he thinks I am quite silly.

He boops me on my nose and rolls his eyes at me.

"I love you too Jared. A whole lot."

"Forever and always, babe."

And with that kind of reassurance, who could even be bothered to worry?

Not me.

Not for a few minutes at least.

CHAPTER TEN.

I've got two weeks left of my junior year of high school and then it's work, Jared, some summertime concerts during the state fair, and zero homework. Jared's speech a couple weeks ago about soaking it all in was well done but I am itching to just be done with school and live a real, full life that I get to design. With Jared.

And probably a dog or two.

Today his family is moving cows and Jared asked if I wanted to come out and help. It surprised me when he asked—not having been invited to do something out there thus far. And while the argument we had after prom about his mom and the fact that she is still talking shit about me, and now my mom as well, surfaces to the forefront of my mind often, I don't want to allow that to keep me from *trying* with them. They are his family and I will be damned if I am the sole reason for a weird relationship. I refuse to look back in a decade and think "I could have done more" if things don't get better.

I am all city-girl with the desire to be a-lot-country. I love the entire aspect of it. The cows, the corn shucking, the dirt, and the work. So, when Jared asked, I immediately said yes—jumping on the chance to be helpful and spend time on their ranch.

Goals for this adventure: show Darla I can do more than just gain weight and ruin her life, watch my boyfriend work those tan muscles, hang out with a whole lot of mama cows.

That sounds like a great day, if you ask me.

I don't know what all I will be able to do to help but I am willing to do almost anything. They have about two-hundred head of black angus cows that calved earlier in the year and so now it's time to put them all out to a bigger area to eat and roam and live their little bovine lives.

Jared picked me up on his way to their ranch and we're currently listening to a randomly shuffled, but also carefully curated, playlist he put together. He does that constantly—makes playlists or CD's for us. I've got a few in my car right now that he made for me. Little scribbles adorn the bright orange or silver tops, things like "luv u hunny" and "4ever". We both are very much music people. We listen to various genres and enjoy new findings. Both of us sing and dance and act out the best car-band shows together. It's one of my favorite things that we do together—music.

I know people talk about the honeymoon phase in each relationship, but I swear, it's been almost nine months and I can't imagine ever feeling less in love or less impressed than I do right now looking at him. I know that isn't a long time in the grand scheme of things, *so* many things could change and grow and alter. But right now... life feels so right by his side.

I don't know if it's the square toed cowboy boots with a million and one scuffs on them, or if it's the grungy neon orange t-shirt that he got at his prom a few years ago with some sort of...

What? What is that?

I squint as if that will make my twenty-twenty corrected vision somehow better.

"Is that a bucket of apples on your shirt?" I push his shoulder forward a bit to get a better view of the back of it. "It is! Why in the world is your prom shirt apple themed?"

"It was a weird Apple of Your Eye theme," he says as he readjusts to his original relaxed position.

No ten and two here, not for Jared. More like twelve and gear shift, or Trystan's leg.

I shake my head, laughing at the total randomness of that theme. Small town schools really do the most sometimes, so I can imagine it wasn't as lame as I'm picturing.

I go back to my ogling. Taking in the strength of his muscles running from his left hand that he has on the steering wheel up to his, unfortunately for me, covered shoulder. His skin is already four shades darker than mine. I blame my genetics, but also the fact that I hate bugs and heat, so pale I will stay. I take in his strong neck...

Is that a weird compliment?

I don't care if it is, he's got a good-looking neck. I make my way up from there, his freshly chapstick-ed lips are moving along to the song playing—*Living In A Bubble* by Eiffel 65. Jared is like my own, less chaotic Eminem sometimes, keeping up with the fast-paced songs.

I take notice of his strong, very German nose that I am utterly infatuated with.

I love a good nose.

And when I get to his hidden but perfectly blue eyes, I see my reflection in his black framed, polarized sunglasses.

My cheeks warm. "Oh, hey there." I give a sheepish smile.

"What are you staring at?" he asks with a laugh and a shake of his head, turning back to the road.

"I was just checking you out."

"Why?" As if he can't fathom why I, his girlfriend, would find him, my hot boyfriend, to be a total babe.

"Uhm... because you're hot and I'm a seventeen-year-old girl?"

"You're insane. And cute," he says with a wink.

I don't even deign to verbally respond, instead scoffing at his words. I roll my eyes and turn the music back up.

I'm a frump of a girl. I don't know if it's the happiness or the birth control or just life and aging and hormones, but I have definitely put on some pounds. Pounds that I had most certainly not been missing in the first place. Weight that clearly have been noticed by people—Darla.

Jared turns the music completely off rather abruptly. I turn my head from where I was looking out my window to look at him. He looks at me for a moment, silent and lips in a thin line, before refocusing on the road ahead.

"I'm sorry, did you roll your eyes at me for calling you cute?" he finally asks, shock dripping off each word.

"Well, yes," I say quietly and slowly. And then in an attempt to avoid a minor lecture I add, "You need your eyes checked."

I laugh at myself depreciation. He does not.

"You need to be nicer to yourself." He shoots me a glare.

"Such wise words for a small-town boy, Jare," I say with far too much attitude. "Careful or I'll start telling people you're actually a genius and then they'll wonder even more than they do what you're doing with someone like me."

Once it's started it can't be stopped, it seems. Insecurities are a real bitch. And boy, do they seem to make me one too.

I feel the car slow down, pulling me out of my internal argument.

"What are you doing?"

He pulls off to the side of the highway into a small driveway that leads to a pasture. The land is currently holding some very pretty, red cows and a rather picturesque windmill. He throws his car in park and turns his body to face me completely as he removes his sunglasses, setting them on top of his head.

"I mean, are we getting in the backseat or what because that's cool with me," I say excitedly, ignoring the tension.

If I ignore it, it won't exist. Right?

I don't love that it's broad daylight, but I guess he has seen it all before. I look up at him to give him a wink and pause my hand halfway to the door handle.

"Why... are you glaring at me?"

He's sitting there with his back against his door, arms crossed over his chest, and eyes narrowed. A very serious face for a very fun boy.

"Do not talk poorly about yourself Trystan Victoria Joann."

Whoa... Middle names. He's pissed.

"Uh excuse you," I say, crossing my own arms. "I am not your child, or *a* child for that matter. Don't talk to me like that."

"Then don't talk to yourself like that." He gives a jerk of his chin towards me.

"Jared, it's not a big deal." I settle my hands in my lap. "Or a secret that I've gained a million poun-"

"Trystan," he cuts me off. "I'm not kidding. Enough." His features soften but stay firm all at once. "You're beautiful."

"Well yeah, you ha-"

"No. No." He waves my words off. "I don't *have* to do anything."

His face lets the hardness fall entirely and he reaches across the center of the car, grabbing my hands in his. I turn my body to face him too, a little annoyed that he kept interrupting me but also a little embarrassed because *how seventeen can I be?*

Very, apparently.

"Jared, it's fine. I get it. I'm pretty, you love me. Can we go?"

I'm now incredibly uncomfortable with the atmosphere. I didn't say anything in a way to gain some compliments from Jared. The words just escaped my big fat mouth. I've always been self-conscious, not ever *loathing* myself but not ever fully loving myself, I suppose. The comments I have heard for as long as I can remember are always floating around my head. The ones from family to acquaintances, friends or even their parents, to classmates. It's always about how loud I am or how I need to chill. The ones about how big my calves are or how thick my eyebrows were before I started getting them waxed. How "extra" I am in every sense of the word. That kind of shit means something to a girl, at any age. But I guess the feeling of being not enough or being too much in the wrong ways—it has gotten worse recently. I don't know why.

Well, maybe I do.

He moves one hand to grab my chin and tilt my head up so I'm looking into his crystal blue eyes.

"It's not fine. You're incredible and I hate that you think you're not. You're brain, your heart, your humor, your body. Trystan, you hold more beauty in and out of you than I ever thought possible in one person. Why are you all of a sudden being so mean to yourself?"

I turn my head away and look down, completely embarrassed at this point. Still having nothing to say.

"Tell me this is not about what my mother said?" The way he asks tells me he knows the answer to that already.

"I think that would be lying," I say sadly, ducking my head even more.

"Tryst."

I don't look up at him or do much of anything, really. The embarrassment is double sided. On one side I am upset with myself for even letting her words eat at me the way that they do. And on the other... I hate that there is anything about me she feels that is unworthy for her son. I feel my eyes start to burn, my vision blurring slightly.

"Jesus... baby. Look at me."

I slowly look up at Jared now. Bless him and his beautiful determination. Jared has moved slightly, with one leg bent so his knee rests on the center console. His upper body is facing me fully and leaning forward, his face is hovering above the middle of the car. I mirror his position, getting closer to him. He has both of my hands in both of his. It's like his eyes are seeing right into my soul—his blue dancing with my brown.

"Listen to me, honey. And listen carefully and closely. Not because I won't say it again—because I will. I will say this every day, any day, always and forever. But listen closely because I need you to hear me." He gives me a small but genuine smile. "You... *You* are courageous. You are... I hate the word beautiful all of a sudden because it doesn't even come close to encompassing the full measure of beauty you hold. But until I Google it or create a new word for it, beautiful will have to hold. You are beautiful, Trystan. Inside and out. From the way your hair gets a little frizzy when it's supposed to rain. The way your cheek gets that little red mark right under the outer corner of your eye when you're getting upset. To the way you flick your middle nail under your thumb nail when you're anxious or being impatient or too far into your own head. The way you let your real, loud, gorgeous laugh out sometimes when it's not even that funny to anyone but you and then your cheeks turn red because you think you should be embarrassed by that wonderful sound—when really it is *actual* music to my ears. The he way your hips look in those jeans today, and your black yoga pants any other day. You are the only thing I see, ever. In my dreams. In my thoughts. Hell, sometimes when you're sitting right next to me, I still find myself thinking about you like I haven't seen you in days. You have me enraptured. You are the beginning and the end for me, Trystan. Every single part of you."

I open my mouth but quickly shut it again as Jared holds his hand up.

"Do not ever let the words of anyone, especially my awful mother, to ever allow doubt to creep into that wonderful brain of yours. I am unworthy of you—but I'll be damned if I ever let you go because of it. If that makes me selfish, then so be it. Knowing all of that only makes me want to work that much harder to deserve you. You are my world. Frizzy hair, red cheeks, beautiful soft tummy. All of you. I love every atom, every fiber, every freckle, every ounce of *you*."

"That's a lot to love," I say with a huff of a laugh as I try to digest so much kindness.

I attempt to rein in the few rogue tears that are making it past my wall. Even in front of a boy as loving and kind and patient as this one, I don't want to be seen as *overly emotional*.

Even though that's exactly what I am.

The tears don't go unnoticed, of course.

"Don't do that. Don't hide your tears or your flaws or your feelings from me. I'm here for it all, honey. Everything you are is everything I love. Even if I don't like it... In this moment 'it' being the wall you brick up on occasion. I love it regardless because it's a part of you. I wish for it to come down, but I love it all the same."

"You're wonderful and I'm the undeserving one Jared. I don't know what else to say to anything you just said except," I reach up to cup his cheek in my hand. "Thank you. I'll try to be kinder to myself."

We both lean in for a kiss. And then, in the brightest hour of the day, unashamed and madly in love, we joined every atom and flaw in the backseat of a Lincoln Continental and Jared showed me again how much he loves every single ounce of me.

Regardless of our slight detour Jared and I pulled up to the ranch right on time. Though, that didn't seem to stop the glare we received from Darla.

From far away she seems harmless. The extremely sun-tanned skin that is wrinkled from the rays, the short stature and seemingly calm, uncaring, demeanor. First glance and you think "what damage could she possibly cause?"

So much.

She's got on a pair of bootcut wranglers over a pair of scuffed up boots. A dark brown Carhartt zip-up hoodie over a simple gray shirt. Even though I can't see through the black sunglasses she's wearing, I can feel the unimpressed look she's giving us. Or maybe it's just for me. In the eight months Jared and I have been together I've been here a handful of times. It seems I have frequented it less and less with each passing month, but I think we all understand why.

It is a true bummer though. I love it here—minus the gut-wrenching tension flowing from his mother. The house is beautiful and quaint. The shops are large and filled with memories of years passed. Cattle chutes and random bits of weathered equipment are spread out amongst the vast land. The ground bounces between tall weeds and green grass and light brown dirt mixed with sand. The Badlands encase the entire thing.

The vibe is so strained as we walk up to the house. We don't go inside, instead hanging out on the front cement steps while we wait for Todd to come outside with orders for everyone.

Todd is Jared's stepdad and he's great. He's the typical rancher—tan and wrinkled. Short in height but big in hard work. Any time I have seen him, he is in skinny Wrangler jeans, worn boots, with a button up shirt and a cowboy hat that he has got to be decades old. Todd is kind and welcoming, quiet, and it always blows my mind that someone who makes everyone feel so good could be paired with someone who seems to hate every fiber of my being. Todd isn't a hugger, but when I see him I am always greeted with a genuine smile and a kind hello.

The most that is said as we stand with Darla is a simple, and less than enthused, hello. Jared is annoyed already and I do my best to not look mad. Kerry drove out here before we did. When he walks out of the house with Todd the tension lessens ever so slightly.

Things aren't awful with Kerry, this week at least, but I wouldn't call him my friend anymore.

"Here's the plan," Todd starts with a nod towards the boys after saying hi. "Jared and Kerry will take the four-wheelers and meet us at the gate. Mom and I will get in the side by side and follow. When we get there, Jared can get the gate open and we'll start wrangling the girls up to move 'em across the road. Questions?" He looks around the four of them, seeming to pass over me even though he said hello a minute ago.

I feel a twinge of disappointment. Jared gives me a sympathetic half glance and no one voices any concerns. With that, Todd nods once more and walks on, his boots kicking up dust as he goes. But as everyone disperses, I look at Jared whose focus is still on me with a look that you would see on someone watching a lost puppy flounder around on an abandoned street corner.

'Im sor-" he begins.

"What the-" I say at the same time.

He lets me go first, "I didn't think I'd be driving a four-wheeler by any means, but I didn't think I'd be sitting here at the house, waiting for you guys either I guess." Disappointment laced in every word. "You did tell them I would be here, right?"

"Yes," he assures me. "I don't know what's going on, but I'll go talk to Todd. He was happy to say yes to you helping. I think he is just used to it being the four of us. Hang on." He squeezes my hand before letting go and jogging after Todd.

I stand there, alone and sad, trying to not feel sorry for myself but finding it a bit difficult.

I wouldn't have come along if I had known I'd feel like I was unwelcome. That's why I don't usually come out here in the first place. And I don't want to think Todd ignored me intentionally... but man.

This sucks.

I could ride along or open gates or something. I'm not used to this kind of job but I'm a quick learner and I am definitely capable of following directions.

"I am not useless," I say to myself under my breath.

"Okay, so-"

"Ah!" I turn around with my hands to my chest. "Oh my gosh, Jared. You scared me."

He closes the distance between us and laughs an apology.

"So... Do I get to help? I don't want to be in the way-"

"You're not in the way. He just got busy in his head and unintentionally forgot to give you a job. But," he grabs my hand. "Since Kerry already left and there's only so many things to do..."

I take a step back, releasing his hand. "My job is nonexistent, isn't it?"

"You'll drive the pick-up." He looks down, avoiding my eyes, at the rocks he's pushing around with his feet. "And you'll just kind of hang back on the road and wait for us to move them." He finishes, with a quick glance at my face and then back to the ground again.

I'd avoid me too right now.

"So... I'll sit in a pick-up on the side of the road and... watch you guys move cows?" I ask, not even trying to hide the disappointment I'm feeling.

I don't need to tell him I am pissed—he knows. And maybe I don't have the right to be so upset? I don't know. But I do know that I am, in fact, incredibly upset.

I got up early for this.

I made the effort to get off of work for this.

I had been looking forward to this day for over a week, and not even just the moving cow's part. I wanted to be useful. To help Jared's family and to be included and involved in something that shows hard work and effort. That shows that *I* am capable and willing to do those things.

And instead—here I'll be... Sitting in a pick-up, alone, doing nothing but watching them work as a unit.

The sting of rejection hurts like a bitch.

And I just know it in my gut that Darla has something to do with my duties, or lack thereof.

That woman is small but powerful.

"Tryst... I'm sorry honey. I hate that you're bummed. I really got to go, though." He explains, looking around the lot.

He gestures to the four-wheeler and pick-up that we'll be in and on—separately. Everyone else is already gone, surely waiting for us down the road.

"Follow me and I'll show you where to hang out, okay?"

"Yeah, sure," I say quietly.

I'm pouting and I don't even care to hide it.

Jared grabs my hand and kisses my knuckles. "I'm sorry Trystan. We'll leave as soon as we're done and go do something fun. Won't even stay for supper." he says, his voice filled with hope.

I give him a placating smile in return. "It's okay. I understand."

Neither of us believe that.

He sets me up in the pick-up and he gets himself going on the four-wheeler. He gives me the Top Gun hand signal with his finger pointing up and swirls it around in a circle.

"Roll out, babe! Follow me!" He yells.

I let myself breathe out a small laugh. It isn't so much that I'm mad at Jared. I'm just bummed beyond repair. This day was supposed to be a step in a good direction. Instead, it ended up being another power move of Darla's to show me where my place is among them.

Obsolete.

So, no. I'm not mad at Jared. Darla though? Darla can pound sand today.

Still, the view of Jared straddling the four-wheeler in his jeans and sweatshirt he grabbed from the backseat of Stella, with a gray baseball cap he snagged from his brother and his shades pulled down over his eyes... Even if I had been mad at him, I wouldn't be anymore.

Holy smokes, does this pick-up have AC?

The next few hours are quite a bore for me—to no one's surprise. I had little cell phone reception while I waited around. I filled my time with listening to the FM radio, bouncing between a country station and a classic rock one. I played about twenty-one games of solitaire on my phone. By the time we were all back at the house and everything was put away and cleaned up, I was unhappily in a foul mood and prepared to sulk the whole way back to town.

Jared was hot and sweaty, even though the weather today had been lovely, so before we could do anything cool, we had to go back to his apartment so he could shower. I immediately changed out of my jeans that it turns out I didn't need to wear today, making my sour mood worse as I slid on my black leggings. Jared put on a different pair of jeans after he got out of the shower, these ones clean, and a heathered blue Hurley shirt.

"What do you want to do? Ice cream, a movie, dinner? Anything specific?" he asks as he walks over to where I'm at on the edge of his bed, a red towel in his hand drying his clean hair.

"I think I'm too crabby for a date. I kind of just want to go home," I say cautiously.

We had grabbed my car on the way back into town earlier and now I wish I would have just stayed home instead of following him here. The fifteen-minute drive alone did nothing to better my irritation.

"No, no. I'm sorry you're crabby but let's fix it." His eyes are wide as he throws the towel into a corner.

I sit on the edge of his bed, his navy-blue comforter serving as something to keep my fingers busy. We haven't talked much since leaving his parent's house—the drive to my house was quiet. He was tired and felt gross, I was pissed and in my feelings. Then we got to his place and he hopped in the shower.

"I know you're trying to be nice, but I'm honestly really irritated about today, and I don't want to fight with you so I'm going to go home. It's fine, Jared."

I move to get up, but he stops with me by gently pushing on my shoulders until I'm sitting again.

"No," he says firmly, standing in front of me. "Trystan. I know you're upset but I don't know what you want me to do about today other than fix tonight. I can't go back in time."

"I'm not asking you to," I say defensively.

He doesn't get it. And honestly, I'm glad he doesn't because I would hate if he understood how I'm feeling firsthand—if someone made him feel the way his mom makes me feel.

I throw my hands up in front of me in frustration. "No, I'm not fighting with you about this. Ugh!" I hang my head in my hands, elbows resting on my legs close to my knees. "I don't know why your mom hates me, Jared," I whisper.

I feel so defeated.

"Babe. She doesn-"

I snap my gaze to his. "Don't. Don't lie. She said five words to me today. Five. She didn't even look at me when she said half of them. She walked around me like I was carrying some sort of plague. I have never felt so dismissed and so unwelcome."

At this point if I don't leave, he's going to hear all of my feelings on this matter, and I am horribly afraid that it will be too much—for *both* of us.

It's as if there is a box in my brain. It's labeled "Things We Don't Let Out" and it's filed in chronological order. All of the slights and comments and looks. The feelings that arise in me with every one of them. The things I wish I could say to her but choose not to out of respect for Jared. It all sits in this thick cardboard box. A bronze name plate on the lid. A thick metal chain wrapped like an "X" around the whole thing. It screams "Don't open me, I'm messy" and so I leave it alone. Never going too far into my feelings to ever open it. Because if I did, if I said the things that I think about Darla... You can't take shit like that back.

I move to get up. Jared stops me, *again*, and gets on his knees to settle in between my legs. Grabbing my wrists, he gently holds them down on top of my legs, grounding me to him like jumper cables on a car battery. My head is still hanging low, and my eyes are stinging with unshed tears.

"I don't want to fight, Jared." My voice is barely a whisper at this point. "I don't want to fight."

"Baby. Look at me."

I shake my head.

"Trystan please. Tell me what all is going on in that beautiful head of yours."

I stay quiet.

"Don't open me," the box says.

"Please," he pleads.

Fuck it, I guess.

"I don't know. I just feel like... I don't know, Jared. My mom *loves* you and your mom can't even half-like me?"

After a minute of my silence Jared tells me, "Keep going. Talk to me. Please."

"I know I've said it before, and we've had this conversation but look at it long term Jare." The tears my eyes were holding start to break free. "If she hates me now, what will she be like in a couple years if we get a place together? Or when you propose? Or when we get married and have kids? Will she ever learn to just be nice? Or will it always be like it was today?" My eyes meet his finally. "I just sat in a pick-up for three hours and I'm still exhausted by how horrible she was to me. I didn't do anything wrong. I don't deserve this."

At this point the tears are sliding down my face and Jared's gaze is more concerned than I have ever seen.

"I can't expect you to choose me over your own mother... but gosh, Jared, I can't live my life hated by that woman for forever."

And I mean it. I can't be disliked by someone who is, and should be, infinitely important to the man I love.

A cough sounds from behind Jared and we both snap our eyes to the door.

"When you're done being a bitch about my mom, maybe you should think about how you treated her from the beginning and then you'd know why she hates you," Kerry says.

Out loud. He said that out loud.

At least he said it to my face this time.

Too stunned to speak I simply just stare at Kerry. I'm physically shaking at this point and Jared looks like he might actually kill his brother.

"Kerry if you don't shut th-"

"No. *You* shut up, Jared. How can you let this... *girl*," he spits out the word like it's disgusting and vile, "talk about your own mom like that? She's done everything for us and you just-"

"I'm sorry, what exactly did I do to her? Or is it to you that I offended?" I interject, genuinely curious now.

And also, incredibly furious.

"You know," he says pointedly, narrowing his dark blue eyes at me.

This boy was your friend a year ago. What is happening?

I jerk my head back like I have been slapped. "Clearly, I don't because I've been racking my brain for months and coming up with nothing, Kerry. Enlighten me."

I take the smallest step in front of Jared, both of us by his bed a good few yards away from Kerry. The three of us are all squared shoulders and wide stances. I may only be seventeen, Kerry a couple years older than Jared, but I am most definitely not afraid of this guy. Not in the slightest.

This grown man who runs to his *mommy* about the problems he has with his brother and his brother's girlfriend.

I might not love confrontation but that doesn't mean I'm not good at it.

"Speak your mind Kerry, you seem to have the answers. What's the problem?" I tilt my head to the side, inviting this fight. Heck—now I've got welcome, warm, open arms. A very much "bring it on", borderline unhinged sort of air about me.

Jared moves to my side and takes my hand while he puts his other one in the front pocket of his jeans. We both wait on Kerry.

"That day that you came to the softball lunch? You were invited by who?" Kerry asks with disdain.

Jared and I share a look of pure annoyance, him rolling his eyes and me trying to not laugh at the audacity.

"Me, Trystan. Me. *I* invited *you*. And who did you hang out with and end up going out with?"

Jared and I both are looking at Kerry like he has three heads at this point.

"Are you fucking kidding me?" Jared almost yells as he lets go of my hand and takes a step forward. "Kerry you can't be serious! We *all* hung out last summer! We were both friends with her."

"So, because I'm dating your brother and not you, your mother has an issue with me?"

"Well, she didn't appreciate how you acted that day." It's the way he's saying all of this... As though it's something he's been working on since September. Like, his plan to ruin things is coming to a head. But I won't let him win. Not this.

"She didn't or *you* didn't?" I ask, crossing my arms in front of me.

"Both." Kerry crosses his arms back.

"You can't seriously be telling me that you and your mother were, and are, pissed at me for having a crush, that wasn't a secret at all mind you, for months, and then acting on that crush when you, my supposed *friend*, invited me to a family and *friends* lunch? Did you ever ask me out and I missed it, Kerry? Did I ever give you any indication that I wanted to be more than friends with you? Did I sneak around and hide the feelings I had for Jared?"

"No but-"

"No, no." I wave my index finger at Kerry. "You don't get to have any 'buts' in this conversation. Are you telling me that for nine fucking months your grown mother and your own grown ass have been talking shit behind my back about how much of a *fat whore* you think I am for dating your brother?!"

I have moved on from pissed and settled into a very heavy outrage. I feel desperately angry and just absolutely exhausted. So much so that I've unknowingly put myself less than a yard from Kerry, my feet having carried me here without my direct knowledge, and Jared has wrapped an arm around my waist to prevent me from closing the distance further.

These people have no idea how reined in I keep my crazy apparently.

To Kerry's credit he doesn't so much as shift or flinch.

That annoys me even more.

"I'm telling you that what you did hurt me, and that my mom knows that and agrees with me on it."

"Of course, she does, you fucking baby!" Jared yells from right behind me. "Get out of my room Kerry. Now. And do not ever call my girlfriend a bitch again. Don't think I didn't hear that earlier. Jealousy is unbecoming. Tell *your* mother to mind her business."

Jared pushes his way in front of me, positioning himself between his brother and me.

Fair.

"I'll tell *our* mother that your little *girlfriend*," he spits, "has been spending the night here and we'll see how that goes for you since mom pays half our rent Jared."

What??

"Fuck you, Kerry."

"Fuck both of you."

And with that Kerry walks out, slamming the door to Jared's room behind him. I step back until my knees hit the bed. Jared's pacing the room with his hands locked behind his neck, his breathing erratic.

I still can't believe that just happened.

"Your adult brother and grown mother," I seem to not be able to move past the fact that two above-eighteen individuals have been doing this, "have been having gossip sessions about us, about me, for the entirety of our relationship."

Jared continues pacing.

"Jared," I say, needing him to focus.

He's refusing to even look at me at this point, his eyes open wide and a light sheen of sweat now on his forehead.

"Jared!" I say a little louder.

Still nothing from him. It's as if his brain has shut off all functions pertaining to anything outside of itself.

"JARED!" I yell from the bed.

That got his attention.

"I'll figure this out. It's-it's fine. It won't stay a problem." He doesn't look like he believes that any more than I do but the pain in his eyes is hitting me square in my chest.

I get up and walk to him, placing my hands on his sides to pull him to me. He unlocks his fingers from behind his head and brings them up to cup my cheeks. We stay there like that, looking each other in the eyes like we'll find the answers behind them somewhere—just searching for what to do next.

Because sure we don't *need* his mom's permission to date. We don't *need* her approval of us or me or this love between us.

But are we okay with that?

I don't know that I am.

"I'll fix this," he whispers.

"I know." It's all I can say to not restart his panic. But we can both taste the lies on our tongues.

Our foreheads meet and while I know in my heart that he will try his hardest to fix this, whatever *this* is, I also know in my heart that it won't be without a whole lot of hurt. And for some reason I don't think I'll be the one untouched by that hurt.

And I *really* don't believe that Jared won't be damaged in the process too.

But I'll be damned if a cranky toddler of a man and a mean girl of a woman take the "try" out of my heart. Not without a fight.

CHAPTER ELEVEN.

School is out for the summer, my junior year having come to an end. My time is now split between working more and seeing Jared more. It helps that the scheduling manager likes me and Jared—scheduling us together on a regular basis.

I knew I'm likable.

We keep our hands and lips to ourselves—mostly. I took a low-on-the-pole management position recently, so our breaks now are one after the other. But we make do. Lucky for us, we are not running short on time spent together these days, so I don't complain.

Much.

"Oh, there you are, sweet boyfriend of mine," I say, batting my lashes at him as I exit the door at the back of the store.

It's beautiful out today. A little warm for my personal preference, but lovely. Jared looks up with a smile on his face from the bench he's sitting on while he takes a drag of the cigarette he's smoking. His turquoise work-shirt seems so bright in front of the red wall behind him. The small break area we are in has a bench on one side of the red paneled fence structure that keeps this area private. A couple giant dumpsters block the view from the parking lot. It's a nice reprieve from the noise of inside, and a breath of fresh air—well, on the pleasant-weather days.

"Would you like one?" he asks, offering me the pack.

"Sure, thank you."

It's a nasty habit, I'm aware. But here we are.

He lights my cigarette for me, as he usually does, before handing it to me as I sit next to him. I bring it to my lips, inhaling the minty nicotine, and when I peek at Jared from the side, I notice he's still smiling at me.

"What are you smirking at me for?"

"I just really am so lucky Trystan." He leans in for a kiss. "Thank you."

"For what?" I scoff.

My bright fuchsia shirt looks almost intentional next to Jared's blue today. Like we planned to coordinate nicely with each other.

"For loving me." He gives me a sad kind of smile that doesn't reach his eyes.

We both look forward again, knowing he doesn't want any sort of deep conversation taking place at work. Where I would love nothing more than to dissect and analyze every letter that he speaks... Jared much prefers not doing any of that.

"We have tomorrow off!" I exclaim around my cigarette dangling from my lips while I unnecessarily fix the thick ponytail on the back of my head—just to have something to do. "Let's go for a cruise. Spend the day in the car and have lunch somewhere in the Hills."

"That sounds perfect. I've gotta get back inside."

Jared kisses the top of my head, lingering there just a little longer than normal. He's had a weird couple of weeks.

Okay—months.

We have been good, Jared and I. Random, and small spats here and there. Usually due to one of us being tired and crabby and overreacting to something small.

Okay, that's usually me.

But his brother has started acting super weird around him and I again when we're together at their apartment. The feelings from the fight last month seem to be lingering for all parties involved.

I've definitely backed off on the sleepovers. Not that they ever got to a place that was inappropriate, but it was a point of contention amongst them—or rather *us*, so to try and avoid causing more issues Jared and I decided to lessen them nonetheless. Not completely, though. We are both *almost* adults, and his brother can get bent if he thinks he can whine enough to dictate our lives entirely. In the same breath though, I don't want to be the cause of every argument or on a regular basis... So, bending on some things is something I will suck up doing.

I haven't seen his mother much—not since they moved cows. She showed up, unannounced might I add, to Jared and Kerry's apartment with random bags of groceries a week or so ago. Outsider looking in—sure, that's fucking nice. Insider's point of view?

Can you spell "manipulation"?

It's like she thinks doing things unexpectedly—like buying groceries or cleaning their carpets, which she did a few days ago, gives her the right to literally just walk in. No knocking or calling or even a text announcing her arrival. Maybe it's just me but I find it to be incredibly disrespectful. I keep that opinion to myself. Or I try to. My face gives me away like eighty-nine percent of the time.

I know she is their mom and, while Jared never confirmed it and I absolutely did not ask, might be paying some of their rent... To not even knock before entering their home?

It's weird, right?

I'm spending the night at Jared's apartment tonight. It makes sense since we're leaving first thing for our adventure day-date. Kerry has locked himself away in his room, which is his normal now, so I'm not concerned about anything going wrong in the moment. He usually waits a few days to weeks before throwing a fit. I'm making spaghetti for the three of us, an attempt to mend bridges or whatever, so I'm currently standing in their kitchen working on the sauce while the garlic bread bakes in the oven. I've got a pot of boiling water and noodles going on a front burner with a saucepan on the burner next to it. The smell of the garlic and parsley and parmesan emanating from the oven is making my stomach grumble.

As I set the wooden spoon on to the glassy, black stovetop, keeping the half-moon shape of sauce in one spot on the paper towel I put there, I feel a set of strong arms wrap around my waist and my breath catches like it does when he's near.

"I can't decide which smells better. You," Jared says into my neck, "or the garlic bread." He takes a big inhale, his exhale tickling me.

"Well, I would say I hope it's me, but I love garlic bread more than myself I think, so I'm going with the bread."

He leans the side of his head against the side of mine, resting his chin on my shoulder. "I love this song."

I've got the 90's Country playlist playing on Pandora over a bright yellow Bluetooth speaker that always sits on the top of their silver fridge. Currently *Rope the Moon* by John Michael Montgomery is playing.

Jared starts to sway with the music, in turn making me sway with him. Eventually, he grabs the spoon I had picked back up to stir the sauce out of my hand and sets in on the counter.

"Hey!" I object. "The paper towel to hold the messy spoon is ov-"

Jared spins me around by my elbow to face him, stopping my protest mid word. He grabs one of my hands with his and places his other one on my lower back. My free hand settles on his chest, and we find the rhythm together. We stay quiet, soaking in the words and the music. Each other.

As the song comes to an end, I lift my head off of his chest and look up to find his eyes already on me—like they seem to always be. I quietly look away, laying my head back on his chest. The song has switched to *Friends in Low Places* by Garth Brooks, but our pace stays slow and steady.

"Why are you still staring at the top of my head?" I mumble into Jared's shirt.

"Maybe I found some gray hair."

"What?!" I freeze.

He laughs as he forces my body back into a swaying rhythm.

"Trystan," he whispers into my hair, his tone changing completely from the joking one it was a moment ago.

My heart stutters. I noticed at work earlier that his vibe was just kind of *off*. He's still being kind of weird tonight, not grumpy or mean. More like... sad? Somber? We haven't talked much since we got here—he's been cleaning and I've been cooking.

After a moment of waiting for him to continue I look up at him.

His hair is a little longer than usual—he mentioned needing a haircut soon and I make a mental note to remind him on his next day off. His eyes seem heavy tonight. Weighed down. Perhaps it's his black T-shirt and gray sweatpants that are dimming his usual light.

"Jared? Are you okay?"

He shakes his head like he's trying to shake a thought free.

"I'm fine. Sorry, I just," he lets loose a breath. "I just love you. And I love this—you cooking, me cleaning. You're so special to me."

"Not going to lie. You're kind of freaking me out," I reply, . "But I love you too. And also, the bread is going to burn so we've got to break a part, at least momentarily."

A soft laugh escapes him as we take a step away from each other. He's looking at me like... Like we're the only two people in this space. Not just in this room—but in this very moment. Like we're alone entirely. No bread in the oven or counters littered with random pieces of mail. No crabby brother a few yards away, probably pouting behind his white door. He's looking at me like it's just him and me in this weird little void of space and time.

Jared leans down and kisses my forehead, then my nose, then my mouth. And without another word we let go of each other completely. He moves to grab the pan out of the oven with a green oven mitt and I finish putting the rest of supper together. He knocks on Kerry's door and let's him know the food is ready. Kerry grumbles a thank you as he takes it into his room. Neither of us bring up whatever dark cloud is currently looming over us for the rest of the evening.

Jared must have woken up quite a while ago because his spot on the bed is now cold. I'm totally seizing the opportunity for more space and a cool spot on the bed, having now spread out like a bed hog. I move to grab my phone and glance to the door and give out a little shriek.

"Jared! You scared me!" I say with a hand to my now rapidly beating heart. "What are you doing just standing there like a little weirdo watching me?"

He's in the door frame, all tan and tall and handsome, his hair a little damp and ruffled. He has his head and shoulder resting against the frame with his arms crossed against his chest and legs crossed at his ankles. He's already dressed and ready to go for today—light blue jeans and a white T-shirt from Old Navy.

"You talk in your sleep. Did you know that?" He is also wearing an incredibly ornery and unfairly attractive smirk.

Oh no.

My cheeks warm a bit. "Yes..." I admit. "I'm aware. I didn't say anything weird, did I?"

"You didn't *say* anything weird."

Relief washes over me but I see his smile turn a bit wicked. My relief is short lived.

"But you did scream 'fuck you' at the top of your lungs at like two-thirty this morning," he says through a laugh.

My eyes widen and I run my hands down my face.

"No... I didn't..." I say wishfully.

He pushes off the door frame and takes a step towards me.

"You absolutely did."

Another step, his hands now in his pockets with his thumbs out. He's a picture of cool, calm, and collected—as if I am not melting into his bed from embarrassment.

"Kerry came rushing in a minute later to check on you. We had a good laugh while you just laid there—peaceful once more. Blissfully unaware of the near heart attack you gave me."

I pull the blue covers over my head now. I've always had little bouts of chatter in my sleep—so claims my mother. But until now it's been just me in the bed while it happens. Just my mom or other family members to bear witness of it from halfway across the house. Easily debunked and wholly denied on my part.

Until now, apparently.

I feel the bed dip down.

"But, it's okay," I hear from outside of the comforter-cave I've made. "I haven't laughed with my brother like that in a while. So really, I should say thank you."

Jared is now towering over me on his hands and knees, completely caging me in. I pull the covers down to just below my nose to look at him—trying to gauge his next move.

"So, thank you," he says with an even bigger smile.

Jared plops a kiss to my exposed nose, nudging the blanket down further and kissing my lips next. Before I have the chance to say a single word, he's got me laughing and screaming at him to stop tickling me. We laugh and laugh, cuddling for a few moments when he relents.

The two of us do some little spot cleaning after I get dressed, getting ready to be gone for the whole day.

"Let's run through Black Hills Coffee for breakfast?" I suggest as we buckle our seatbelts.

"Definitely."

He's glowing today—his usual light shining like a beacon to my soul. I hum happily to myself at the calm air in the car.

"I love you," I say as he pulls his car onto the main road.

It's beautiful today. Sunny, a warm seventy-four degrees already at 8:30 in the morning. Blue skies and a nice calm breeze.

"I love you too, honey."

I hold his hand the entire day—so thankful for him and this chance at love.

So grateful for the laughter Jared got to share with Kerry, even if it was at my expense.

Thankful for Jared.

CHAPTER TWELVE.

eight months later.

LATE WINTER 2011.

The February weather in South Dakota is dicey at best. You really do need to plan for all four seasons in one day. Honestly, every month in the Midwest is incredibly unsure at any given moment.

Today for example. Before I left for school, more than halfway through my senior year now, I grabbed a sweatshirt and a jacket to go over my T-shirt. Black yoga pants continue to be my pants of choice these days, regardless of the time of year, as are my sandals. My dark hair had started the day flowing down my back, frizzy and crazy but doable. However, now that it is after noon and the school's HVAC system is just as confused by the weather as we are, it is sweltering in this library and my free period is becoming absolutely miserable. So, my thick mop of hair is now not-so-neatly placed atop my head in what my mom calls a 'crazy person bun'.

As I sit here attempting to do some homework despite the heat, I keep finding myself lost in thought. Looking at me you would think I am just blankly staring at the wall of gray desktop computers and matching keyboards on top of the white countertop. Three of the black rolling armchairs are occupied by students doing, what I assume, is homework.

In reality, I'm not seeing any of that. My eyes might as well be shut off at the moment—my brain lost in thought.

Thoughts about Jared.

Jared and I have been together for about a year and a half now, and while it has had its downs—the highs far outweigh the lows.

He got a new job doing administrative work for the business his mom opened this winter. It's a cleaning business—residential and commercial. It seems to be doing quite well, though I steer clear of getting too involved where Darla is concerned anymore. I would be lying if I said I was one-hundred percent in love with Jared working for Darla, working closely with Kerry who holds the same position as he does. It seems to be just one more thing for her to control and for Kerry to report back to her on. But I don't say any of that.

Things with Kerry have been rather stable the last nine months or so. That chunk of time hasn't gone without some unenjoyable moments, though.

On New Year's Day for example, reining in Two Thousand and Eleven, Jared and I had plans to spend it at his place. We were going to cook and watch some movies and probably not make it to midnight, but we were going to give it our best shot. A nice night in, out of the snow and away from noise. Instead, what we actually ended up doing was putting together furniture in the new office Darla had acquired.

With Kerry and Darla.

I don't think either of them were too pleased when I strolled in through the door trailing behind Jared. Both of us covered in snowflakes and huffing warm air into our cold hands, laughing as we turned to face the other and wipe melting snow off of each other's faces. You would think that they would have been *happy* to have an extra pair of hands to assist. The glares and silent treatment told a different story—they were undeniably unimpressed. But I did what I could to be helpful and pleasant and at the end of the day that says more about me than her.

That's what my mom said at least.

Now it is February and I've got about three months left of high school. The senioritis is real. The itch to be done and out of here and have even a shred more of freedom is insane. My plan, so far, is to continue working at McDonald's for the time being. I don't have any idea on what I want to be when I grow up—or where I want to be. My only true, tangible goal...

Happiness.

Prom is coming up quickly and Jared and I discussed it briefly a few weeks ago but he got really weird and cagey during the conversation. I dropped it and haven't brought it up since. Tonight, we are going on a little date and I'm planning on bringing it up then. I don't know if he feels out of place now that he is almost twenty or if it's something else. I can understand if he doesn't want to go to a dance with a bunch of teenagers again. I just don't get the feeling that it's that simple.

I'm sitting with my mom in the living room waiting for Jared to pick me up for supper.

"Where are you guys going out to eat at?" my mom asks me.

She's currently watching Rachel Ray on the Food Network. She's got on a pair of light blue jeans today and a Minnesota Twins T-shirt. Even though she will take mental notes on the Dutch oven pot roast recipe Rachel is working on right now, we both know she won't be putting the knowledge to use. She's more of a crockpot or spaghetti kind of gal, my mom. And I love her for it.

"I think we are going to Olive Garden tonight. I didn't ask when we talked earlier," I respond from the other end of the couch. My freshly highlighted hair is pulled up into a less-messy-than-usual bun and I opted for comfort over cute tonight, as though that is anything new. It's not. My leggings and a nice, loose army green long sleeve shirt are quite the staple 'fit these days.

She nods, eyes still on the tv. "What movie will you guys see? How to Train Your Dragon looks cute."

Her eyes land on mine as I roll them.

"Yes mother, we will go see a cartoon. On a date." I laugh as she rolls her eyes back at me, being a child just to be one because we absolutely *would* go see a cartoon if it looked good. "No, we are going to see Shutter Island."

"Oh, gotta love Leo."

"Amen to that, ma."

A moment later Jared is knocking while opening the front door, like he always does at this point. He heads straight to my mom to say hi to her first, also like he always does.

"Hey Tracy!" he says with his big, infectious grin. "Where's Mikey?"

Before my mom can answer Michael is bounding down the hallway and into Jared's open arms. Mike has grown what feels like a full five feet in the last few months and I can't help but wonder silently about what will happen when he is too big to jump into Jared's arms like this.

Who am I kidding? My sweet baby brother will be thirty and still lunging into almost forty-five-year-old Jared's arms like he does now. Whether Jared will be able to hold his ground like he does currently... that will be a different story.

"Okay, okay. Let the man breathe, Mikey," I say, ready to get out of here and get going.

It isn't like I haven't seen Jared lately. With him working his new job now, us no longer working together, I don't see him as much I was used to.

I just miss him.

"I'll bring you back some of that bread you like from Olive Garden, Tracy." He throws my mom another grin over his shoulder as he grabs my hand, pulling me out the door.

"You look beautiful tonight, babe." Jared spins me around in front of his car before bringing me in for a kiss.

"Can we go to prom?" I blurt out.

That... was not how I wanted to ask that.

I am met with silence and guilt-filled blue eyes. I take a step back and towards the passenger door of his car, waving my hand in the air like it can erase the tension that question caused.

Or the tears lining my eyes.

"Never mind! It's totally fine. We don't need to go." My voice cracks.

"Babe, get in and we will talk about it, okay?" he says as he goes around me and opens my door.

I don't look at him from my seat as we pull out of the driveway and head down the street. I watch as the houses go by, the neighborhood kids play in their driveways, the dads washing their vehicles. I expected him to say no, to not want to go. And I don't mean to act like a disappointed brat but... senior prom? If he can't go, I don't know that I WANT to go. Well, yes I do know. I don't want to go without him.

Jared takes my hand and rests both his and mine on my leg.

"Listen, Try-"

"Jare, if you-"

We look at each other, both wearing sad smiles. I look away first, giving him the go ahead.

"Tryst, I can't afford prom this year," he rushes out.

The way he said that has my heart breaking. And not because we aren't going to prom. He sounds so... embarrassed. He should never feel that way around me. And now I hate myself for making him feel bad when I'm sure he's felt bad just enough on his own.

I shove my feelings aside and try to be reassuring. "It's okay, Jare. We don't need to go."

Because it *is* okay. He is an adult with adult bills and an adult job and a not-adult-yet girlfriend.

"I should have thought about that. I'm sorry I even asked. It's okay, really. We went last year, and I only talk to like two people at my school anyways at this point. I don't need to go this year."

And I really mean it. I wanted to go with Jared, for *us*. Another memory for us to share.

"I'm so sorry, Trystan. With my car and the apartment and my mom being-" he cuts himself off. "Well, never mind about her but I just can't swing it and I'm sorry."

His eyes are so sad as he looks at me, the guilt there is evident.

I squeeze his hand in mine. "Jared, it really is okay. I'm fine with not going. Truly." I hope he believes me because I really do mean it. And now I am more interested in something else he almost didn't say. "But what were you going to say about your mom?" I ask as carefully as possible.

"It's nothing, she's just being... watchful."

"Like, she's watching you?" I try to keep the judgment and annoyance clear from my voice.

Tread carefully, Tryst.

He gives a slow nod. "Yeah, I guess. Watching me. Watching how I'm spending my money."

"Why would she think she needs to do that?"

Jared shrugs slightly before answering me. "I think Kerry is talking about me to her again. Or still. About the TV in my room or the new bedroom set I got. I don't know, really. My shit is getting paid, so I don't know what difference it makes to her. I just don't want to add fuel to the fire so I'm choosing to be more mindful I guess about the things I'm doing that might get back to her."

I reply with a small nod, facing forward and dropping it. For now. It isn't *really* my business—his finances. And I don't trust his mom's opinion on anything at all at this point, I keep that to myself though. Darla is his mom—I try to stay respectful when it comes to my thoughts and feelings about things that don't necessarily affect me.

Our moods are lighter by the time we sit down to eat. Supper was perfect and the mind-mess of a movie afterwards was a wild ride, distracting us both wholly. Jared and I are sitting in his car down the block from my parents' house, kissing a little before he finishes dropping me off.

"I could get in my car and meet you at your house, stay the night if you want?" I suggest, batting my lashes a little extra.

Jared runs a hand through his hair as he sits back in his seat.

"I would love that, really," his tone carrying a hint of apology. He turns his head to look at me as I smooth down my hair and check my face in the visor mirror. "But my mom is coming over first thing in the morning for one of her cleaning sprees." He finishes his sentence with an eye roll.

"No worries, we have all weekend to hang out," I say with as little disappointment in my tone as I can manage.

"I'm sorry she keeps getting in the way of things," he says solemnly.

I take his hand in mine and turn my body to face him, resting my knee against the center console. "It's okay, Jare. We have forever."

"And always."

He brings the back of my hand to his mouth and kisses it as he finishes the drive to my house. When he walks away from my front door and waves one last time, I can't help but find myself feeling a little extra bitterness towards Darla tonight.

I also can't help but question if Jared is keeping something from me.

Again.

CHAPTER THIRTEEN.

SUMMER 2011.

I graduated today.

I.

Graduated.

Today.

Gosh, I have been wanting to be done with high school since I was fourteen. From the beginning—I was ready to be done. And now I finally am. It's a blissful relief.

My parents, Mikey, and Jared all sat together in a spot where I could find them easily. Beth couldn't make it, she's visiting her grandparents in North Dakota. I held my tears at bay until I looked up and made eye contact with my mom. Then I totally lost it, sniveling and crying like a damn baby.

Why?

I have no idea.

Emotions run high in times of change, I suppose.

Today was an extra special ocassion, so it called for an extra special outfit. I got some new jeans that look almost exactly like every other pair I have ever owned—dark blue, flared at the ankle, tight on my butt. My top is a beautiful and unlike my typical style—navy-blue baby-doll style shirt. Puffy and sheer sleeves that hit three quarters the way down my arm, with little pink flowers scattered all over it. I got some super cute blue wedge heals to wear, and I straightened my hair that is currently a nice shade of chocolate brown with pops of golden highlights throughout. The event of today plus the way I feel about how I look... I've never felt so damn good.

I don't wear heeled shoes. Ever. That was made very clear to myself and everyone else in the event center that housed the graduation ceremony when I tripped as I made my way to the stage while names were being called.

Mortified.

Very much a Lizzie McGuire meets Gracie Lou Freebush moment.

Pictures were taken after everything was said and done and then my family, Jared and I all went out to Applebee's for supper followed by Armadillos Ice Cream Shoppe for dessert.

It was the perfect day.

Until it wasn't.

The plan, for *weeks*, was that after the ceremony and the photos and the supper and celebration, merriment commencing complete—I would go to Jared's and stay the night.

Standard.

Normal.

Typical for an eighteen-year-old girl and an almost twenty-year-old boyfriend who has his own place. That's what one would think. Right?

Wrong.

Kerry was in a mood today. A mood that I, for one, have never seen on him. Which says something considering the arguments I have witnessed and been a part of over the last year and a half. Even the summer before while we were friends and hung out all the time, I saw plenty of his moods then.

Today though... He was volatile. Borderline threatening. And that was all before we even got to their apartment. It got so bad through texting that Jared told me to stay in the car when we eventually did arrive at their place. And so I did, respecting the fact that they are family and I'm not.

I don't have a clue what Kerry was so bent out of shape over. But the next thing I know, Jared is slamming the front door just to have Kerry throw it open again. Jared isn't halfway to his car before he turns back around and I sit there, windows up, listening to them scream at each other.

If I could have sunk down into my seat any further, I would have become one with the fake leather.

What I gathered from their screaming match was that Kerry is tired of me being there, using their "resources" as he said, when I don't live there or pay rent. It is "their" apartment, not mine. And "how dare" I continue to stay over when Kerry and Darla both have made it clear that it is inappropriate, in their unstable minds.

Jared came to my defense the entire time, bless him. Pointing out that I buy groceries. I clean the apartment. I don't invade Kerry's space. I don't leave anything laying around or take advantage of anything they provide.

None of it mattered to Kerry, though. He didn't bat an eye as his gaze landed on me, sobbing in the car. That might have hurt worse than any of the words he has spewed—the way he looked through me like I was nothing and no one.

I am still in tears, just totally shaken and shaking, by the time a very pissed off Jared gets in his car. He slams his door and runs his fingers through his hair, pulling at the stands. And from the disheveled state of it, I would wager to bet that this isn't the first, or even twelfth time, he's done so with those gorgeous brown locks.

"Jared?" I ask incredibly cautiously and quietly.

His eyes meet mine and I don't find the bright, vibrant color I had looked into not two hours ago. His eyes change with his mood, I've noticed. And the color of clothes he wears. Right now, staring back at me with a look that lands somewhere between heartbroken and begging, they're this sort of sad blue. The kind of deep, dark blue you'd find in the deepest parts of an ocean. A place that isn't ventured and visited by even the bravest of creatures.

"Jare..." I say again as I reach for his arm, squeezing just below his elbow. Not in question, but in comfort.

Jared says nothing to me as he puts his car in reverse and pulls out of their driveway. We quickly leave the cul-de-sac with no plans, no music to aid the discomfort. After a few moments of silence, both of us going through our own feelings and thoughts, Jared parks on top of Skyline Road and takes the biggest breath his lungs can handle.

The view in front of us is one we have seen together a million times. A brick wall that sits three feet high and is comprised of various shades of brown and tan and gray stones is what separates a hill side and this parking lot. Beyond it is the city. It's still light out but when the sun goes down, it's all building silhouettes and streetlights from up here. Headlights and nightlife flash in the dark at night. This is one of our favorite spots to end up at after a leisurely drive around town, or in the middle of a beautiful day with nothing to do.

Or after a horrific fight with a crazy person.

"This has got to be the loudest silence like, ever," I say lightly, still not looking at the man to my left. "We should look into some sort of Guinness record or something."

After Jared's continued silence, making me more nervous than anything, I work up the courage to look at him. I turn my head and find that he's already looking at me. His knuckles are no longer white like they were while he drove us here. His breathing has levelled out a little bit, it seems. But his eyes... The slight line of tears threaten to crush me entirely.

My heart is breaking for this boy that I love.

I stay quiet, knowing he needs to find the words himself without being rushed.

I need him to find those words quick though.

"Trystan." He reaches over, brushing away the rogue tear from my own cheek. I lean into his touch, closing my eyes.

"How do you feel about camping out in your car tonight?" I can't help but want to lighten this mood—this dark cloud.

Storm Kerry. That is what I will call this mess.

We both lean forward, pulled towards each other. Our foreheads meet above the center console and our fingers lace together.

"Which parking lot should we set up camp at?" he asks, doing his best too.

A small bit of hope ignites in his eyes and I promise to do my best to keep it there. But, after trying and failing to be okay with sleeping in a car in a Walmart parking lot on the night that I graduated high school... I finally call my mom.

I feel so overwhelmingly defeated. Almost *lost* in a way. And while I would like to believe I can tough it out and just deal with this uncomfortable sleeping situation—it turns out I am a wimp.

"Trystan? Are you okay?" Her voice is pure panic and sleep.

I should have texted her or called Craig first.

"I'm fine, mom. Nothing is wrong. But listen... and don't freak out, okay?"

She is going to be so pissed. And not at me or Jared.

"Well, now I am freaking out! What is going on?!"

I give her the story, leaving out some of the details that would tempt the woman to drive her angry ass to Darla's or Kerry's houses. When I finish relaying the events, she lets out such a defeated sigh, joining me in the discomfort. She hates this for me, I know. But she also really hates this for Jared. Her family growing up wasn't picturesque. She has a soft spot for him, and his life, and the struggles that come with having a family that can make it all a bit tough.

"Come home. Both of you," she says, quickly adding, "He is sleeping on the couch, Trystan. I don't need Mike asking questions in the morning."

I can almost hear her run her hand down her face.

Same, mom.

After spending the night in the same basement, but not the same room, I wake to find Jared already awake and upstairs talking to my mom. I try to sneak up quietly so I can eavesdrop.

No shame in my game.

But, alas, the noisy stairs give me away.

"Just come up all the way, dear. We know you're there."

I make my way the rest of the way up the stairs. As I round the corner I find Jared, his bright blue shirt and gray sweatpants that he grabbed in a hurry last night while Kerry screamed at him, looking extra cute. My mom with her green slicky pants and gray sweatshirt make me huff a sigh of bother. They are both sitting comfortably at the kitchen table, two pals. Steam wafts up from the coffee mugs in front of each of them and a pink box of donuts is plopped in the middle of the table.

"Craig must have got up early and grabbed donuts?" I ask no one in particular as I take an open seat opposite Jared.

My nods and Jared sips his coffee before saying, "Your mom and I were just talking about yesterday. You and I need to maybe talk some more, I know. But for the day, can we just be two happy people and go on a day-date?"

The hope in his still-sad eyes give me only one choice.

"I love a good day-date," I answer, reaching inside the box for a maple bacon donut.

His smile tells me how much he needs calm today.

So, calm he shall get.

Even if I am a raging pool of fire on the inside over yesterday's bull shit.

After a long day on the road going through the hills and stopping at any and every shop that we could find, we are both a few dollars lighter and a few random trinkets richer.

Kerry is out of the house for the day, some sort of bike marathon that has been on their kitchen calendar for months. With that being so, we both felt comfortable coming to Jared's place to rest for a bit before he takes me home.

We are currently sitting shoulder to shoulder with our legs out, our backs leaned up against his dark walnut headboard. 8 Seconds is playing on his television, one of his favorite movies. We have open packages of various fudge, taffy, and roasted nuts spread out around us.

"I did a project for school on the poem Cody Lambert wrote. *Cowboy Is His Name,*" Jared says as the poem is recited in the movie.

I nod my head while I set my water on the table next to me. It's not that I don't care. I do. And it's also not like I haven't tried all day to not bring up yesterday or blow my fuse finally. But after a day of small talk and ignoring the heavy feeling that is nearly choking me...

"Jare..." I say carefully. "Can we talk about yesterday? Please."

Today has been lovely, really. But not having spoken about the fight he had with his brother and the way things seem to not be progressing in a positive way on that front, I can't keep pretending there isn't a dysfunctional elephant sitting in the middle of this apartment.

With the heaviest sigh and a sag of his shoulders, Jared reaches for the remote and mutes the movie. We both go about closing up snacks and moving them out of our way, repositioning ourselves so that we are facing each other, legs crossed and knees touching. His hands clasped together with his elbows resting near his knees. My hands are pressed together between where my legs cross in an effort to keep me from fidgeting too much.

We both sit there for a moment, just looking at each other. This isn't my story, not really. It's not my family, though someday I have plans for them to be. But regardless, I wait for Jared to start and when he does... my heart breaks.

"My brother and mom are unhappy with the state of my life apparently. They don't appreciate how much you're here. They don't like what I spend my money on. They don't think I help enough outside of the job duties I signed on for. They both think I'm wasting my life and that you are the reason for why I am living it the way I am."

I feel like I have physically been struck. Kerry himself could have just walked in and thrown the wheel of his stupid bicycle at my face for all I know. I feel myself actually sway with every word out of Jared's mouth as he says them.

Blow by blow, I am stunned into silence.

Which is new for me.

I don't know when I started crying. Was it immediately? Have I been crying for long? Which part got to me? I do know, though, that we are all *very* lucky that Kerry is not within these apartment walls right now.

Finally, after trying and failing to calm the beast, the words come to me. I don't know that they are really the *right* words, but they're what I go with anyways.

"How fucking dare they?" I seethe. "Jared. How. Dare. They." I get up off of his bed to pace around his room like a mad woman. Which I am. "Seriously! Where do they get the audacity from? Why is any of that any of their concern? Are you not doing your job? Are you not living up to what is expected of you per your *real* job description? Have you been reckless? Are *we* being reckless? Am I so fucking horrible that they can't just be happy for you that you're happy?" With each question asked the volume of my voice raises.

And with each question, rhetorical and not, Jared just... sits there. He looks like a statue with how still he is. Fragile, though.

I abruptly stop my frantic walking and spin to look at him.

"You *are* happy, aren't you?" I ask barely above a whisper.

And then my brain floods with everything that could be wrong.

What if I am wrong about everything?

What if, even though I am blissfully in love and happy and hopeful of a beautiful future with this incredible man sitting in front of me, Jared *is* unhappy and doesn't know how to break up with me or end this relationship without some crazy consequences that he thinks might happen?

What if his mom and brother see something I don't see, and they can tell he's miserable and they're only trying to better his situation by putting issues between us?

Okay, crazy, take a seat.

My tears start falling faster as Jared cuts across his bed in one swoop. He strides towards me, his long legs making the small trek even smaller. He grabs my face in his hands and leans down so we are eye to eye as he says to me with lethal calmness and surety, "*You* are the *only* thing in my life that makes me genuinely happy, Trystan Victoria Joann Harper."

And maybe that should scare me. Perhaps being "the only thing" to make someone happy should feel like a startling idea... But it doesn't. Not here. Not with him. And all I can do in this moment is look at him—*really* look at him. I try to hold on to his words. I know he means what he says. I know he hates this as much as I do.

"What do we do Jared?"

Like he can physically feel how defeated I am, or maybe he just feels the same way, he lowers us both to the floor of his room. The sandy colored carpet is soft and cool beneath us. He pulls me in to his lap so that my feet rest on one side of his legs, my hands settle between our chests. I rest my cheek on his shoulder as I tuck my face in to the crook of his neck and his hands alternate with each other between running through my hair and rubbing my back.

"I don't know, Trystan. I don't know what we do. But whatever it is, we do it together."

I inhale sharply, holding back a sob.

Who would blame him if he dumped me? No one.

Not even me.

His family would chill out. His life would be less complicated. And maybe it's selfish of me to not make that call for him. To not leave him and let his family win. But I don't care if it is because this man, he is everything to me. He is my best friend. He is the love of my life. He is it for me.

"Together." I finally say.

They're just two people, Kerry and Darla. What can these two, small people do to the two of us that hold so much love together?

CHAPTER FOURTEEN.

Nine months have come and gone and things with Jared's family are as tumultuous as ever.

I'm not sure who dislikes who more at this point—Darla and me or me and Darla.

Definitely me and Darla.

Jared is still working for his mom's cleaning business with Kerry. The boys are still cohabitating. I am one more snide comment about a sleepover or "she's not welcome here" before I go full psycho on Kerry. For Jared's sake I try to keep it together, I try to be chill and not go out of my way to be petty and cause discord. But after almost a year of just absolute bull shit... I am nearing the edge of fed up.

We got tired of tiptoeing around Kerry's social schedule, which is next to nonexistent, so the days and nights I am over there, we act as if nothing is the matter and just live our lives. Respectfully, of course.

We don't act out of spite. We just do our own thing. Clean up after ourselves. Keep a good volume. It seems to never be good enough though.

February is a busy month for cleaning companies apparently—who knew? Jared has been putting in overtime most weeks. His job leaves us with little time during the day to spend time together. Nights are where we find our "us" time. Which is fine, I'm still at McDonald's and open the store most mornings, evenings and nights are for Jared.

We try to not discuss the issues with his family. When we do talk about it, all we end up doing is getting into a fight like the one we had back in October.

We were on our way to have supper with a friend of Jared's. I don't even remember who, but one of us had brought up Darla and how rude she was over Labor Day weekend.

The next thing I know, I am crying into my hands, sobs just breaking free, while Jared is near-yelling about how he "doesn't know what to do" or how he "doesn't know how to fix what is going on". I finally lost it entirely and told him to pull over or I would jump out of his moving car. I remember my chest feeling like it was going to pop. My legs were shaking so bad I almost bounced out of my seat. My whole body was hot and cold and my head was a mess. He obliged my demand, albeit reluctantly, and the second his car was getting thrown in to park I was already halfway out of it.

I grabbed my phone to call Beth and have her come pick me up, my shaky hands and blurred vision making it a slow process, when

Jared snatched my phone from me and told me that I needed to calm down and just talk to him.

"Talk to you?!" I yelled, not giving a single shit who saw or heard. "Talk to you like you were just *talking* to me!?"

We were most certainly not in a secluded area, very much out in the open and public. He had pulled in to the first parking lot he could, and it happened to be one with a strip mall of open businesses in it. A casino, a restaurant, and a cigarette store. Not to mention the gas station to the right, full of patrons not minding their own business. I wouldn't have either, I'm sure.

Do you think I cared?

"I shouldn't have yelled at you-"

"No, you shouldn't have yelled at *me*! You know who *should* yell at though, Jared?" I yelled while throwing my arms out around me. "That horrible mother of yours! That is who should be on the receiving end of every single one of these stupid arguments! Not me! *Her*!"

With each word came a visible puff of breath, it having been cold out.

By that point, me having lost my damn mind, Jared was just staring at me like I had recently escaped the psych ward. And honestly, I wasn't so sure that that wouldn't be the very place I might be headed with all of this Darla drama.

Grippy sock vacation, here I come.

"I am exhausted, Jare," I said, my voice finally at a normal volume, completely and utterly and simply drained.

"I am too, Trystan," he said with a bite to his words.

"Then what do we do from here?" I asked cautiously.

The thoughts in my head then weren't good ones. They weren't hopeful like they were a year ago. They weren't excited to face this together.

They were very much negative ones about breaking up and being done with this drama.

This awful woman had taken every ounce of my hope from me in that moment.

"What do you want to do, Trystan?" Jared asked.

His tone made me even more angry. "I'm sorry, the attitude you're currently carrying is giving me the impression that you think this is all a *me* issue?" I continued, "And that just simply can't be true. Because last I checked we are on the same team and it is *your* family that are trying to tear us apart—not me."

By that point in the fight my hands had gone slack at my side while I stood a few feet away from where Jared was leaning with his back against his Continental, his arms crossed in front of him. He had his jean clad legs squared and his black jacket unzipped. My head was cocked to the side, my eyes forming little slits as I dared him to keep pushing me in that moment. Realizing this was about to head to a point of no return, we both took a few minutes to calm down.

"I don't think it's a *you* problem," Jared said, going first to break the quiet.

I could tell he was trying to tread carefully.

Good.

"But I do think that you are letting them win every time you get this upset over something they do." He looked up at me finally, his blue eyes meeting my brown ones that absolutely had black mascara tears trailing down my cheeks.

I took a deep breath before replying to his observation.

"So, they can have their opinions and make them known constantly and without repercussions from you," he opened his mouth to object and I held my hand up, stopping him. "But I let out my feelings on them, whether it's quietly or loudly, and I am the one letting them win?" I asked softly, tears still falling from my eyes.

I took some breaths, reining in my tears. I tried to hide my still trembling bottom lip by pulling it between my teeth and looking away from Jared. He must have noticed it though.

He always notices.

As he pushed off of his car and closed the distance between us, he said, "Trystan, I don't know what to tell you anymore other than I love you. I need that to be enough."

Gutted. That was how I was feeling at that moment in time. Gutted and desperate for change. Pissed off that he let it get this far. Mad at myself for being upset with him. Loathing Darla's existence. Embarrassed that the people inside of the stores to my right were getting a show of their lifetime.

"I don't think I can do this anymore, Jared." I said, staring at his chest to avoid his face.

Because I didn't know if it would be enough anymore—our love. What if her hate was too much?

"Baby... No." he begged. "Don't do that. Don't give up. That really would be letting my mom and Kerry win. I love you. You love me. Why can't that be enough for now? We can figure the rest out at some point."

I looked up to meet his gaze and when I did my whole resolve crashed around me. The anger, the resentment, the embarrassment, the hostility. It washed away with the tears running down Jared's face. I swiped one away with my thumb and brought him closer to wrap my arms around his waist.

"I love you too. It's enough," I said, barely above a whisper.

And for that second, in the moment, with tears streaming down both of our faces and our hearts beating for the other person—it had to be enough.

"I'm sorry," he said.

"I'm sorry too," I didn't say.

Now, months after that particularly horrible fight, I am sitting next to a wounded Jared trying to convince him that he needs to get his knee looked at.

"Explain to me again what happened," I tell him from the passenger seat of his car.

I am eyeing his left knee from here for the eightieth time and cursing him silently for being such a boy. Stubborn when injured. Even through his blue jeans I can see the size difference between his injured left knee and his healthy right one.

"I was on the four-wheeler, in the pasture, headed back to the house," he starts, for the third time while driving us around town aimlessly.

He called me while I was hanging with Mike watching Cars. He didn't tell me what happened, but he said he had hurt his knee and was coming to get me to go drive around because he didn't want to just sit at home. I told him that if he hurt his knee that I would come pick him up. His answer to that was a honk of his horn in our driveway.

"I didn't see the dip in the ground as I came up on it and the four-wheeler went to flip forward. I don't know why but my brain told my leg to kick out like a kickstand to stop the flip from happening and then there was a pop and pain and here I am."

"A pop?"

"A pop."

I blink at him slowly. "You need to go in, Jared," I say—also for the third time.

The glare I get in answer tells me enough.

Time to get mean.

"Don't make me call my mom, Jared. She will want to look at your knee herself, putting you in the postion of having to pull your damn pants down in front of her because you can get the leg of your jeans pulled up over your knee. You won't like sitting in my living room in your boxes. And you won't like what she says when she tells you to go in. She is bossier than me. You think you will be able to glare at her when she tells you what I just told you?" I threaten. I raise my eyebrows are him. "No, you won't. And then you'll still end up going in but now you'll have not just me in toe with you—but her as well."

I cross my arms, pleased with the dramatic sigh from Jared, as he turns towards the urgent care on this side of town.

Tracy's medical knowledge makes her a great enforcer, even when she's unaware.

Four hours, a doctor's visit, a referral to the orthopedic office, and an X-ray later—Jared has a broken knee and enough attitude to last him a lifetime. Knowing our children will be just as wild and stubborn is still something I find endearing though.

"Surgery," he repeats to his mom on the phone.

I don't need to actually hear her to know she is being her usual half-supportive self. I don't think she has even asked if he is okay. Not outright at least. I wish I could say it's shocking.

"We got it scheduled for Thursday afternoon." He pauses, Darla talking. "Yes, the Thursday that is in three days." Another pause. "Correct, I will be missing out on branding this year." A sigh accompanies this pause. "Trystan is taking me."

I don't need to even wonder what her response to that statement is. I heard it from over here in the driver's seat while Jared gets to be the passenger home. It was a loud and disgusted, nasally "excuse me?!"

We both look at each other, neither of us surprised nor pleased.

"She is going to take me in, stay for the surgery, take me home, and get me settled," he states firmly.

After what sounded like a bunch of angry and irrational comments Jared lightly tosses his phone in to the back seat.

"That went well then, yeah?" I ask in an effort to ease his pulse back down to a normal rate.

The defeated look he gives me intensifies the bitter fire in my soul. *I hate that woman. Genuinely hate.*

It's surgery day and Darla texted Jared first thing this morning—

> So long as Triston is going to be at the surgery center today I will NOT be

Real mature. Also, not how you spell my name.

"If you want your mom there, I will understand Jared. She's your mom," I say, trying to hide my reluctance at handing him over to her.

Not reluctance about me potentially not being there. Reluctance about the quality-of-care Jared would possibly receive if his mom did go in my stead. Which sounds like I'm high on myself or something—like I think I can do it better than her.

My offer is sincere, though. If he wanted his mom there for this, and I was the only thing in the way of that, then I would excuse myself from the equation and make that happen for him. I don't want that to be the case, clearly. She isn't kind. She wouldn't get him what he needs without him having to ask, and he would refuse to ask because she would be rude about whatever it is he would ask for, and it would just be an absolute mess.

"Absolutely not, Trystan. Don't even think for a second that I wouldn't want you there," he counters, quickly adding, "And let's be real—I don't want her there."

That fills me with both relief and resentment.

And so—here I sit, only thirty minutes in to waiting. My mom is in a chair next to me. Kerry is two waiting rooms down, the ever faithful watchdog.

We are in a quiet surgery center. White walls with swirly black and gray carpet. Black accents throughout—very modern and sleek.

Sterile. The chairs are comfortable, and they have televisions with various weather channels or cartoons playing throughout the three different waiting rooms. Magazines line the small tables in between every few chairs.

"Ms. Harper?"

I look up from my solitaire game on my phone to see a lovely nurse in pale green scrubs coming towards me. I assume her hair matches her beautiful golden eyebrows, but it is hidden by the Finding Nemo scrub cap she has on. I quickly pocket my phone while I go to stand. She holds a hand up to stop me, smiling kindly, so I sit back down.

"He's fine, you don't need to get up. I just have a question."

"Oh, okay, sure. What's up?"

Speaking quietly, "There is a woman on the phone asking for a progress report on Jared. Her name isn't listed on any of his paperwork. I checked. Twice." She winces slightly. "So, I wasn't sure if that was an accident or not. Figured it was best to ask. She says she is his mom."

If this lovely woman had to field that call, I should probably apologize.

Not knowing what to do, because it *wasn't* an accident, I look over to my mom. She's sitting across from me in jeans and a red hoodie, completely unbothered. Jared chose to put me and my mom down as the contact information this morning while doing the paperwork.

"No accident. Darla can come down here herself if she is so concerned," my mom says without looking up from her magazine.

It does not go unnoticed that good ol' Tracy said that loud enough for Kerry one room over to hear her.

I look back to the messenger. The kind, scrub clad lady's name tag says "Shay".

Poor, poor Shay.

Shay's face flashes with surprise before she quickly hides it and says, "Yes, of course. I'll let her know that. I will just pass her message to Jared when he wakes up."

And with that, Shay is walking away. I can only imagine how that conversation will go for her.

"Mom, maybe we should have just let her tell Darla the gist of it?" I ask, setting my phone down on the chair next to me.

Her eyes leave her magazine and meet mine.

"Absolutely not. She could have been here and chose not to out of spite for you and now she can deal with the consequences of that decision."

And that is that, I suppose. Kerry is barely down the hall anyway. He will come down here when the doctor comes out in an hour or so. Darla will be fine.

Shay might not fare so well, though.

An hour and a half later and Jared is happily snowed. Absolutely sedated. And it is the funniest thing I have ever seen.

Surgery went great, everything went as expected and he handled it all perfectly. The four nurses residing over his care are currently going over medications and aftercare information to me while Kerry stands off to the side by the door. My mom stands about halfway between him and I.

Not accidental, that move.

"Will he be in a lot of pain at any point?" I ask whichever one will answer me.

"He has a nerve block in his leg right now that has his knee just completely numbed, basically. That will wear off in about six to eight more hours. As it does his pain will increase and he will become uncomfortable. As long as the pain meds stay fairly on schedule, his knee should be able to ease into it all. So, it is *really* important he stays caught up on his medicine," she says as she hands me the copious amounts of paperwork and prescriptions. This nurse is older, probably around my mom's age. Short, cropped, brightly highlighted hair, slightly smudged mascara on her tan face. Intimidating enough for me to simply nod and grab the paperwork.

I look to my mom for the hundredth time to make sure she also heard everything because this is my first rodeo—she is a seasoned vet of taking care of people. She gives me a smile and a nod, and I go back to watching Jared.

"Trystan, you're so pretty," he slurs.

"You are very happy right now." I laugh. "Let's hope that good feeling stays throughout the next few days."

"I'm taking off," Kerry says from the door. He hasn't spoken a word since we all got back here. And no one has talked to him either.

"I didn't even know you were here, Ker. Bye then," Jared replies without even looking at him, his half open eyes staying on me.

The answering scoff and something resembling "asshole" are all that Kerry gives any of us before he turns around and leaves. I can't wait to deal with that later when I take Jared to their apartment.

Shay pops her head in and says hi to the three of us before giving Jared the message about his mom calling earlier.

Apparently, she called four more times before he finally got out of surgery. Kerry must have texted or called her to relay that information. Like I knew he would, Jared gives zero shits about his mom calling and only apologizes to Shay for how much that must have sucked. She laughs a little and leaves.

Round of applause for Shay.

CHAPTER FIFTEEN.

O nce I get Jared settled in his room, I give him a once over.

His black basketball shorts reveal his swollen and wrapped up knee. His lips look dry, so I hand him his Chapstick. I fluff the two pillows under his head before doing the same, more gently, to the two other ones under his hurt knee.

Television remote, pain meds with the schedule of times to take them, plugged in cell phone that has alarms set up to coordinate with the scheduled medications, two plastic water bottles, and a peanut butter and jelly sandwich all sit within reach of where he lays in his bed.

"I have to go home and shower and stuff, but I will come back in a few hours," I say as I straighten his already straight remote for the fourth time.

I'm nervous to leave but Kerry and I need some space before one of us kills the other. I intentionally didn't bring any shower stuff or clothes so that I would HAVE to leave.

He grabs my hand and pulls me closer to the bed.

"Thank you," he says as he kisses my knuckles. "You're the best."

His sleepy eyes connect to mine, and I smile as I lean down to kiss him.

"Your alarm is set on your phone for the medicine you need to take while I am gone. I love you. Get some sleep."

As I turn around to shut his bedroom door, I see that Jared is already asleep.

It has taken the entire fifteen-minute drive over here to calm my rapid heartrate even a little bit.

When you get a call from your injured, normally stoic, boyfriend at 6:30 in the morning and notice immediately the way he is hysterically begging you to come get him, a heart can only beat so slow in that situation.

I was not prepared for what I found upon entering his room, though.

When I left late last night Jared was fine. The picture of recovery.

"Trystan something is wrong, I need to go back to the surgery center."

Jared is a wreck now. His skin glossy with sweat and lacking in color. He is hunched over, gripping his knee, his injured leg sticking straight out in front of him, tears streaming down his red face. He must have been running his hands through his sweat-wet hair, it is sticking up every which way.

"Yes, okay. My mom is going to meet us there. Let's go," I say while trying to stay cool calm and collected.

I grab his left arm and throw it over my shoulder while putting my right arm around his back to brace him against me. He grabs one of his crutches to use in his right hand as he stands, that left leg unbendable with the bandaging and brace on it.

We stagger out of his room and through the house. It's eerily quiet, barley seven in the morning.

Kerry opens his door with some small amount of aggression. His hair mussed up from sleep and his bare chest moving with each deep breath. When he finds us halfway to the front door, I can tell Jared did not try to get Kerry to help him before he called me, the surprise in his eyes is very telling.

"What the hell is going on? Are you okay?" he asks as he rushes over.

Jared doesn't stop moving so neither do I and when he doesn't reply to a frantic Kerry who is now typing away on his phone, no doubt doing what he does best; relaying information to their mother, I finally answer him.

"He is in a ton of pain and wants to go back to the center so that's where I am taking him," I manage to work out as we exit their door to head down his porch to his car. "Let your mom know if you haven't already, or I can call her if I need to."

I don't wait for a response before closing the driver side door of Jared's car.

I'm not a monster, contrary to Darla's belief. I would want to know if my kid was in pain like this regardless of who I get the information from. I don't look to Kerry before pulling out of the driveway. And because I am not 100% certain that he did or did not tell Darla about the current state of things, my anxious brain convinces itself that I need to call her just in case he doesn't.

Better to be safe than sorry.

I use Jared's phone to call Darla. The chances of her answering for his name far greater than if it were my name on her phone.

"Yeah?"

Rise above, Tryst.

"Jared is in a ton of pain. I am taking him to the surgery center right now," Is all I say.

"Great, obviously I am coming into town now for this," she spits out.

My anger gets the better of me as I say, "If it is an inconvenience then don't bother."

"Ha! I'll be there."

I don't wait to see who hangs up first.

I swallow down, or rather choke on, my anger. My being a bitch is the last thing Jared needs. I send up a prayer that me doing something semi-decent doesn't blow up in our faces in an hour when she arrives.

Foolish girl.

"I will take you home. Clearly you need better care," Darla fires off while the nurses finish explaining that that nerve block wore off and because Jared sleepily ignored one of his pain medicine reminders, shit just hit the fan inside his body. That's the gist of it at least.

"Mom, no. Trystan is taking me home. It isn't her fault that I didn't take my med." He replies. His voice is finally calmer and not so filled with pain.

"I didn't ask, Jared," she states.

My mom is giving everyone room, herself included. She is practically smoking at the ears right now.

I feel almost numb. I know I am mad at Darla. I know I am concerned for Jared. I know I am sad for me. But right now, in this bright, sterile room all I can muster up is nothing. A blanket of faux calm washed over me the second Darla started complaining.

"Kerry can drive your car home with you, and I will follow over." She glares at me and then looks to my mom before saying to her, "And your daughter can go home with you."

They have a stare-off for what feels like an eon before my mom looks at me, smiling sadly. She then looks at Jared and tells him that it's okay and she'll take me home once he gets all checked out and the okay to go.

His responding nod is all he gives before looking over at me and squeezing my hand in his.

The burning fire brewing inside of me is turning to acid in my veins. The quiet that is out of place on the outside is slowing melting away with every snarky comment or rude glare. Do I feel horrible for Jared that he was in immense pain? Obviously. Is it my fault though? Not in the slightest. He shut his alarm off half asleep and missed a dose. It isn't even something that needs to have someone AT fault.

Leave it to Darla to make it out to be something that someone messed up on.

Once we are outside Kerry and I load Jared into the passenger seat of his car.

Kerry and I haven't said much to each other in quite a while so working with him like this is proving to be a bit awkward.

After getting Jared settled, Kerry goes around and gets in the driver's seat. Like the good boy he is, he decides to wait for his mom's go ahead before leaving.

The weather this morning is a bit misty so instead of staying by Jared at the door I climb in the back seat and wait with them, both our moms are still inside.

At least between the three of us we can still act somewhat cordial. We converse about the wet morning and the branding plans the Barns have for this weekend. It is all going well and fine, surprisingly.

Until it isn't.

My mom and Darla exit the surgery center, the former following behind the meaner. Darla doesn't hold the door open for my mom as she follows hot on her heals and they both head toward Darla's pick up.

I feel my fists clench in my lap. All three pairs of eyes in the car solely focus on what is sure to be a shit show a few parking spots down.

Our collective heartrates would power a jet plane.

Through Jared's and my rolled down windows we hear, "If you think you can walk away from me or ignore me after treating my daughter, and myself, with such disgusting disrespect, you have another thing coming, Darla."

My mom is seething.

Darla doesn't respond with anything other than an abrasive laugh as she climbs in to her black two door Toyota pick-up. My mom still right by her, Darla closes her door. Once in and buckled and settled, she must realize mom isn't going anywhere until she shows her some semblance of respect, so she rolls her window down and looks at my mom.

"What do you want Tracy?" she asks.

The three of us are silent. I don't know if any of us are even breathing. Our windows are down, and the radio is off. My hand is on the handle of my door and I'm ready to bolt to my mom in a flash if things somehow get extra crazy.

The last thing we need is for her to pull Darla out of her pickup by her horrible hair and then end up in jail.

By the way my mom's hands keep clenching and relaxing and then clenching again at her sides, I'm not ruling that possibility out entirely.

"I want," she emphasizes greatly, "for you to quit being horrible to my child and show her some damn respect. Or at the very least, respect your son enough to show some remote amount of kindness towards the girl he loves, for Christ's sake!"

My mom has her hands stuffed into the pocket on the front of her red hoodie now.

Smart move, Trace.

"Listen to me now when I say this, and you can relay it to that daughter of yours." Darla's voice is so reminiscent of that of a Disney villain.

And then Darla speaks a sentence that will forever be tattooed in to my very being. The core of me.

"That girl will NEVER be a part of my family."

I think I physically flinched.

Ten words. One sentence. Two seconds in time.

Such small increments in the grand scheme of life.

But for someone who has been wholeheartedly planning on spending the rest of forever, and every forever after that, with the boy cringing in the seat in front of her...

That sentence just broke something so incredibly vital inside of me.

"She could marry him, and I will still not accept her as one of us," she finishes before looking up and down at my mom, like she can see the wound she just caused. "I don't have anything more to say to you." Looking around my mom and to Kerry, completely avoiding me and Jared, she says, "Let's go. Now." And with that she rolls her window up.

My mom stands her ground, unflinching and unmoving.

I catch Kerry's gaze in the rearview mirror as I look forward. What I see in it surprises me. He looks at me with a hint of regret and sadness.

I say nothing to him though, refusing to acknowledge him, as I get out and lean in through Jared's window to kiss him goodbye. I try to hide my trembling hands and quivering bottom lip. The tears in my eyes start to take over.

Now is not the time.

Neither of us exchange words as Kerry, with what looks like reluctance, puts Jared's car in reverse.

I walk to where my mom stands as they exit parking lot, Darla long gone.

"That girl will never be a part of my family" echoing in my brain.

That girl will never be.

I'll never be.

"Get in the car. Let's go home," she says. The defeat in her tone is so familiar, I recognize it immediately.

It is the twin to my own.

I numbly walk around her red Dodge Durango and get in the passenger seat. With buckled seatbelts and absolute quiet we make our way home. She dropped Craig off at Jared's on her way to the surgery center to retrieve my car and take it home. I am suddenly struck with the feeling that my mom maybe knew how bad this all would go.

The silence as my mom drives us home is heavy. Weighted with anger and sadness and worry.

As she pulls into our driveway and we go to get out I tell her I want to go for a drive, clear my head.

"Don't go to Jared's, Trystan," she says, bitterness and caution coating every word.

Not towards me, though.

"I won't. I just want to drive for a bit. Maybe see what Beth is doing. Maybe just go for a walk." I say as I walk to my car.

"Tryst," my mom starts. I don't turn around to look at her. "I'm so sorry, honey."

"I know, mom," I say as I get into my Stratus.

I don't know where I am going or what I am doing. I would normally call Jared and go see him when my heart is this heavy. But I can't do that.

She's there.

"She will never be a part of my family."

How could she say that so confidently? So comfortably? Like it is the end all and be all of decisions where her son and I are concerned?

What is so wrong with me that she has hated me for these last almost two and a half years?

What did I do to her to make her want to hurt me so much?

How is she with hurting Jared so much?

I was not even seventeen when this all started. A kid.

She is a grown woman.

How can she hold so much hate for me?

By the time I show up to Beth's, unannounced, I am a wreck. I am shaking and sobbing and an uncontrollable disaster of "why's" and "what now's".

Thirty minutes and a lot of crying later, Beth and I are sitting on opposite sides of her bright red leather sectional, our normal spots, with pints of ice cream in our hands and a box of Kleenex on the glass coffee table in front of us. I have a pile of snotty, tear-filled tissues in my lap.

The tears are slowing finally when my phone vibrates, and I see a text from Jared.

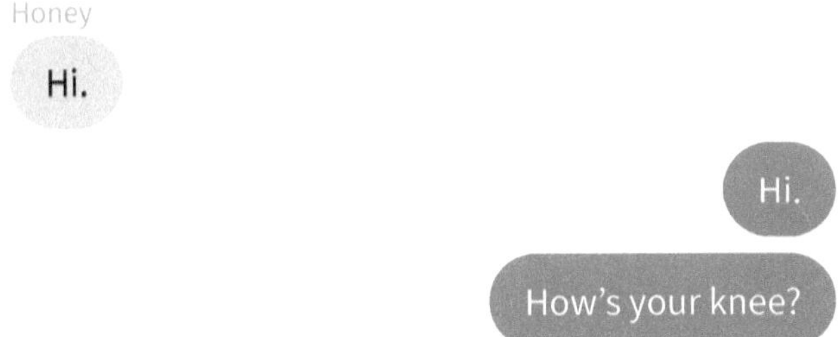

It's fine… sore but the edge is gone.

Good, I'm glad. Make sure you drink some water and eat something if you haven't.

I am finding the energy to even text him next to nonexistent.

I just got a turkey sandwich thrown at me.

Thrown?!

Not literally I guess haha

Not a great time to joke Jare, but sure.

Oh, okay.

Trystan… I can't even start to apologize correctly. What a fucking mess.

It's okay.

No, no it isn't.

None of this is.

I don't reply. I don't know what to say or how to even act right now.

Talk to me, please. Tell me what's going on in that head of yours.

We can talk tomorrow, Jare. You need to eat and get rest.

I wish you were here.

Me too.

I love you Trystan.

Love you too.

I look up at Beth, her face showing every ounce of heartbreak she is feeling for me, and I crumble all over again. I spiral hard.

I'll never be a part of his family.

CHAPTER SIXTEEN.

MAY 2012.

"**I** think I need to move."

My mom audibly chokes on air. I must have surprised her with my declaration.

So, I say it again for her. "I think I need to move."

She looks at me from where she is sitting at the dining room table, a freshly cleaned counter between us. I have on a blue hoodie that I got to represent my high school before graduation last year, black leggings, and a fantastically messy back-to-black bun on top of my head. From where I sit on top of the counter on the other side of the kitchen, eating Ben & Jerry's Chunky Monkey from the carton which has become my only source of food lately, I get the sense that I should have maybe started this conversation in a different way.

Eased into it perhaps.

"Did you hear me or are you having a stroke?" I ask around the spoon full of ice cream that halts halfway to my face.

"No, no. I heard you. But I also think I might be having a stroke because what I think I heard you say is you need to move," she says with a shake of her head. "Like from the counter, you need to move? You haven't been there that long."

I answer her puzzling look with a tilt of my head and a serious gaze, "No, I mean move out of Rapid. Like, *away.*"

"Uh, yeah. Okay. To where?" she asks, tone full of sarcasm, as she makes her way to the kitchen.

Once standing across from me, jeans, and a grey V-neck T-shirt with her auburn hair down and curtaining her face, she crosses her arms over her chest and leans back against the counter.

"Well, I was thinking I would call aunt Hope. See if she would take me in for the summer. Or longer." I shrug my shoulders like it's nothing when really... it's kind of everything.

Aunt Hope lives in a super small town in Nebraska. She and I have always been close. Hope was the one to watch me a ton when my mom was on her own and putting herself through school and working a million jobs when I was but a wee babe. Hope has three other kids, all within five years of me, and a really cool husband. After moving north when I was five or so, my mom and aunt Hope would meet halfway from our house to hers every summer and I would stay in Nebraska for two weeks with her. Those weeks hold some of my most favorite memories.

"Do you think she would say yes? It's just Chance living at the house now."

"I don't know that Hope has it in her to say no to you, so the chances are good," my mom replies with raised eyebrows. Her face softens as she asks, "What about Jared?"

What about Jared?

It has been two months since Jared's surgery. Two months of sneaking around his brother and mother. Two months of avoiding their apartment. Not for their sake, but for mine. Okay, and for theirs. I'm one look or comment away from becoming physical I think. We're all a little scared of me right now.

Jared and I haven't even discussed the things Darla said in the parking lot of the surgery center. I don't know if either of us really knows where to go from here—keeping it simple and easy for now while Jared heals has become my priority.

"I assume we would stay together. It's only an eight-hour drive, easily done in a day and he could come visit. Once I get a job, I could come back up here to visit," I say with a shrug of my shoulders.

If I were to be honest with my mom, and therein myself, I would say that I have no idea what will happen with Jared. With me and Jared. With me. I love him entirely. The thought of leaving without him and doing a long-distance relationship is terrifying and then thinking further down the line, how will life be with his mom?

Will he eventually move away with me?

Will I just have to move back and endure decades of her horribleness?

Will she ever change?

I shove those thoughts away because positivity and optimism are the only options my hurting heart can handle right now.

"I guess you need to call your aunt," my mom says while squeezing my knee. "And Jared," she adds, walking away.

Neither Ben, nor Jerry, are cutting it right now. My nerves are insane. As soon as I got off the phone with aunt Hope, who gave a resounding "hell yeah!" when I asked if I could move in with them in a couple weeks, I called Jared and told him I wanted to hang out if he wasn't busy.

Beings he is currently broken, his words not mine, he is as available as ever. He came and picked me up to go for a cruise around town. Thank goodness it is his left leg that is injured.

A Jared who couldn't drive would be an extra sad Jared.

Now that I sit here though, looking at the handsome boy I love with every fiber of my being, my gut is in knots. My heart is trying to climb its way out of my throat, revolting against the choice I am making.

"I need to tell you something," I finally say, working up the nerve.

Just do it. It'll be fine. Rip the bandaid off.

He looks over at me, his sapphire eyes hidden by his sunglasses. And thank goodness for that. I don't think I could do this while looking directly into his eyes.

"What's up?" He sounds so cheerful, happy.

"Well... I've been thinking,"

He shoots me a worried look now. All I give in return is a tight smile.

"This isn't a good talk, is it?" he asks.

I take his right hand in my left, squeezing it gently, saying nothing for a moment.

"I think," I start, taking a deep breath, "I am going to move to Nebraska."

The way his whole body seemed to melt, like visibly relax, tells me he was thinking something much worse was about to happen. I have been going over it and over it in my head for the last day, since talking to my mom last night, about what his reaction would be. About what he would say and the questions he would ask and the argument we might have.

I never expected what I received.

"Okay."

I jerk back, wanting to release his hand but choosing to attempt to remain equally unfazed.

"Okay?" I question, raising a brow.

"Yeah," he says with a shoulder shrug, as if this is a simple run of the mill conversation.

"Should we go to Applebee's?" "Okay."

"Do you want to watch a movie at my house?" "Okay."

"Should I just extricate my heart for you here in this car and hand it to you now or later for you to run over?" "Okay."

"If that's what you want? Then okay." He brings my hand to his mouth and places a lingering kiss on my knuckles.

I straighten in my seat, using the radio's volume dial as a good excuse to take my hand back. Having my hand in Jared's felt wrong for the first time in over two years and I'm not sure what to do with that.

"Okay," I say.

Okay.

I guess he doesn't mind that I will be moving. To a different state. Without him. Eight hours way.

Okay.

I have never hated a singular word so much.

The next week goes by in a bit of a blur. I've been chatting with aunt Hope about what jobs she thinks I should apply for, and at the same time she has been reassuring me that there isn't a huge rush to apply for anything. It's almost summertime so there will be plenty of options around their tiny town. I put in my two weeks at McDonald's the day after I decided I was leaving for real, they said they were sad to see me go and tried to pry into things pertaining to Jared and I... I left them guessing. Beth and I have spent time together, soaking each other in. I've had movie nights and meals with my family rather than down in my room or out of the house. Jared and I have, well, been Jared and I. Hanging out and talking often, the normality of it all is almost nauseating, really.

Is it too much to ask for him to be devastated?

Right now I am packing things up in my room. I'm not putting everything away, leaving some stuff out and here. It isn't that I am anticipating moving down there and then turning right back around and coming home. Rather—this is still my home. So, I don't *have* to take everything with me. I can take the major stuff and worry about the rest when or if it comes time to worry about it.

I'm folding up my zebra print blanket to put in a box when I hear a knock on the door that separates the basement from the stairs. A second later Jared breezes through my sheet-door and beelines it for me, happy as can be.

"Hey," Jared says as he leans across the box that will house the blankets and pillows that I'm taking. "Packing it all up?" He stands back and surveys my changing bedroom.

"Yeah. I have another week, I know. But I don't want to rush next week to get it all sorted out." I point to the bed before saying, "You can move the suitcase and sit if you want. Or you can help me wrap this stuff?" I motion to the little figurines my grandma has been gifting me since I was a baby.

My personal favorite is the porcelain robin she gave me when I was eight. It sits perched on a small, round music box and the colors of the bird itself are so realistic.

Jared moves to sit on the bed, my black comforter not at all made-up on my matching sheets.

"I think I will just hang out a bit," he says as he sits down.

His face is a little pinched. Light brown eyebrows low, soft mouth pulled down slightly at the corners. But I am in the zone, so I continue about my business, moving on from blankets to wrapping breakables and placing them gently into the cardboard fry box I acquired from work. Not even two minutes later I hear Jared move around and look to see him standing, one hand rubbing his jaw and the other tucked in a jean pocket.

"Actually, I think I'm going to head out."

"Oh, okay. I know this is boring. Sorry," I say over my shoulder.

I don't know which one of us has thrown this wall up between us. It's there though. Seemingly made of something flimsy but substantial nonetheless. He must sense that I'm questioning why he's leaving so abruptly. I don't move to turn around to look at him, focusing on the trinkets in front of me.

"Trystan... this is hard for me," he says to my back.

My eyes are rimmed with tears instantly. We haven't really talked about me moving, or the reasoning behind it, since that day in his car. It isn't that we have been avoiding it, but I suppose maybe we have been. But how do you just say "hey, I'm moving away because your mom broke my heart and also because you kind of let her?" without causing a scene?

"Watching you pack to leave me here," he says. "It isn't easy. I don't want to help you get ready to move eight hours away."

I turn around to face him finally. He has one hand still in his pocket and the other one running through his hair now. A bulky black knee brace clings tightly to his blue jeans. His orange Hurley T-shirt feels so off from the current mood in this suddenly too-small, dark room.

"I'm sorry," I mutter, unsure of what else there is to say.

It really isn't that I don't *want* to discuss Nebraska—I'm looking forward to the change. *I think.* It isn't even that I don't want to discuss Darla—though I really don't. I just don't know what will happen if I open that floodgate of feelings and emotions and thoughts. And with Jared's birthday in four days and then me moving in seven... When will the time be right to even talk about such heavy things?

"You don't need to be sorry," he says as he crosses the room and puts his arms around my waist.

I place my hands on his chest and meet his gaze.

"I don't want to make you sad," I say, tears now slowly falling down my face.

Jared's hand goes to the back of my head, tanging his fingers in my hair as he gently nudges me to his chest, resting his chin on top.

"I don't know what to do here, Trystan. I don't want you to leave. I don't want to *not* support you. I'm lost." He lets out a heavy sigh.

I don't say anything, again not knowing what to do here. After a few long moments of silence, I pull up to meet his sad blue eyes.

"I can stop packing for today. Let's go for a drive or something."

He smiles his smile, a little less sad than a second ago, and we go. I ditch my packing and we both leave our heavy hearts with the half packed boxes in my room.

CHAPTER SEVENTEEN.

"Why do you think he hasn't told me not to go?" I ask Beth.

She called me, crying, this morning, an absolute mess. In between the sobs I gathered that she was beyond upset that I was leaving for Nebraska in four days and that even though we have seen each other almost every day since I told her I was moving, it isn't enough. So, I quickly dragged myself out of bed, brushed my teeth, dressed in my best leggings and baggy T-shirt, threw my hair in to the messiest bun on top of my head, and headed out the door.

Beth takes a sip of her coke that I picked up from McDonald's on my way over to her apartment, thinking it over. "I don't know, babe. I think he just wants to support you," she says while looking at me over her black aviator sunglasses.

The balcony at her apartment got furnished by her dad, Little Jack. The love he has for his sweet "Lizzie girl" is unmatched. He came to town from North Dakota one day a few weeks ago, grabbed Beth, went to Tractor Supply like the farm boy he is, and bought her whatever she wanted for her porch. Very standard Little Jack behavior. She walked out of there with a cute dark green L shaped couch, a matching set of chairs, a round glass table to go in front. He even sprung for the woven rug that has at least seven different colors in it, pinks and blues and nearly anything in between. Very chic—very Beth.

I glance at her from where I'm propped up in the corner of the couch, my legs taking up one side of the L. Her bright blonde hair flows to her collar bone in a straight glossy sheet today. She's got on yesterday's make-up and mustard yellow sweatpants. A black sports bra shows off her fake-tan-out-of-a-bag—signature summer-Beth vibes. A black sports bra shows off her fake-tan-out-of-a-bag.

Gosh, I am going to miss her.

I voice the thought that I have yet to say aloud, making me feel guilty for even asking. "I just feel like he should be fighting for me to stay a little bit, no?"

I set my soda down and get up. I begin pacing around her porch, pulling my hair out of the bun it is in and sliding the neon pink scrunchy on to my wrist.

Knowing my spiral will be safe here... "Like, does he not care that I am moving? Does he think I will chicken out and not go? Does he think I'll get down there and just turn around and come home?"

I have got to look like a total spaz to anyone that might be witnessing this lovely meltdown of mine. I'm flinging my hands around with every question and thought while I circle Beth and her furniture. I pause my flailing and drop my hands, facing my best friend and locking my bleary brown eyes with her worried green ones. She pulls her glasses off her face to look at me with nothing between us. From here I can see the perfect ring of gold that lines her pupil.

"Does he want me to break up with him, so he doesn't have to do it himself and him letting me leave without a fight is just his way of getting us there?"

There it is.

I sit on one of her chairs, the cushion warm from the sun that has been shining on it. I curl my feet under me and rest my face in my hands. After a long bout of nothing from Beth I look up at her and find her already watching me. Tears are lining her eyes—my empathetic and beautiful, kind friend.

She says in a quiet voice, "I don't know, Tryst. I wish I did."

We both begin to cry then, as she moves to sit with me in a chair that isn't big enough for both of us. She settles into my lap, looping her arms around my neck and putting her forehead to mine.

"I will miss you so much," I say, straightening my head up and wiping salty trails of tears from my face.

"You have no idea how much I'll miss you," she says, doing the same to her face. "You need to just talk to Jared, Trystan. Your feelings are valid, and you both deserve to have them voiced. That's the advice you would give me at least." She finishes with a sad, wet wink.

She's not wrong. Word for word, almost.

"Can we go watch Pitch Perfect and order Qdoba?" I sniff and try to smile.

"You had me at Pitch Perfect, snookums."

CHAPTER EIGHTEEN.

It is Jared's twenty-first birthday today. While I feel a smidge of guilt for him choosing me over going buck wild tonight like a standard twenty-one-year-old... I don't feel bad enough to try to convince him to change his mind. And, while I am all for him doing his own thing, I wouldn't be able to go out with him. Birthday's are important to me. Celebrating the day he was brought into this world, celebrating him and feeling blessed that he is reaching a new year... Well, call me old fashioned, but I want to spend that day with him. Plus, he says he doesn't really like the idea of going out and getting wasted.

Will that change when I'm gone?

He invited his brother, and I patted myself on the back for not making a snide comment about it at this point. It's the small victories, I suppose. A few of his friends from high school are in town this weekend so they came as well. He also invited Beth, thank goodness. I don't know if it was all for me or if he genuinely wanted her there, but you won't hear me complaining. We went and bowled a few rounds, had some drinks and ate supper as a group, before coming back to Jared and Kerry's apartment.

So, here we all sit. Jared's friends, Keith and Quincy, are playing on the X-Box in the living room. Kerry is scrolling on his phone in one of the chairs on the patio in his basketball shorts and T-shirt that he changed in to when we got back here. Beth, looking extra cute in her leggings and bright pink tank top, is talking to Devin on the loveseat. Devin kicked her ass in bowling and I think Beth might have a thing for him now.

Love that for her.

"Spend the day with me tomorrow," Jared whispers into my ear from behind me.

We're sitting on the floor of his patio, his back propped up against the railing with me leaned back against his chest and settled in between his legs. He has one knee propped up supporting one of his arms and I've got my legs in front of us next to his injured, almost healed, one. I relish in the view that is his jeans and my leggings together.

I turn my head to look up and behind me, catching his eyes. "You don't have to tell me twice," I say with a smile. "I'm in."

He leans forward and presses a kiss to my cheek. "A hills day-date sounds perfect before you leave," he murmurs into my hair.

And just like that—three words threaten to ruin my whole night. I say nothing back, tightening my grip on his forearm that he has laid over my chest and humming a generic response.

"Before you leave."

Our adventure in the hills was lovely today—it usually is. We stopped at every rock shop we passed, like we always do on these trips. We ate lunch at a little inn that sits in a small crevice of a hill. We listened to all of our favorite songs and laughed when either of us missed notes.

It was perfect.

We stayed out all day and now the sun is setting in front of us. The fact that I leave the day after tomorrow, and the weight of my decision, is starting to feel heavier and heavier with every minute.

Jared brought us to our spot on top of Skyline Drive, the same place we always sit and watch the horizon when the mood strikes. We got out to watch the sun go down together. The different shades of blue, sapphire to cerulean, with the contrasting blood orange and marigold that then meet the dark horizon of the city—it's magic. Even with the lights from the streets and buildings below, it's still beautiful.

"Are you sad that I'm leaving?" I ask from beside Jared.

Both of us have our legs dangling over the side of the short wall, his arm around my back and me leaning my shoulder into him. I don't make to look up at him, but I feel his gaze move to me.

"Am I sad? Trystan, you can't be serious," he says, sounding annoyed and surprised by my question.

I look up now, meeting his eyes. He is, in fact, irritated. I scoot away, not hiding the surprise on my face. He removes his arm from behind me and slides out further so that we can look straight on at each other instead of up and down.

Or maybe he moved to get away from me.

"Yes, I'm serious." I cross my arms over my chest. "Why does that question annoy you?"

"Because it's insane," he says, his voice a little louder than it was a moment ago. "Do you honestly think I am fine with you moving? Like it doesn't affect me? Do you think I want you gone? Do you think I want you to move away?" He stands up and shoves his hands in to the pocket of his dark blue hoodie.

"Well, this is the first you have said any of that so excuse me for thinking you maybe don't give a shit about the situation." I stay seated. "I don't know if you think you have been acting otherwise but from where I've been the last two weeks, you haven't seemed to care at all that I am about to live eight hours away from you."

He scoffs, *actually scoffs*, at me. His eyes are wide and his mouth is open, shock radiating from him.

Then his eyes narrow on me. "This is ridiculous."

"My feelings are ridiculous?" I ask as I get to my feet, crossing my arms.

He must have realized how that came out because he removes his hands from his pocket and runs them down his face before looking at me with pleading eyes.

"I don't want to fight with you when you leave in a day, Trystan."

"It isn't like I said anything to start a fight, Jared."

Fight with me. Fight for me.

My arms stay crossed, even as he walks the few feet over to where I stand.

"I don't *want* you to leave. But I don't want to be the reason you don't do something you want to do." His voice is more calm, his face softer.

"You'll miss me though, yeah?" I ask, looking up at him from under wet lashes. "Like, you aren't happy I'm leaving, are you?" My voice sounds so small, so sad.

Jared reaches out to hold my hands, coming to stand in my space. His lips meet my forehead, the toes of our shoes slightly overlap with proximity. Our hands are clasped together between us at our chests. His breathing is slow and mine feels pained.

"I will miss you every second you are gone, honey."

"I'm sad I'm going," I admit.

"I am too," he replies, his lips still on my skin.

I'd never noticed, until that moment, how sad I actually am. About it all.

The day is finally here. It feels like the last two weeks, maybe months, have lasted two years, but here we are. My car is packed to the brim with shit that I probably won't need but am bringing with just in case.

Like my musical robin.

"Call me every time you stop for gas or bathroom or snacks. Every time, Trystan Victoria Joann," my mom says, standing in front of my car.

Tears well up in her eyes, though she won't allow them to fall until she is safely tucked away in the privacy of her room or the bathroom. She's stoic, that mom of mine.

"Yes, mother, I will call you each time I put this car in to park," I say as I tap the hood twice.

Craig walks up to my mom, placing his arm around her shoulders and pulling her in to him.

"You gave her this lecture already, Trace. Three times," he says with a laugh and a wink at me.

She gives him a light shove and moves out from under his arm. Once she stands in front of me and we look at each other, my own eyes start to burn.

"I will call you. All the time," I say, my voice breaking slightly.

Our hug is quick but tight and I wait until I am pulling out of their driveway before I let any tears fall. I have never not lived with my mom before. I didn't realize how much that would affect me until I saw how much it affected her. I let myself cry the entire way to Jared's apartment, missing my mom already.

I haven't seen Kerry since Jared's birthday, even then the exchanges we had then were brief and robotic at best. I think at this point we both just don't know how to be around each other. I don't see his car in the open garage as I pull in the driveway, and I let out a sigh of relief at that. I notice his bike is missing too, he must be out in the hills somewhere.

Good—he doesn't need to see me leave.

He doesn't need to be a witness to their victory.

Jared is sitting on his porch waiting for me, grey sweatpants and a gray T-shirt on. Perfect color for a shit day. He has his elbows resting on his knees and his hands clasped tightly in front of him.

"You should have seen my mom before I got in my car," I say as I get out. "She was absolutely distraught."

I'm clearly trying to stall the inevitable and he knows it. It seems he isn't quick to stop me though, so I continue.

"Even Craig made fun of her a little bit. The overbearing mother hen." I let out a forced laugh.

"I'm sure she'll just miss you," he says solemnly as I reach where he is sitting.

I take up the spot next to him and mirror his position.

"I know. I'll miss her too," I don't look at him.

We sit like that for few minutes. Quiet, not touching but close—together.

"Tell me not to go."

I see his head turn quickly to face me but I keep mine forward, avoiding meeting his eyes.

"Tell me not to go," I whisper again.

He gets up and moves to squat in front of me. I don't look him in the eyes as his broad shoulders come in to view, then his face. I find a spot between his nose and his lips and focus on that. He's so handsome. I memorize that part on him in this moment—the freckles there and the way the lines from his frowning mouth wrap around it fully.

Skype will not do this boy justice.

"I can't do that, Trystan."

I look down at that, focusing now on a small piece of dirt between my feet. "You *could*. You could tell me to stay. That you love me and that we will figure it all out."

Finally I look up. His eyes... Man. They are so blue—like glowing ice. And worried—they look so worried. But about what, I haven't a clue. Because he won't tell me anything beyond the fact that he loves me. And I haven't asked until yesterday.

"You could tell me to stay here with you for forever and that we can overcome it all and that love will be enough, that *we* will be enough."

My eyes are filled with tears, his with concern.

"I can't do that. I don't want to be the person who stops you from doing something you want to do," he says quietly.

As I move to stand up, he does the same. We're eye level now, me standing on a step above him.

"Okay," I say, forcing myself to be just that—*okay.*

There's that stupid word again.

He reaches out and grabs my hand. I don't stop him, but I don't meet him in the middle or squeeze his hand back.

He knows. He knows that what his mom did and said has broken me, that she has shattered a fundamental part of who I am—who I was. And I don't know if he is choosing to just not voice that knowledge, to not acknowledge that hurt, or if he doesn't realize how deep that crack is. Blissful ignorance maybe? Like, if we don't discuss it, it's fine? His silence on everything though... I can feel the ache deepen to a new low.

"I'll text you and stuff," I say numbly when we reach my car, hand in hand. I stop at my door and we both turn so that we are facing each other. He grabs my other hand with his.

"Call me when you get to your aunts, too," he says.

I guess that's that then.

Why am I even upset? *I* made this choice. The rational part of me knows that. Knows that *I* am *choosing* this route. That *I* am choosing to run. That I, me alone, have made this decision. So why am I suddenly so mad at the man standing in front of me? I'm not super pleased with myself either right now.

But in the same breath—why won't he fight for me? Why did he simply yield to me leaving? He says he doesn't *want* me to leave but yet he isn't telling me not to go. We're both making choices that I don't we understand.

We kiss for a long moment, soaking in the sun and warmth—soaking in each other. I can taste the tears on our lips as we break apart, not even trying anymore to stop them from falling.

"I love you, Jared," I say with a shaky voice.

He reaches up and swipes his thumbs across my cheeks.

"I love you too, Trystan." His own voice giving a small shake. "Forever."

"And always," I barely get out.

He holds me close for another minute, my head on his chest and my heart in his hands.

I call Beth as I get on the interstate, broken. And I know she cries tears of her own for me as I leave Rapid City.

As I leave my home.

As I leave my family and my best friend.

As I leave my heart on the front steps of a west side apartment with a boy who didn't tell me to stay with him like I so badly wanted him to.

Taylor Swift doesn't even make an appearance for the first sixty-eight miles.

CHAPTER NINETEEN.

In the last six days, thirteen hours, and... forty-seven minutes, Nebraska has welcomed me with open arms and an obscene amount of humidity. My hair has never been bigger—and not in a fun way.

"So, did you get the job?" my mom asks on the phone for the second time, bringing me back to our conversation and away from the picture of Jared and I that I have been staring at.

The picture sits tucked in a frame that I picked up at Walmart a couple of days after moving here. My aunt Hope and I went to pick up groceries and I wanted to print some photos of my parents and Mikey, Beth, and Jared. I pinned the majority of the pictures on a cork board that I also got that day. Neon colored pins adorn it all over like a map leading you to the most important people in my life.

Mike on his first day of kindergarten in his navy-blue T-shirt with an American flag on it, holding the straps of his bright red backpack, smiling his perfect little kid smile at my mom behind the camera. My mom and Craig playing Guitar Hero in the living room on our dark blue sectional, both matching accidentally in their light gray Air Force T-shirts—which is so on brand for them. Multiple pictures of Beth and I, but my favorite sits front and center.

It was Senior Skip Day. Somehow both of our schools had SKD on the same day that year. We decided to go to Cabela's and try on fishing hats.

Do we fish? No. Did that stop us? Obviously not.

From there we ventured to Reptile Gardens and then got ice cream even though we are both a little lactose intolerant, but also masochists. The picture is of her and I when we got back to my parents' house. My mom insisted on us putting on our brand new, tags still on, matching hats. We opted for light brown instead of dark or green and I remember feeling so silly and young and fun for our choice in attire and activities on a day when most kids in our classes were getting drunk at the lake or going on wild excursions. Not us though. Shopping for fishing hats we lost almost immediately and walking around a zoo looking at reptiles. That is very much *us*.

And then there is the one of Jared and I that I framed. The frame is a matte silver, two glossy hearts on the top right corner that intertwine. The picture itself is perfection in my absolutely biased opinion. Beth snapped it on her phone before we went into the bowling alley for Jared's birthday. I've got on dark jeans and black flip flops with a dark blue V-neck T-shirt. I straightened my black hair before going out, it's all shiny and hanging past my chest. Jared has on some light blue jeans and white vans with a heather gray crew neck shirt that I got him for his birthday. The picture we posed for before this one was a good one—smile at the camera, his arm around my shoulders, mine around his waist. But then she captured this one too...

I had turned towards Jared thinking we were done with the photo op. I put both of my arms around his waist, holding him close to me, and he pulled me in tighter with one of his arms around my shoulders, his other hand holding my arm just above my elbow. I put my forehead to his chest and smiled, closing my eyes. Jared kissed the top of my head, resting his lips there, closing his own eyes.

I remember feeling just so in love and happy and excited to celebrate the man I love.

I make a mental note to thank my best friend for this photo later tonight when we are on the phone.

"Hello?" I hear, remembering I am supposed to be talking to my mom. "Earth to Trystan?"

I shake my head like I can physically shake off the dark cloud that I have been shouldering for almost a week.

"Yes, sorry. Uh, what did you say?"

I turn from my dresser and take a seat on the edge of my bed. I'm in my cousin's room so it came fully furnished. An old, light brown six drawer dresser, a matching end table that sits by the queen sized bed. This bed has only a frame and creaks horribly any time you get on or off of it. But oh, is she comfortable. The sheets are white, and the blankets are handmade. A quilt my aunt's mother-in-law made forever ago full of color and flowers and random swatches of fabric. The second blanket is one my aunt crocheted, an afghan. It's zig-zag rows of maroon and ivory. On top of the dresser is the television and my Wii with an assortment of Bath & Body Works lotions my aunt stockpiles, amongst other random things. And then, of course, the picture of Jared and I looking blissfully ignorant of the dark cloud above us—in love.

"I'm going to pretend my feelings aren't hurt about being ignored," mom jests. "I asked if you got the job at the restaurant you interviewed for?"

"Oh, right. Yes. I did. *Souvenir's*. I start in two days."

"Oh, honey! That is great news!"

"Totally," I say trying and failing to match her enthusiasm.

It isn't that I'm not excited to have a job. I'm relieved and happy and looking forward to it, really. My aunt and uncle are so easy to live with and I have cousins a plenty in the immediate area to spend time with. A couple of them play baseball, so I have already taken to going to games.

It's just...

I miss Jared and I don't know if he misses me.

I mean, he has says he does, right? But like...

Ugh! Get a grip Trystan. He misses you like he says he does and it's all fine.

It's fine.

"Ma, I got to get going. I have stuff I need to get done before tomorrow," I say, hoping she doesn't smell the lie from all the way up north.

I don't have anything to get done. Maybe paint my nails.

"Okay, sure honey. I'll talk to you later. I love you."

"I love you too."

And with that I am left alone to my overwhelmingly loud thoughts.

I settle on my bed, legs crossed under me, with a bottle of hot pink nail polish and the remote to my Wii. I toggle to Netflix and turn on Gilmore Girls—currently on season four.

Rory just got done having the most awkward conversation with Dean on the street. He invited her to his wedding and even though I know how that all ends, I still find myself surprised at the small bit of momentary hope that I feel for them each time I watch this. Hope that even though they broke up they can still be friends. That they can learn to love each other in a different way. Because I think when you love someone the way they loved each other, wholly and irrevocably, a friendship at some point is almost necessary. How do they go about their lives without each other after everything they went through?

My phone vibrates from next to me while I finish up my toenails and I grab it knowing who it is already.

Hunny Pie

I laugh internally at what he changed his contact name to before I left.

Hunny Pie

My mom just said the weirdest thing to me.

Intrigue.

I refrain from being snarky and stop myself from typing out *"anything semi decent would be surprising."*

> What's that?

> She said I've been different lately.

> Like, lately as in?

Loving this for me already.

> She said the last week...

> She said I haven't been as moody, and also not as talkative. But really, I just miss you so I think I'm quieter now.

> But I guess at least she isn't fighting with me anymore or being a bitch.

I feel my heart stutter as I set my phone down on my bed.

So... Now that I'm not there to cause a rift, his mom is being nicer to him? Have I really been *the* catalyst this entire time and I was just too young and dumb to realize that it is, in fact, *me* that has been *the* problem?

I can't have been that blind, right?

No way...

But what if...

What if I really am the sole problem preventing Jared and Darla and then Kerry from having a good, loving, respect filled relation-ship?

It all hits me like a truck. A big, mean, snarky truck with hateful eyes and bad hair. And I know what I need to do—it's nothing I haven't been fully aware of for a long while. I may be one to rush into things or rather, away from things. But this... I can't be the reason for this anymore. It isn't fair to Jared.

Can I call you in fifteen?

Definitely.

My mind spirals. If I really have been the only thing standing between Jared and Darla having a good relationship, or even just a simply *calm* relationship, what am I doing, other than being selfish, by continuing to be the issue? I don't enjoy this—the volatile atmosphere between all of us. It strains things between Jared and I, and it clearly affects him in his heart when it comes to his mom. Why wouldn't it? He loves her, despite all of the bull shit. And he should, Darla is his mom and even I respect that much of her.

I may not respect her, but I can respect the fact that Darla is Jared's mom and at the end of the day that isn't something that should be messed with.

Right?

So, the fact that I seem to be the one thing that can draw them apart, cause strife and hard feelings... What am I supposed to do with that knowledge? It isn't like me moving was meant to be a sort of science experiment. I hadn't been meaning to test a theory that I hadn't even been thinking about.

Unless... Had I been? Did I know all along that me leaving would mend something between them? Or at the very least that take away one piece of an unstable equation?

What does that mean for Jared and I? I can't ignore the fact that he seems happier now that I'm not there to cause issues.

His voice is brighter on phone calls. His face seems less stressed on Skype. He mentioned he is getting better sleep lately.

I clearly am not the only one that sees that. His mom bringing up his sunnier disposition today says enough.

Me gone = a happier Jared.

I stand from my bed, only a couple minutes having passed since Jared's last text. I look around my room, my head spinning and my heart breaking.

I have to break up with Jared.

Oh no.

I can't morally, knowingly stand in the way of Jared having a good relationship with his mom.

Without another thought I grab my phone and shove it in the pocket of my leggings and head upstairs.

"I'll be back. I'm going to go drive around and talk to Jared," I tell my aunt as I walk through the kitchen.

Hope Jelinek stands at five feet ten inches and rocks the cutest highlighted pixie cut. Skinny and long and tone—a knockout. Her eyes are the prettiest shade of icy blue and her personality could rival the sunshine for how good she makes people feel.

Leaning against the counter by the sink with a paper plate full of microwaved shredded cheese and tortilla chip nachos she says to me, "Okay, sweet pea. I'll be here."

Her kitchen is newly remodeled. Tuscan style orange tiles on the floor. The same brown, wooden cupboards line the walls up high and below the white counter. An island with a flat top stovetop next to a double sink sits to the left of where you can walk from the living room to the mud room that houses the side door in and out of the house. She stands facing the island, back to the counter, next to the second double sink. I look out the small window that sits slightly behind her and see that the sun has started to go down. The sky is painted a light pink and I quickly remind my feet to keep moving.

I park my car by the baseball field and leave it running. It may be getting dark but here in Nebraska that does not equate to cooler temperatures or less humidity.

Or less bugs.

So, in my car, air conditioned and insect-less, I will remain.

I didn't notice my hands shaking until I grabbed my phone from the passenger seat. Now while I stare at my lock screen, the same picture of Jared and I from his birthday that is printed and framed in my room, I see how nervous I am.

Who wouldn't be?

I'm about to break up with the man I love for reasons that have nothing to directly do with him and I. I'm sick to my stomach over this whole thing. I'm making the choice, yes. But this choice isn't *for* me. This is for him—for the relationship I know he wishes he had with his mom.

Without giving myself more time to think about it, to question what the hell I'm doing, I press his name on my favorites list and wait for Jared to pick up.

I don't have to wait long.

"Hey babe." I can hear the smile in his voice.

"Hey," I say. "I need to talk to you about something."

"Oh, okay. Shoot, what's up?" His tone is still light and hopeful.

"I think," I loose a breath, "I think we need to break up."

Silence.

More silence.

"Jared?" I whisper.

Unshed tears line my eyes and the lump in my throat grows. An ache takes up residence in my chest.

"Yeah, I'm here," he says just as quietly.

I give him more time, fixating on the peridot rosary hanging from my rearview mirror. I found it in a box when I was twelve, it belonged to my great grandma once upon a time.

I try not to overthink his silence. Try and fail.

Does he not care? Is he busy playing a video game or something? I mean, surely he is about to start asking why or telling me no or he will do something that might resemble putting up a fight... right?

"Okay."

I can't have heard that correctly. I blink a few times before finding my voice.

"Okay?" I ask slowly.

"Sounds like you made your mind up. So yeah, okay." His tone is clipped but also not and-

What the fuck?

"Okay?"

That's it?

Damn near three years, a million firsts, a lot of "I love you's" and "forever and always" and he simply says "okay"?

"Okay... I guess I'll let you go then," I manage to get out through sheer will and determination to not completely implode on the phone right now.

After hanging up, I sit here and feel shocked. If I were to hear this story second hand, I would call bull shit. This is simply unreal. But as it is, I just sat front row to this disaster—it is as real as the mosquito currently trying to fight its way into my car.

I think I must have blacked out for a couple minutes, driving to my aunts in blind despair. Before I know it, I'm walking back in to her house. I couldn't tell you who hung up first or if anything more was said. *"Okay"* is on repeat inside of my head. That word is all I remember right now of the English language.

I am numbly meandering, aiming for the stairs that lead to my room—to my bed. To what I hope is a small bit of sanctuary. I am so focused on not being focused that I don't even see Hope standing by the stairs with a basket of clean towels.

"Hey sweet pea, you okay?" Her voice sounds like she's under water but that's silly because there she is, standing at the doorway to the stairs.

I don't know when I started crying again but the floodgates have opened completely, and I don't think it will stop any time soon. I walk straight into aunt Hope's open arms, nearly collapsing to the floor. She says nothing as I cry into her. She just lets me break.

So, I do.

I cry.

And cry.

And cry.

Hope doesn't say a word.

Hope.

I am clinging to Hope. My entire heart has just shattered in to a million and one pieces. My whole world has been spun upside down. And here I am—clinging to Hope. Only, there is no hope to be found anywhere near me.

CHAPTER TWENTY.

You know that scene in Legally Blonde where Elle Woods is lying in bed eating chocolate and she's watching a movie? And the main male character in that movie tells his love interest that he loves her? And then Elle yells "liar!" and throws the box of chocolates at the television? She looks all disheveled and sad and broken. Puffy and unwashed.

That's me.

Minus the throwing because your girl isn't wasteful.

Here I sit, propped up against the wall that my bed is against, pillows aplenty. The afghan laying across my outstretched and crossed legs is providing some much needed weight. Copious amounts of half empty plastic water bottles litter the area around my bed and bedside table. And a bag of mixed chocolates take up residence in my lap.

Dove, obviously.

The Wedding Date has been on repeat for the last eight days. Something about Dermot Mulroney is so comforting.

And hot.

Eight days.

It's been just over a week since Jared and I broke up. Eight miserable, sad, lonely days. We have talked a few times, just via text. The majority of them are me telling him that I hate this and that I miss him and that I'm sorry and I wish things were different already.

I lied to him and I hate myself every second for it.

He eventually asked me why I ended things. I knew, or rather hoped, that if I were to be honest with him that he would tell me I'm stupid and that the real reason is invalid and ludicrous, and all would be fixed and remedied.

So instead of being honest and telling him it's because of his mom and the fact that I seem to be the main culprit to their unhealthy relationship, I went with bull shit.

"It isn't either of us. I just live so far away and I think it's best if we both just see what it's like to not have the other person to depend on or expect anything from. Blah blah blah."

Lies.

And whether he bought them or not—I don't know. But he hasn't pushed it since.

In the last few days I have realized I have a very small circle. Minuscule, really. Beth, my aunt, and my mom. That pretty much sums it up now that Jared isn't in it. And honestly, I don't really want to talk to anyone other than Jared.

Alone on an island.

So, in my sad and lonely, mentally unstable state... I have made friends with Bob. Bob is a gentle fella. He doesn't do much during the daylight hours—like me. He's quiet and listens when I talk.

Doesn't hardly judge me while I sob—at least not out loud. He's easy to get to considering he lives here. In this house... In the bathroom... In between where the bottom of the wall doesn't quite meet the concrete floor. He's very relaxed, and I think equally as lonely as I am.

Bob is a spider. A daddy-long-legs to be precise. And he keeps me company while I cry-sing Julie Roberts' 'Break Down Here' in the shower.

I should maybe be institutionalized.

Am I mildly depressed? Absolutely.

Do I think I have made huge mistakes by moving here and then dumping the man I have loved for almost three years, and still love today, via a phone call? You bet.

Is it weird and unhealthy that Bob the Spider has become something I depend on daily?

Let's skip that one.

Alas, heartbreak doesn't get you out of work so as my phone rings with my alarm, I realize it's time to brush my teeth and get ready for hosting.

Once in my car, hair brushed and teeth clean, I let out a sigh. It does nothing to alleviate the crushing pressure on my chest, but it was a valiant effort. As I exit town, a Cubby's gas station to my left and an endless highway in front of me and to my right, I pick up my phone and click *"Don't Forget Me"* on my favorite's list.

The line rings for what feels like eons.

"Oh my gosh," I gasp to myself as the line stops ringing.

This can't be real life.

"What? Are you okay?" Beth asks in her worried voice.

It is no secret she is concerned about me.

"I'm at an intersection on the way to work, right?"

"Yes?" she drawls.

"There's a gas station right here, I'm right outside of town. Guess the name. Go ahead," I say, in utter disbelief.

My knuckles have gone white. My heart rate has gone up. I crack my neck waiting for Beth to answer, squeezing my eyes shut for an almost dangerous number of seconds.

"Um... Hard Rock Gas?" She laughs at herself.

"Ha." Unamused I say, "It's literally named *Jared's*, Beth. Spelled just like Jared. My-" I cut myself off, painfully aware that I can't say that. "Well, not my Jared anymore I guess."

Ouch. That stung.

I wish I could slam my head into my steering wheel without any consequences.

"You're shitting my dick."

"I absolutely wish I was."

How have I not noticed this before today?

Like she heard my thought, or maybe I said it out loud, she says, "You *have* been in, like, a daze since the," a gentle pause, "incident," she finishes quietly.

"Yes, but have I been so bad that I have driven by this place at least a dozen times since moving down here three weeks ago, and have been in such a funk that I haven't noticed that giant name in lights?" I ask, my breath quickening and my heart pounding.

She starts laughing. Actually laughing. And honestly. I can't blame her. I would laugh at me too if I weren't so miserably heartbroken. If I hadn't forgotten how it feels to *want* to laugh.

"This is punishment. It has to be."

A long stretch of silence passes. Self-loathing on my end, utter unknowing how to proceed on Beth's, I'm sure.

"I did the right thing, right?"

Silence.

"Beth." I breathe out. "Did I fuck up my entire life?"

The panic is hitting big time and I have got to get it together before I pull into the parking garage or my coworkers will know that the cool, calm, collected façade I have been playing at work is just that—a façade.

Fake.

Unreal.

Untrue.

I am certifiable.

An absolute basket case.

Finally, Beth's soft voice breaks through. "Not your entire life babe. No. I just don't know if breaking up with Jared was the right call or not."

"But-" I start.

"No," she interrupts gently. "I know. I know why you did it. And it's honorable. But Trystan? You guys were electric."

"So electric that all he said was 'okay', Beth? That's it."

He said 'okay' when I told him I was moving. He said 'okay' when I told him we should break up.

What I would give at this point to never have to hear someone say that word to me again.

There was no fight. Just like when his mom declared that I would never be a part of their family—there was no fight. Jared didn't fight for me...

"Someone who wants to spend the rest of forever with you wouldn't just let you go like that," I continue, my voice breaking. "He wouldn't have just let me go like that."

"I don't know, babe." She sounds so solemn. "I wish I had the answers for you because I know you're dying inside over this. But I don't."

"I wish I hated him, Beth. It would be so easy to be angry with him for breaking my heart." I wipe tears from my face, my fingers mirroring the windshield wiper blades removing the falling rain from my view. "But instead, I can only blame myself for that shattered, half beating organ inside me."

"I love you, Tryst."

"Love you too, B. I gotta go, I'm at work."

How did I go from blissfully happy and in love, with an irritating semi-in-law family presence, to miserable and still in love and lonely in a matter of weeks?

I opted to work a double today, figured the extra cash and the lack of time to think and sulk would be lovely. What I didn't anticipate was the walk to my car after twelve hours, up the five flights of stairs to the top of the parking garage that sits next to the hotel *Souvenir's* is in.

"My feeeeeeet," I grumble to myself while I reach the top, my little red car now in sight.

I freeze as the heavy door to the stairs slams from behind me.

Something else I didn't think I would endure today; the flat tire greeting me on the rear passenger side of my car.

"Noooooo," I plea as I drag my aching feet the rest of the way. I look up to the dark, wet sky. "What did I do to you, huh? Why? I let him go *for* him! I broke my fucking heart *for* him! I let her win, consequences for myself be damned! What did I do wrong here, huh!?"

As I look to the Heavens, begging God to let me in on his game plan, I force myself to hold my tears at bay. I square my shoulders and focus on the tangible task ahead. I can change a fucking tire—easy.

I have, thankfully, known how to change a tire since I learned how to drive. It was a requirement per my parents. And thank goodness because the clouds are continuing to roll in and I do not need to be caught in another bout of this storm on the top of a giant building after twelve hours of working on my feet and faking a smile.

Someone has got to be messing with me.

And with that thought... I get caught in a storm, on the top of a high parking garage, after working for twelve hours, while changing a tire on my car.

Trying to change a tire on my car, actually.

The lug nut is stuck. I don't know how or why or really what to do at this point. All I know is the stupid thing is stuck to the other stupid thing and I'm at a loss.

In general, really.

I put my whole body in to trying to get the last bolt off. I try everything I can think of. And as the rain starts to come down even harder and colder, I decide it's a sign. For what? I'm not sure.

Hilary Duff made being caught in the rain look way nicer.

A sign that I did in fact ruin my life by moving here and dumping my boyfriend?

A sign that God is mad at me for some undisclosed reason?

A sign, perhaps, that I should have checked a weather report and maybe parked on floor four?

I must be a sight to behold.

While the rain comes down... I lie here on my back, eyes closed, salt from my tears mixing with the fresh water from the clouds. My messy bun is now extra messy and soaked, the pieces that have escaped it are stuck to my face and neck. My black button-up long-sleeve shirt is now untucked and unbuttoned to just below my chest. I am thoroughly drenched. My black slacks that were dirty with mustard and spilled soda are now getting washed clean. And my feet, bare since the moment I stepped on to the second flight of stairs, rest next to the round-toed black work shoes I curse at all day.

I hate this. All of it.

I hate that I am depressed.

I hate that the only two people to really, truly blame is Darla and myself.

I hate that at almost 20 years old I am sad and lonely and questioning whether or not I just made the biggest mistake of my life.

In the middle of my very own rom-com-worthy meltdown, I think I hear someone say something from a distance. I choose to ignore it.

If it is even real.

"Miss?" I hear, this time a little louder.

I crack open an eye, someone *is* speaking.

"Miss?!"

Oh yeah, someone is definitely yelling now.

"MA'AM!!"

With that holler, I sit up in a jolt and look around. I spot a bald-headed man with skin the color of the iced oat milk latte I had this morning leaning out a window across the street, his view level with the top floor of the garage.

I point to my chest in question.

"Yes, you." He points back at me. "Are you okay?" he yells.

Oh yeah, definitely a sight to be held.

Certifiable.

After reassuring the man I am perfectly fine and not planning on jumping off any high buildings in the near future—*debatable*—a guy I work with, with impeccable timing, makes his way to his car that is parked next to mine. Chivalry is not dead, I realize, as he helps me change my tire.

Before I know it, I am finally headed back to the safety of my bed.

Back to Dermot and Bob and the box of tissues that I remind myself to replenish soon.

CHAPTER
TWENTY-ONE.

My neck hurts like I have been viciously attacked. My feet... *oh my feet*. It's as if I've had them folded in half for seventy-two hours, stuffed in to my shoes. *And my back.* My back feels like it has carried the weight of three elephants across the African jungle with no rest.

And at this point I must be hallucinating because of the pain.

There is no way that the six-foot two-inch, tanned, muscled, chestnut haired boy I love with every fiber of my being is sitting on the porch of my aunt Hope's Victorian era home.

The porch is my favorite part of this house. It is weathered and white. Wraps around two sides of their home and sits a few feet off the ground, lattice fencing covering anything underneath. My aunt has it decorated with a couple hanging planters full of petunias of assorted colors—reds, purples, white with pink in the center. She has a small, yellow metal bistro style table with two matching chairs off to the left of the four wide stairs that take you on to the porch.

To the right is the front door that they never use—don't ask me why, I haven't a clue. The whole thing is quite picturesque.

And there, in the middle of the top step of the porch, looking handsome as ever in light blue jeans and the same old gray T-shirt I saw him in the last time I saw him in person, sits Jared.

My Jared.

I pull my car up the curb in front of the house and start to get out, moving quickly and spastically. I grab my phone from where it sits on the passenger seat, and I can't help the huge smile gracing my face.

I think I almost had forgotten how to genuinely smile.

"Trystan," he says with a smile as I make my way, work uniform and gross hair forgotten, around the grass to the concrete strip that leads to the steps.

"Trystan." But this time he sounds like he's further away from me as I take a step towards the porch.

I narrow my eyes and pick up my pace. I reach out to him, six feet away. Now four, a yard... My chest gets tight and the panic sets in.

"Trystan!"

I snap my eyes open and just like that I am in my room, the open ceiling staring back at me along with my aunt's concerned icy-blue stare.

"Your alarm has been going off for fifteen minutes, sweet pea," she says as she takes a step back.

It was a dream. He isn't here. He didn't come for me.

Why would he?

I hold it together until Hope is halfway up the stairs and out of view.

I make it another fifteen minutes before I call in to work.

I manage to get to the bathroom, brush my teeth, say hi to Bob, shoot my mom a text so she doesn't try to call me and hear the desperately sad voice I have been trying to conceal from her, all before I collapse back in to bed.

Dermot has my attention for all of seven minutes before I am fast asleep—chasing that dream, the man, and the false reality it comes with.

Jared isn't coming back for you.

I'll never be his again.

CHAPTER TWENTY-TWO.

August in Nebraska is even more unenjoyable than June in Nebraska. The way in which my leggings stick to my butt by the time I walk down the concrete path from my aunt's house to my car is an absolutely disgusting feeling.

I miss South Dakota.

I miss my mom. I miss Mikey. I miss Beth fucking Stanton with my whole heart. I miss the less-wet ninety-degree weather.

I miss Jared.

We are still very much broken up. I have remained single, my heart needing more time to heal than his, apparently.

That isn't to say that there haven't been other boys in the two months since that horrid phone call in the baseball field parking lot.

When you're bleeding out, don't you try to at least stop the bleed? Even if it's a small brown Band-Aid on a gaping chest wound, you try to do what you can to alleviate any part of the pain.

That's what I have been doing with Xavier from work. Trying to staunch the pain. It has been working efficiently enough. I haven't called out of work to lay in bed and hope to rot since I started seeing him. "Seeing him" in the most casual of ways.

Band-aid casual.

Jared, however, didn't seem to have too much trouble bandaging his wound.

Caitie is her name. Jared started dating Caitie not two weeks after the demise of my relationship with him.

I know all of this due to two reasons.

Rapid City is small enough that word travels fast and people like to update you on your ex.

And Jared himself told me.

How kind.

I don't know how most people do post-breakup life when a giant catalyst to never speak again is not present. We never had an all-out brawl. He didn't cheat on me and vice versa. There was no major conflict between *just* the two of us to end things over.

I do know that the fact that Jared and I still talk every single day, at least once, is incredibly unhealthy and absolutely the way I need it to be, or I *will* go fully catatonic.

Today I am covering the coffee kiosk that's across the lobby of the hotel *Souvenir's* resides in. The raspberry white chocolate iced mocha I made for myself is dripping water on to the stainless-steel counter I'm sitting next to. The hum of the ice machine and the other appliances is the only noise outside of my head.

Today is so slow.

I grab a towel from behind me, not moving from where I am seated on a black stool, to wipe up the moisture from my drink and then use as a coaster.

Jared

That sucks. Maybe they'll let you close early though.

Yeah, maybe.

What are you doing tonight?

Idiot, why ask him that?

Just hanging out.

Cool cool.

Here's the thing—Jared is my best friend. Does it absolutely hurt like hell to still be talking to him without all of the "I love you" shit? Yes.

Does the friend he is to me make me think that it is worth the pain? Also, yes.

So, even though I want to cease to exist every time one of our meaningless conversations end without the "love you", I will push through that pain because he is worth it to me. He always has been.

Beth's grandma died yesterday. I'm coming home tomorrow for the weekend to be with her and go to the funeral Monday.

That sucks for Beth. Nice that you can come up for her.

Are we going to see each other at all?

My boss did in fact let me close the kiosk early and go home. It's a Thursday night in a small, sleepy town and while I could call a cousin, or Xavier, to find something to do... I am instead lying in bed after my shower and checking my phone every thirteen seconds like that will make him reply to my text from hours ago.

"Fuck it," I say to myself.

I grab my phone and stand up from my bed, my wet hair wrapped up in a white towel and a red one covering my body. As the phone starts to ring, I realize something.

I don't have the right to call Jared like this anymore. Who am I to think it's okay to be upset that he didn't respond to my text two hours ago? I am not his girlfriend. And what if he's with him new *girlfriend*? He owes me nothing. I freed him from his obligation to me two months ago now. And he *is* probably with his new girlfriend and here I am calling him like some sad, heartbroken fool that is still in love with him.

Because I am all of those things.

Desperate much?

Yes. Very.

"Hey," I hear a second after the ringing stops.

"Hi," I manage to squeak out of my suddenly tight throat.

"You okay?" Jared asks.

"In the lightest of ways, sure."

"Okay," he drawls out.

"Listen," I start. "I know I don't have a right to be upset about you not texting me back earlier but I am and I just need to talk to you about it because I am fucking sad and I miss you and I know you have a girlfriend now but we were together for almost three years and so the fact that you have replaced me so quickly has me a complete mess and I just don't understand any of it Jared." I take a large breath.

Oh, so we are doing this *then, huh?*

After a long moment of silence, I begin again. "Jar-"

"I don't want to talk about Caitie. It will just hurt you more. All I can say is that I am sorry you're having a hard time with," he pauses and takes an audible sigh, "all of this."

"Am I the only one having a hard with this? I am crazy to think that we should have mattered more?" I whisper.

I feel like I am in some horrible fever dream. This can't be my life right now.

He loved me, right? I didn't imagine that?

"Of course I *am* having a hard time with this, Trystan. But it isn't like you haven't been seeing anyone else either."

"Sleeping with a random boy from work to keep myself from driving my car off the bridge that I have to cross every time I go into the city is completely different than you having someone you call your girlfriend, Jared."

"Don't say shit like that. It isn't funny."

"I'm not trying to be funny," I snap.

Neither of us speaks after that, both of us not knowing what to say.

Listen... I'm not suicidal in the serious, *you need to be alarmed, lock me up, and hire a therapist* kind of way. I don't *want* to die. Not really. I just...

I am so fucking sad.

And while I may not have the right, while I may be out of line, I ask anyways... "I get it if you don't want to see me. And I'm sorry that you don't. But I would like to see you in person at least one last time this weekend when I'm back. Even if it's just to say goodbye to you Jared."

"Okay."

Learn a new word J.

"I guess I'll talk to you tomorrow then." Relief washes over me.

"Drive safe, Trystan.

CHAPTER TWENTY-THREE.

"**Y**es, I am pulling in now" I reassure my mom as I park my car at Beth's place.

The drive home was quiet and sad. Much like the last long drive I made when I was going south.

And south I went...

It was eight hours of the Julie Roberts playlist on Pandora. Only Beth and my mom calling to check in on how the drive was going, one person loudly missing from that group. I filled my soul with a lot of Honey BBQ Fritos, beef jerky, and Mountain Dew. I only cried twice.

Progress.

I hear a loud squeal from behind me as I grab my duffel bag out of the backseat. Beth must have been watching for me out her front window.

"You're here!" she yells at me as she bounds down her driveway.

She lives in the same apartment villa as Jared and Kerry. A few blocks from each other, but the front of their buildings is almost identical. I feel my chest tighten and force myself to focus my attention on my now brunette best friend.

"I'm here." I try to smile genuinely but she can see right through it. Her extra-long-lasting hug proof of that.

I pick my bag back up from where I dropped it on the pavement and follow Beth inside. The air is so much more livable up here—not as humid. But even still... I feel like I'm suffocating.

The whole way into town, and then through it, to get to Beth's I searched every driver's side window of a white car for his face. It didn't matter if it wasn't the same kind of car. If it was white, he might be in it.

Even walking the short distance from outside and into the cool air of Beth's home, I kept looking around like I might see him lurking in a shadow or sitting at the end of the street.

After settling my things in to Beth's guest room, the two of us sit in our respective spots on her couch—the red cushions providing comfort.

We talk about her grandma and Beth's memories with her. She was a great lady, kind and empathetic. Much like my sweet, grieving friend. We order Chinese takeout and turn on Pitch Perfect—our usual. The movie serves more as background noise while we scroll on our phones.

"Jared and I are meeting up at the L tomorrow," I say, aiming for nonchalance, from the corner of the couch I occupy.

"When did that get decided?"

"Just now." I hold up my phone so she can read the texts Jared and I just exchanged.

"What is the," she pauses with a finger tapping her chin, humming. "Goal? Yeah, what is the goal of meeting up with him tomorrow? Do you want him back? Do you want to be done and never talk to him again? Do you want back-up to kick his ass for moving on so quickly because I'm there for that." She wiggles her dark brows at me.

"We are not beating him up, Stanton," I say with an eye roll.

Everyone should have a friend like Beth. Or at least *be* a friend like Beth.

"We should," she mumbles with her own answering eye roll.

After a minute of thought I tell her, "I don't know what my goal is. I just know that I need to see him."

"Fair enough, babe."

The L parking lot is just like it sounds—a parking lot in the shape of an L. It sits next to a couple tennis courts on the corner of one of the busier roads here in town. There isn't much special about it other than the fact that it is public, and anyone can just be on it, whenever. Behind it is the creek that runs through town casting a nice dull roaring sound.

It's after dark now as I pull into the L. I tried to keep myself busy today so that I didn't dwell entirely on tonight and the magnitude of my choices thus far—or show up five hours early. Alas, my stomach has felt like it houses a cement block, and my heart hasn't slowed its incessant beating since I awoke at Beth's house thirteen hours ago.

I really tried, too. When I woke up, I wasted no time in self-pity. I got up, washed my unruly dark hair, brushed my teeth, made Beth and I some eggs and toast. I called my mom and set up a lunch date. I then attended aforementioned lunch date where she grilled me for an hour and a half.

"I just want to know what happened."

"Mom, I already told you what happened. I felt like the distance wasn't working so I broke up with him."

"I'm not trying to call you a liar Trystan, but do you think I am stupid?"

"No, mom. I don't think you are stupid. I just don't know what you want me to tell you."

"The truth would be nice." She threw an eye roll in there for emphasis.

"Mom, I would rather just not talk about this. It's over, it's done, he has a girlfri-"

"Don't get me started on that whole thing," my mom said as she picked her water up to take a sip. She continued a moment later, "I don't care what you say about him having a new girlfriend. He loves you. I know it. He is trying to move on because men can't be alone. It's stupid but it's true. He loves you and you love him, and I just simply do not understand what happened and why you broke up with him."

And that was all *before* the spinach artichoke dip showed up to our booth at Chili's.

I don't know why I am keeping the truth from her.

His mom sucks less without me around and I would rather be the one to choose between her and me instead of having Jared do it.

Either way I end up destroyed.

The digital clock in my car turns to ten—the time we decided on. And while I didn't think it was scientifically possible, my already rapid heart rate doubles.

I see headlights to my right, through my passenger window, my breathing now becoming choppy. I try to not over think it all.

I fail.

What am I doing here? Am I going to beg him to take me back? Am I going to get out and receive a box of my things? Is he going to yell at me and tell me how much he hates me? Is he going to get out and thank me for making his life easier by removing myself from it?

My breathing is erratic, my heart the same, and I can feel the tip of my nose start to tingle like it does when I'm hyperventilating. My legs are shaking uncontrollably while I sit here, white knuckles gripping my steering wheel.

I am having a panic attack.

Fantastic.

I've had these on occasion. Once when I went to donate blood at a school fundraiser and had to leave before I got stuck by the needle. It took me a solid hour to feel like I could drive again. Another time was when I got caught smoking cigarettes the summer before I turned seventeen and I thought my mom would never stop being disappointed in me. I hyperventilated on the floor by our dining room table for what felt like forever.

I try to count to ten, to tap my fingers together while doing so, but each time I get distracted by the tingling that is spreading to my cheeks, to my lips. I rub my palms down my black leggings' clad thighs. Anything outside of this car is now null and void, the thoughts in my brain are the only things real right now.

He hates me or he doesn't, and I don't know which is worse.

Little does he know—he can't possibly hate me more than I hate myself.

I jump at the knock that sounds on my driver's side window. I look to my left as Jared pulls my door open and ducks his head into my car, grabbing my hands and pulling them to his chest. His calloused fingers feel so familiar. Like home and heartbreak all at once. I'm not buckled at this point, so it doesn't take much for my body to go to his—like it has for years.

"Trystan, you gotta breathe. Look at me right here." He motions to his eyes with two fingers.

I look everywhere but his eyes. His perfect, expressive, blue eyes.

They probably show how much he doesn't care about you anymore.

"Trystan, come on. Look at me, right here." His voice is more serious now as he motions to his eyes again.

I do as he says and meet his gaze, crumbling the second I see the warmth there.

What's worse? He hates my very existence for breaking up with him or he doesn't care at all about any of it?

"I'm. So. Sorry," I say between sobs.

"I know, I know. I need you to breathe though, baby. I need you to calm down and just focus on me and breathe with me. It's okay.

Okay? It's okay." His voice gets softer with every word, his hand holding mine loosens slightly.

We sit there for a few long minutes. Each breath he takes, I try to mirror. Neither of us breaking eye contact, nor the hands we're holding. Eventually my breathing evens out to an acceptable rate.

"I'm sorry. I don't know why I thought I needed to see you. I knew it wasn't a good idea." My words come out breathless still.

Jared smiles weakly at me, squatting next to where I sit in my car still.

He is so beautiful. With only a few streetlights illuminating us, I take in Jared for the first time in over two months.

His russet hair looks like it's freshly cut—sitting short and crisp. His face is tanner than when I saw him last. He has on a simple gray T-shirt, jeans, and white vans. He looks maybe a little thinner. All in all, the same Jared I saw in June.

And then there is me... I have absolutely lost weight. And not in a healthy way. Chain smoking cigarettes on the daily, a diet of Mountain Dew and eating actual food once a day, and general sadness did wonders for my waist size.

Two out of ten—would not recommend.

I drag my gaze back up to his face. I have my legs out of my car, facing Jared straight on. He's got his feet under him and is squatting in front of me, his arms resting on my knees. The creek, our breathing, and the cars on the surrounding streets provide the only sounds this late at night.

"It's good to see you," he says, squeezing my hands with his before standing up and stepping back a few paces.

I follow him, standing up and shutting my door. I focus on a rock that sits next to my feet as I take up a spot by my car. Neither of us say anything. The awkwardness is heavy in the air, weighing down every thought in my brain. I finally look up to Jared's face and find that his eyes are on me.

"I'm sorry," I say, barely above a whisper.

"I know, Tryst." He takes a step towards me, only a yard or so between us now.

I can smell his favorite, my favorite, cologne from here—True American Eagle. I relish in knowing his scent still. Thankful that at least that hasn't changed.

"Let's go for a drive," he says, nodding his chin towards his Continental.

He doesn't wait for a reply before going around the front of my car to the passenger side of his, opening the door and waiting for me to decide.

Not much of a choice there.

His car smells like I remember.

Black Ice.

We don't talk as we drive around the darkened city, lights of houses and buildings and tall posts reflecting off windows and cars. Both of our windows are rolled down and the sound of the local country radio station is a dull background noise.

We make it to almost twenty minutes of just silence between us before Jared speaks first.

"I don't know what to do here, Tryst."

I nod slowly, even though I don't know to which part he is specifically referring to. He continues driving and like in the past I let him work his way through what he needs to say.

"I love you. That hasn't changed. But I *am* with Caitie now."

His emphasis on the last sentence cause tears to form in my eyes.

"It wouldn't be fair to her to just dump her because of..."

I see from my peripheral that Jared looks over at me while he pauses before looking back at the road ahead and going on.

"I don't want to not talk to you anymore, Trystan. I don't want to never see you again and not have you in my life. But right now, I can't just *dump* Caitie." He takes a breath, his knuckles turning a bright white against his steering wheel. "And honestly, I'm kind of pissed about this whole thing still." His voice turns cold.

At me.

I turn my head to look at him now. His squared shoulders, both hands on the wheel, his eyes unmoving from in front of him.

"I'm sorry, Jared. I really am," I say before looking away. "I would take it all back in an instant," I whisper, more to myself.

Jared turns the car right and takes a road I know well. We drive up the winding street to the top of Skyline Drive and he parks in our usual spot.

I guess it isn't ours anymore.

We sit in more quiet, all four windows down now and the music turned completely off. The cars on the street below the cliffside are the only noise beyond the breathing between us. I unbuckle my seatbelt and open my door. The feeling of suffocation becoming unbearable. I make my way over to the short brick wall while listening to Jared do the same from behind me before taking up the spot next to me.

Three months ago he would have sat six inches closer, his arm would have been around my shoulders, his fingers wrapped up in my hair, with my body leaning closely in to his.

Tonight though... The distance between us is loud and silent all at once.

"Sometimes," I begin, clearing my throat before going on. I stare ahead, watching the faint white light of the stars in the horizon glimmer. "Sometimes I think no one in my life really knows me. Like at all, honestly. Not Beth or my mom. And that's my fault. I think I show what I believe people want form me, or what they expect me to be. Good or bad. Whether it's a loud or quiet laugh, bad jokes to lighten the mood, a resting bitch face and standoffish attitude, or a welcoming warm charming smile. Whatever they assume me to be—I become. I feel like I have conditioned myself over the last few years to believe I know what someone thinks of me and then to give them that version of myself."

I look over at Jared. His eyes are wholly on me, his face solemn but warm. His hands rest lightly clasped together in his lap as he leans forward slightly—like he needs to see my face while I speak. Turning back to the night sky I continue on, my voice surprisingly steady. I allow myself to smile, albeit sadly, not needing to hide anything here—not from him.

"But then there's been *you*. And you know me—to my very center, I think. And what happens," I turn to look at him once more and he sits up straight. "What happens when you decide that you don't even like me anymore? You are no longer bound to me by a romantic attachment. You could just, like, *go*. And no one would question it. No one would probably even blame you because of what a mess I have made of us."

His crystal blue eyes are too much for me to handle, nearly shutting me up completely. So, before I decide to just leap off the edge of this hill, I divert my gaze once more and face forward. I feel Jared's eyes still focused on me, though.

"I just need you to promise me something. Even though I don't deserve it at this point. I need you to make this deal with me, okay?"

I turn around towards the parking lot behind us and stand up, pacing in front of Jared who turns around to face me. Walking back and forth between Jared and his car, my hands pulling at my messy bun over and over before eventually falling slack at my sides. The next sentence sticks to my tongue like a bittersweet candy.

"I will take you as my friend. It will be the hardest thing I might ever truly choose to endure in my life. It might suck the very hope from my bones—the little bit left anyways. I honestly might die a little bit inside. But I will take you any way I can get you. And if you are serious about where you are at, who you are with—and my choices are either love you without you or love you with a one-hundredth of you... I will choose you. In any form or percentage or variable—I will choose you every single time."

I pause my pacing to stand in front of Jared, placing my hands on my hips and squaring my shoulders.

"Promise me that you will never disappear," I beg, knowing it might be too much to even ask for. "That if you ever need to, or want to, no longer have a one-hundredth of *me*, that you will tell me goodbye. Whether it's to respect a girlfriend's wishes of us not talking anymore, or maybe you just decided you don't want to be my friend anymore—whatever the reasoning. Promise me right here, right now, that you will allow me the chance to say goodbye to you one last time. Because the thought of a world in which I live without you is unbearably devastating." My voice cracks, I take a deep breath before continuing, "But a world in which I live without even getting a *chance* to say goodbye to you..." I shake my head. "Don't ever not say goodbye to me, please. Don't leave me like that."

I'm fully crying now, tears and snot and gasping breaths breaking free. From the spot he is perched on the short wall, high above the city life and hours into the night, Jared locks eyes with me, hurt and heartache heavy in his gaze.

"I promise I will never leave you like that, Trystan. Forever."

I can feel my shriveled, barely beating heart change. I can feel a small breath of life that Jared's promise gave me rattle it a bit. Then, slowly and quickly all at once, metal walls erect around a piece of me—my heart. Thick chains made of iron criss cross over each side, locks at every juncture clicking shut. A mote appears around the base of it all, empty and hollow and dark.

No matter where I go or where Jared goes, no matter who or what or why or when or how, that spot inside of me is *his*. It still beats and it isn't broken—not really. It's hidden and protected and safe and will never be anyone else's—no one's but his. But it *is* different now. Guarded. A little sore from the new changes made.

It's as I watch the tears form in his own eyes that I say on a sob, "Always."

After the crying ceased and the mood lightened enough to fit back into a car, we finish our drive back to where my car is parked. We sit in slightly tense silence for a few minutes before I shut his radio off completely, unbuckle my seatbelt and turn my body to face him.

"Earlier you said you are pissed at me."

Jared unbuckles and turns to face me as well, leaning back against his door and propping an elbow on his steering wheel.

"Yes," he says gruffly.

"Explain."

"Not much to explain there. I'm pissed about how you did things."

"Okay," I drawl. "Do you think I am not pissed at you?"

His face shows surprise. "Why are you mad at me?"

"Well, it isn't like you really tried to stop me from breaking up with you."

"What would you have had me do, Trystan?" His voice is tight, and his jaw clenched.

"Oh, I don't know. Fight for me? Tell me no? You could have drove your happy ass down to Nebraska and demanded answers or tried to get me to take it all back. You did nothing. You literally said 'okay' and did nothing!" My voice is suddenly two volumes louder than it should be in a car and the second my ears register that I turn towards my door and get out.

"Don't! Don't you do that!" Jared yells as he gets out as well. "Don't you dare turn away from me and just walk away!" He rounds the hood of his car to stand between me and mine.

"I didn't want to yell at you inside your car, *Jared*!" I cross my arms over my chest.

"Well, we are outside now, *Trystan*. Go right ahead!" He throws his hands in the air before shoving them into his pants pockets.

And so I do.

"I would have fucking died for you! I would have walked through fire for you. Turned myself inside out and then outside in for you. I would have moved mountains and oceans and deserts for you, Jared. I would have burned bridges and robbed banks and stole the fucking moon for you! I would have never let you just dump me over the phone without some sort of fight afterwards." My voice goes from bitter and angry to defeated and miserable. "And I would have *never—never* started dating someone not even two weeks after being with you. It took me almost two months to even just kiss another person, Jared. You had a full-fledged girlfriend in a matter of days."

The silence that follows is deafening.

I loved him. I loved him so much that I still love him. So much that I will suffer through a friendship with him to avoid losing him altogether.

He loved me enough to let me go? But isn't that what I did in the first place? Why we are where we are...

"Trystan..." Jared says so slowly it hurts me.

He takes a tentative step towards me and I don't step away. So he takes another, and another. Then he is standing right in front of me.

"I don't know what to say to you other than I'm sorry."

"I know, Jared. That's the problem. I know you're sorry. And so am I. I love you and you know that—I don't think that will ever change. And I will be your friend as long as you'll have me because of that love. But don't think for a second that you're the only one pissed off here. I am beyond angry with you, yes. I wish you had fought for me—for us. So, I'm mad at you too. But I *hate* me." My finger goes from pointing at his chest to pointing at my own.

"You're mad that I broke your heart?"

He nods slightly, his face sad and his eyes narrowed.

"I'm mad that I broke my heart, too."

I move around him, avoiding any sort of physical touch not wanting the torture, and walk to my car. He doesn't move to follow or even pivot to watch as I get in silently and drive away in the night. He stands still, facing away from me, hands in his pockets and hang hanging down in defeat.

I would have sold my very soul and bones for that boy.

He couldn't even string together five words when I said we were done?

I deserved at least seven.

"Please don't do this. I love you."

CHAPTER TWENTY-FOUR.

a year-ish later.

SUMMER 2013.

"**A**lright. Enough is enough."

The sudden sound of my newly now-ex best friends voice waking me up is jarring to say the least. A grumbled "get out" escapes me while I pull my black and gray striped comforter over my head.

"I will do no such thing. We are done with this, Trystan. Get up, get dressed, get outside—*live*," Beth demands.

I poke my head above my blanket, barely uncovering my eyes. It's dark in my room as there are only storm windows that let in little light thanks to the purple curtains hanging up in here. I can see Beth standing, short and angry, by my dresser. Her hands are on her hips, an old white T-shirt hanging low enough to almost cover her hot pink athletic shorts. Her hair is blonde again and up in a bun. Her tanned, make-up free face in a scowl.

"Get. Up. Now."

"Beth, I love you but if you don't get out in the next thirteen seconds, I will break up with you." The blanket muffles my words.

That is short lived though, as Beth yanks the comforter off me and my bed entirely. In my long black T-shirt and neon green boy-shorts I flatten myself to my bed and glare at my arch nemesis.

"It's time to rejoin the living, Trystan. I can't watch you wither away anymore. Enough of this. It has been a year."

A year. A whole year of being Jared's friend and not his girlfriend. A whole year of just living my life day by day and trying to not crumple into nothingness. A year of trying to stay afloat and just be fine.

I wouldn't say I have withered away, technically. I go to work regularly—back at McDonald's as a manager again. The conversation asking for my job back was unpleasant.

"We all took bets on how long it would be until you came back," one of my managers said when I came in nine months ago asking if I could get my job back.

I didn't ask who won the bet. Fuck them.

I hang out with Beth a lot. Only at her place—not risking the chance at running in to Jared and Caitie in public.

I do some things... kind of.

Maybe it's the fact that I have lost forty pounds since the break up, though I am nowhere near complaining. The weight loss is purely due to the copious amounts of cigarettes I continue to inhale daily and the lack of food present in my diet but here we are.

"I am fine. I am not withered. I am just tired," I say, convincing no one in this room.

Beth takes a seat on the edge of my bed next to my legs and without looking at me says quietly, "I'm worried about you. It's been over a year and you don't seem to be getting better. I just want you to be happy again."

The hitch in her voice wakes me up the rest of the way. I sit up and wrap my arms around her from her side, resting my cheek on her tiny shoulder.

"I'll get dressed and let you take me out for breakfast."

I feel her head whip to my direction and her hands come up to clutch my wrist at her front.

"It's one in the afternoon so you'll have to settle for tacos but get up. Let's go!"

The smile in her voice causes a lump to form in my throat. I am so grateful for her.

"You keep my wild, B."

"You keep me safe, my girl," Beth says with a wink.

Since moving back to Rapid City after my failed small-town Nebraska run, I have resumed life to near normal. It's July and I have been single for a year and a month and have slowly been hating it less and less. Really, I have been hating *myself* less and less.

I can tell I am doing better by small things. I've started to notice when it's been however long since a sad-Jared-thought has crossed my mind. At first it would be something like an entire length of a song in the car that I hadn't thought of him when I normally would have. Then it would be the whole fifteen-minute drive to work that his name didn't echo in my mind. A whole shift, or a movie would go by that I hadn't longed for him to be next to me. Before I knew it, a few weeks ago an entire day went by where he wasn't on the forefront of my brain. Of course, upon realizing *that* as I laid down to go to sleep that night—he occupied my mind for the next four days without reprieve.

Progress is progress though.

That progress is currently being threatened, as is my nonexistent criminal record, as I sit here in a slightly secluded booth at the back of the store I work at. The red cushions are cold and the white table between myself and *Kristin* would do little to save her from my clenched fists if suddenly I stopped practicing self control.

Kristin is a mean girl by all definitions. She is maybe five foot six and has dull, lifeless brown hair that is always in a horrendously tight ponytail. Her brown eyes are pinched and annoyed, always. She is pasty and pale and just honestly so vile.

She maybe isn't those last few things... But even if she looked like Tyra freaking Banks—I would loathe her entirely.

The daggers I am shooting her with my eyes are clearly making her uncomfortable.

Wish I cared.

She moves her body side to side, fidgeting with the name tag that she's holding in her hands. Our manager, Theresa, sits next to her on the inside of the booth with her purple button up shirt perfectly ironed. Her long acrylic hot pink nails drum on the table next to her notepad and pen. Her red, blonde, brown mutli-toned hair is pulled up into the same small bun it always is, and her green eyes, sitting on her tan and freckled face, show the kindness and understanding she doesn't actually possess.

Mean Girl Number Two—but she doesn't take sides.

I roll my eyes at my inner thoughts, not giving a single shit if they can see the disdain bubbling off me.

"Listen, girls," Theresa starts, her voice high pitched and nasally. "I know there has been some turmoil recently. Since Trystan came back, really. But we need to figure out how to keep it off of the work floor."

"Then she," I shoot my gaze to Kristin. "Needs to stop talking shit about me when I am not here. And she needs to stop talking to her little friends, right in front of me, about Jared and Caitie and how they go on double dates and hang out constantly." I do my best to make my voice extra annoying and mousy, mimicking Kristin, before I look back at Theresa.

"Oh, Kristin," she drawls. "You aren't doing that intention-ally, are you?"

"Of course, she is!" I say at the same time as Kristin says in her whiny, grating voice, "Would it matter if I am?"

Theresa sighs loudly. She acts like this is so inconvenient for her but really, she loves the drama. It's her favorite pastime.

"It *would* matter if you were doing it on purpose. That is unprofessional and fairly unkind. Trystan and Jared's, uh, relationship," Kristin scoffs and rolls her own eyes. "It's not something that anyone needs to be making more difficult than it already is."

I clench my fists in my lap hard enough to feel pain in my palms, my light blue nails digging in to the skin. But my face portrays quiet vengeance and wrath under the fake smile.

"Oh, no. It's okay Theresa. Jared and I are great." I look to Kristin. "Our relationship is invaluable, and we talk nearly every day," I say sweetly.

And it isn't a lie. Jared and I *are* great. Myself on my own? Not so much. But our friendship is thriving. We text and call each other. Not constantly like it was pre-breakup, and not as often as it was immediately post-breakup—but we still talk frequently. That hasn't stopped in the year we've not been together. In the last month since I have "come back to the living", as Beth puts it, Jared has even popped into the hookah lounge we go to a few times a week to smoke with us.

Was it intensely horrible for me on the inside? Yes.

Did that stop us from having a nice time? No.

Growth. Or something like it.

"Caitie and Jared are happy and in love and you need to get a grip on reality and back off," Kristin spits from across the table, crossing her arms over her small chest.

Lap dog.

"Let's settle this so we can move on, girls," Theresa says.

"Here's what we are going to do, Kristin. I won't speak *to* or *about* you outside of meaningless work encounters. *You*," I emphasize while leaning forward, setting my clasped hands in front of me and locking eyes with Kristin. "Will be done trying to bait me. You will be done trying to goad me into a fight with you about your dear, sweet friend Caitie. You will stop talking about me to *our* coworkers. You will stop relaying bull shit information to Caitie because I can guarantee when she gossips to Jared, Kerry, or their horrible mother, Jared already fucking knows whatever it is that you think is such valuable information."

The rage in her face scrunches her features even more than usual.

"I love how Jared pities you."

I try to hide my flinch. Theresa doesn't.

"You think you two are such good friends, but if you heard the things we *all* say about you... You're pathetic and he hates you. It's laughable. You..." She moves to set her own hands on the table, near mine. "You are nothing to him but a joke."

I can't stop the tears then. I can play mean and vicious when the opportunity strikes but fuck... Kristin is out for blood today and I no longer have it in me to hold back the tears. Not after the week I have had dealing with her and her bull shit.

"Go cry to him about this and see what happens," she taunts.

"Enough, Kristin." Theresa moves her pen and notepad around for the eightieth time.

I don't try to stop the tears from falling—not anymore. They can see them. They don't make me weak. I'm not weak. I am strong and good and even if Kristin is spitting out the truth with malicious intent... I will rise above and show her honesty and realness. She won't know what those two things are—having nothing but a mean spirit.

"You have no idea how hard the last year has been for me. You have no idea how hard the two and half years before that were for me either. You know nothing about Jared and me. You will stop being so horrible to me, Kristin. Not because of anything I will do but simply because I do not deserve it. *Be. Done.*"

My tears splash on to my pink button up shirt forming small dark spots. Theresa sits across from me watching carefully, a look of empathy gracing her face. Kristin's bully-façade takes a back seat to a look I would equate to guilt if I thought she could genuinely feel that.

Kristin says nothing as Theresa wraps up our "meeting" and dismisses us both for the remainder of our shifts. The three of us walk to the office where Kristin pretends to be busy looking over the time off binder. I grab my things, not smiling or bidding anyone else goodbye, but allowing everyone to see my red rimmed eyes and somber face as I make my way to my car.

I give myself one cigarette before I pick up my phone and press Jared's name in my contacts list.

Jared picks up on the second ring, happy as can be. "Hey Tryst. What's up?"

"Do you hate my guts?"

"What?" he asks, genuine confusion present in his voice.

"Do you sit around a room with your girlfriend and her friends and talk shit about me? Are you pretending to be my friend so you can just use whatever I say when we talk as like, ammunition or something? The punchline to some new jokes? Am I a joke to you Jared?" My voice raises in volume with every word, my heartbeat with it.

"Okay, so first, please settle down a little bit. I can hear your breathing and you don't need to have an attack at two in the afternoon on this beautiful July day, Tryst. Okay?"

"I'm fine," I say tightly, counting to ten in my head.

"Right," Jared drawls, knowing I am far from fine. "And two, none of what you just asked me is anywhere near true. Of course, you aren't a joke to me. Where is that even coming from?"

I can't help the snark in my tone when I say, "Why, your new *bestie*—Kristin."

Loud silence emanates from the other end of this call.

"Trystan, Kristin is a lying brat. She thrives off drama. Whatever she said to you is bull shit."

Which I already knew in my heart but wow—she knew just where to strike today.

I sit with his words for a moment before saying, "Okay then. Thanks for picking up."

"Yeah, of course. You okay now?"

"Yes, I'm fine. I'll talk to you later Jare."

I end the call as I hear him say his goodbye, not waiting for him to finish. Because I'm pissed and I don't know if I one-hundred percent believe him that at least Caitie and Kristin aren't talking shit about me in front of him. I know his mom and Caitie do together. I've seen the shitty comments on Facebook that they toss at one another about me.

A post from Darla or Caitie about how "peaceful their supper was" or how "nice and smooth" moving cows went. One will post it and the other will comment something about how lucky they all are that Jared upgraded.

Yes, that happened. Had to beg Beth to not comment back and then take my mom's car keys away so she wouldn't drive to Jared's house.

And when Jared found out about these instances... Well, he said he was sorry and told me he told them to stop.

They didn't.

I give myself a few minutes in the parking lot to be pissed. To rage internally before I pull another cigarette from the box, dialing Beth's number.

"*I'm fine*" I repeat to myself in my head the whole time.

CHAPTER TWENTY-FIVE.

August in South Dakota is much more tolerable than August in Nebraska. While Nebraska Two Thousand and Twelve was a total failure, South Dakota Two Thousand and Thirteen is looking up—finally.

Tonight is not a night for sadness or depression—but instead Gary Allen and friends. A good time that I deserve because I can't hate myself for forever.

Well... Can't I?

"You look sad again," Tanner says from beside me, bumping his shoulder into mine.

Standing at a tall six foot four inches, high and tight light brown hair, light brown eyes to match, and a handsome baby face—that is Tanner. Beth met him earlier in June on a dating app, but it turns out he was meant to be our new friend instead of her new boyfriend. So, here the three of us sit, four of Tanners military buddies behind us, in the silver metal stands at the concert arena for the state fair.

"I'm fine," I reply with a smile and a shoulder bump of my own. "Really, I'm okay."

"It's okay to still miss him but listen, babe," Tanner says while hooking his arm around my shoulders and pulling me close.

Tanner knows all. The drama, heartbreak, sadness. I don't know how he infiltrated his goofy self into my heart like he did, but I am so glad he took up residence there.

"It isn't even that. I just talked to him an hour ago." I laugh at my situation. "I'm fine, seriously. I miss him but not like, in a soul crushing way anymore. It's just..." I lean my head on Tanner's shoulder, "We loved this song. We listened to it constantly. He put it on a CD he made for me when we had first started dating, for my birthday. So, it's just bumming me out a little."

'The One' by Gary Allen. Gary is up on stage, clad in dark Wrangler jeans and brown boots with a brown T-shirt and white cowboy hat, singing his incredibly talented heart out to everyone here.

"Alright, listen sweetheart," Tanner leans in putting his mouth to my ear so only I can hear him. "You need new memories to old songs to make them okay again, so here's what we are going to do." He takes my hand in his, his arm still around my shoulders. "I am going to serenade the shit out of you right here, right now. From here on out when you hear this song or any of the other ones tonight that make you sad, my sultry singing will outweigh your heartache. Yeah?" Tanner leans back to look down at me, raising his eyebrows.

"Yeah," I say with a genuine smile. "Serenade me, Tan-Man."

And he does. The rest of the concert is him and Beth and even his buddies behind us, and eventually me, singing to and with each other. Not erasing the memories I already have with Gary Allen and Jared. But the new memories with my friends are like a layer or two of white primer over a bright pink wall. The pink is still there underneath the splotchy white, but it's not as blinding.

CHAPTER TWENTY-SIX.

I am going on a date tonight. A real, full fledge, date. I have been out with boys in the last couple months. I have mingled and moved on in physical ways in the last year. But I haven't been asked out, picked up, and on a wined and dined kind of date yet.

I could puke I am so nervous. More nervous than an almost twenty-one-year-old should be but here we are, sweaty palms and leaden stomach.

Ethan Anderson, twenty-six, single dad of a two-year-old girl, truck driver for a cattle company in Wyoming.

That's what his profile on Fish-A-Plenty said, anyways.

Ethan is due to pick me up any second for our date. He is taking me to lunch and then we are going four-wheeling in the hills where his parents own a cabin. I'm sitting outside of Beth's apartment, having gotten ready here while she was out and about. I straightened my dark hair and put on the standard make-up with some extra bronzer and brown eyeshadow. I've got on a black Jack Daniels t-shirt and dark blue jean-shorts with my black flip-flops. Beth's fake-tan-out-of-a-bag is doing wonders for my pale Irish skin.

I'm checking my phone for literally anything from anyone for the four-hundredth time as I see an old, light blue Suburban looking thing pull into the cul-de-sac with an incredibly handsome, bearded driver. From the pictures on the dating app we met on I can confidently say that is my date—Ethan.

He pulls into Beth's driveway, waving and smiling, before getting out and meeting me halfway as I walk to him. The awkwardness is palpable. We shake hands and small laughs escape both of us.

"Trystan?" he asks.

"Yep, that's me. Ethan?"

"You bet," he says, flashing a pearly white smile at me.

We drop our hands, his going to his front jeans pockets and mine hanging loose at my sides.

He is handsome. Light brown hair cut short, chocolate brown eyes with the longest and darkest eye lashes I have ever seen. He's got to be like, five foot eleven maybe. Strong looking arms, tan skin. He has on a tan Browning T-shirt with blue jeans and brown work boots. A scruffy but charming beard hangs about an inch long on his face.

A good 'ol boy, I think.

"You ready to go?" he asks me.

I nod my yes and follow him around his vehicle to where he holds the door open for me.

"This is a cool... truck?" I hedge, unsure of what to call his vehicle. It's not one I've seen before.

"Yeah, thanks." Ethan lets out a small chuckle while going around the front and getting into his seat. "It's a 1975 Jeep Wagoneer."

I'm not really knowledgeable on the car front. But I am knowledgeable on the boys-who-like-their-cars front and so I tell him how cool I think it is, noting the pride in his voice.

The day with Ethan was incredible. He took me to a small diner in the hills where we each ordered a hamburger and fries. The food was great, and the conversation was simple and easy and flowed wonderfully.

After we ate, we drove the winding curves and bends of The Black Hills to his parents' cabin. That was where we got out of his Jeep and spent almost three hours exploring the surrounding area on his family's four-wheeler. I have never gone riding like that—just for fun. It had rained the two days prior, so the "roads" were thick with mud.

As was my hair by the end up our date. I didn't care though. I didn't think about Jared all day. I hadn't compared Ethan to him or missed him or had even a moment where I had a sad thought enter my mind.

It was the perfect first date.

When he brought me back to Beth's, she was home and came out to her driveway to meet Ethan. It went *so* well. I shouldn't have been nervous about that, but I was. Beth liked Jared a lot. She liked me and Jared together. Even after everything she was still a Jared Fan. But to my happy surprise she seemed elated to meet Ethan. As I recapped the events of the day, her and I sitting on her patio furniture and drinking homemade margaritas, she seemed genuinely excited for me. No mention of Jared or the last year between us.

"So, you like, like this Ethan guy then?"

"Honestly, Beth," I say looking down at my margarita and smiling, "I really, really like this Ethan guy. I know it was only today, but it *was* all day."

"That smile looks good on you, Tryst."

I look up to see her own smile.

"He's coming over tomorrow to hang out after work. I hope that's okay?"

"I told you to use this place like it's yours. Just like I keep telling you to move in with me, but here we are." The sass in her voice and the laughter in her eyes makes me giggle.

Or maybe it's the tequila.

"You're the best, babe."

"Just shout me out at your wedding someday," she says, raising her salt rimmed, green tinted drink at me.

I laugh and roll my eyes at her. Little soon to be talking about a wedding, no?

CHAPTER TWENTY-SEVEN.

Some would call me impulsive.

Borderline psychotic.

Beth called me "marginally problematic."

"In need of an intervention or therapy."

Actually, therapy would probably do wonders.

I wouldn't really be able to argue with those people, honestly. Especially now as I drive Ethan's blue Wagoneer through the small streets of Gillette, Wyoming.

I've never been to Wyoming.

First impression—*it's fine.*

Second impression—*what the fuck am I doing with my life?*

If you had told me a month ago that I would be moving to Wyoming with a boy I have only known for that small amount of time, I would have laughed at you. Yet here I am—engaged, the future Mrs. Ethan Anderson and stepmom to a sweet girl named Birdie.

How did I get here?

a month ago.

"I think..." Ethan says on a breath while lying next to me naked as the day he was born, "I love you."

Am I that *good?*

My heart skips a beat. I love that word. "Love". I love that feeling and that emotion and that sentence. It's been so long since I have felt loved like this—the way Ethan has shown me lately.

It's been three days since our first date.

Yes, three.

"I think I love you too, Ethan," I say, surprising myself with such a declaration.

But I do. I think I love Ethan Garrett Anderson.

In only three days!?

We roll over to face each other, his arm draping over my middle and pulling my soft stomach to his flat body.

"I have to go back to Wyoming next month. I took leave to come sort shit out with my ex-wife but that's over by the end of September."

His gaze meets mine as I draw small circles on his shoulder. Ethan raises his dark brows in a silent question.

"What?" I ask, thinking he's going to maybe ask what we do from here.

"Come back with me."

I blink a few times, the question he just posed taking a moment to sink in. And at some point, I will probably reevaluate why my answer didn't take longer to form. Why I so quickly am going to jump headfirst into this entire thing? Some day in therapy I am sure this situation will come up and I will laugh at myself. But right now...

"Okay."

That evening, Ethan at his parents house with his daughter, I am sitting with Beth in her living room. We're watching reruns of Tabitha Takes Over while scrolling on our phones. Beth wasn't super stoked about my news when I told her what Ethan and I discussed this morning. She never outright tells me I am an impulsive idiot, but I get the feeling she is less than impressed in this situation.

"You're mad."

She looks up from her phone and meets my questioning eyes. Her green stare is anything but warm right now.

"What are you doing?"

"What do you mean?" I ask.

"What. Are. You. Doing?"

"Expand, Beth. Let it out."

I sit up from my relaxed position and cross my legs under me. Beth does the same, both of us setting our phones down.

"This is stupid, Trystan. You haven't even known him a week. *What are you doing*?"

"Beth, I know it seems crazy. I know that it probably actually *is* crazy. But do you know the last time I have felt even an ounce of the peace I felt this morning when Ethan was telling me he loves me and that he wants me to move in with him?"

"Of course, you felt peace! You had just gotten your rocks off like four times, Trystan. A fucking scorpion would feel peaceful by that point. But that doesn't mean that that scorpion should make any sudden and drastic decisions about its entire life!" She throws her hands up in the air and lets out a large sigh. "This is insane... You're not even twenty-one. He's got a two-year-old and an ex-wife. You want to deal with all of that, cute kid or not, and move all the way to bum-fuck Wyoming? That's two hours away. It's not eight like Nebraska was, but Trystan. What are you doing here? Is this a cry for help? Are you sad again and I just haven't seen it?"

I get up now, annoyed by the suffocating opinions and judgement being thrown at me.

What sucks completely is that she isn't wrong. *What am I doing?* I don't *think* I'm sad again. I wouldn't jump into something like this if I still loved Jared like that—I wouldn't have it in me to do so. I *have* been feeling restless lately—like I need to keep doing something and keep moving and keep just... *going*. And sure, this is fast. Like, *really* fast. But it isn't like I don't know that. So as long as I can recognize that, the quick pace and mildly reckless behavior on my part, then at least I'm being self-aware right? And if I am being self-aware then I can't possibly be going in to this blindly...

Right?

"I am moving to Wyoming with Ethan in a few weeks. I am going to get a part time job and take care of Birdie on the weeks she is with us. I hope that you find it in you to support me and continue to love me. I need you in my life. You don't have to agree with me, Lord knows we don't always see eye to eye, but I need you, Beth. Please. Try to understand and just be happy for me."

Beth stands up from the couch and walks to where I am near the TV. She grabs my hands, squeezing them twice, while giving me her best-effort smile, looking me in the eyes.

"You keep me safe, Trystan. I'll keep you wild."

As we stand there, embracing one another, her words continue to sound off in my head.

"What are you doing, Trystan?"

present.

And that is how I got here, pulling Ethan's Jeep into the driveway of his little Wyoming home. My belongings are with him in my car. I don't know why we swapped vehicles, something about him wanting to see how Salsa did on the two-hour drive. I won't complain though, I love Ducky. Ethan, like me, appreciates a good vehicle name. He chose Ducky for his Jeep when he first got it a few years ago.

His house is cute—small but charming. A bungalow style layout with a lot of off white everywhere. A typical rental style color scheme. It's fully furnished, he's been here for about six months now.

After the small tour Ethan gave me, we settled on the gray pleather couch to watch a Twilight marathon. I told him how excited I am for the next one to come out around my birthday, so when he saw this was playing, he turned it on.

He's so thoughtful.

It's been five months now since Ethan brought me to Wyoming with him. Five months of being completely alone nearly every day and night. Five months of me solely taking care of Birdie when we have her. I love that girl more than I thought possible, but even so, doing it all alone has been exhausting. I spent my twenty-first birthday by myself watching the new Twilight movie on Pay-Per-View. We spent Thanksgiving here, Taco Bell was the main course. We spent Christmas with his family so Birdie could be with her grandparents. I visited Rapid City by myself once after my birthday. It was then that I started to feel the weight of the mistake I had made.

You would think I could just leave. That I could just give Ethan his ring back, pack my things, and go. But no. Not because he won't let me, don't get the completely wrong idea.

I won't let me.

How embarrassing would it be to go home, tail tucked between my legs, head bowed like a loser? Everyone—Mom, Beth, Jared fucking Barns... was right. This was a bad idea. It was too much, too fast. And now here I am—sad and alone, *again*, and wishing I could go back in time and say no when he asked me to move with him.

I think I love him, even still. But the fact that I don't *know* is pretty indicative of an embarrassing lapse in judgement.

We can't go on like this. He is never home. And then when he is, I am pissed that he isn't ever here outside of that moment. So, then we fight. He wants nothing more than to hunt and reload his stupid ammunition when he is home. So, then we fight about that. It's all just fighting at this point.

But I guess that explains why I'm here, in this bathroom, crying into a brown bath towel. Ethan is in his little reloading room, avoiding me and my emotions.

We can't keep doing this.

A few moments go by and I sigh as I stand in the doorway to Ethan's man-room. I lean my shoulder on to the frame and cross my arms while I watch him ignore my existence.

Quietly I finally tell him, "We can't do this anymore. *I* can't. I think I need to go."

"I hate to say it, but I think you're right."

"You gonna turn around and at least look at me while we break up?"

I am trying to rein in my anger, my heart isn't breaking like I think it should be. Instead, all I feel is irritation and annoyance towards this man who I don't even know.

Ethan finally swivels around on his little red stool. His eyes meet mine, neither of us move to go to one another. We don't say anything for a long while.

"Do you want help packing?"

I scoff, rolling my eyes, and walk away.

I had already packed the majority of my things before going to talk to him. But as I walk the rest out of my things to my car, Ethan watching from the living room behind me, I pass Birdie's room and actually register it all in that moment. That's when I feel it—the breaking.

Through a tight throat and the tears that in retrospect should have been for Ethan and I but aren't, I turn to him and say, "Please don't let Bird think I don't love her."

His eyes soften and he shows the first sign of emotion he has had tonight. Or for the last few months, truly.

"She will know, Trystan. That you love her." Ethan grabs the bag I am carrying, takes it to my car and returns to stand in front of me.

I'm still staring at Birdie's room. I take in the pinks and purples that cover every inch. I walk in and pick up the neon orange stuffed unicorn she picked out at Walmart with me that last time she was here.

Gosh, had I known that would be the last time I would ever get to hug her and tell her how wonderfully brilliant she is...

I give the plushy a good squeeze, breathing in the scent of that sweet girl. I hate this. I don't know that I will even miss Ethan. How do you miss someone you don't know? But Birdie... Fuck. I saw her more than I saw him. We bonded. She quickly became my little bestie.

I did not think this part of things through. But you can't stay with a man you don't like simply because you're in love with his baby.

I walk to where Ethan is, his hands in the pockets of his worn and mud-stained jeans, and stop in front of him. He reaches out and wraps me in a hug, his arms staying high around my shoulders. I wrap mine around his small waist and we both give each other and ourselves this moment.

"It wasn't all bad, right?" he mumbles into my bun.

"It wasn't *all* bad."

"I *am* sorry."

"I'm sorry too, Ethan." I sniffle at the thought of Birdie.

We let each other go. I don't look back at where he is standing on his porch as I pull out of the driveway. I don't wave. I don't stop for fuel. I simply go. I drive and drive and end up in Beth's guest room two hours later—sad and hurting all over again. But not broken, no. Not this time.

CHAPTER TWENTY-EIGHT.

As quickly as the Ethan Anderson chapter of my life had started—it ended.

What. A. Ride.

The hardest part for me is not seeing Birdie ever again. That little sweet pea and I had started to become besties and I will miss her golden hair and chocolate brown eyes for the rest of my life, I think.

I'm sitting in the driveway of my parents' home, my belongings now back inside my room exactly where they were five months ago the last time I left. I had my hair cut yesterday so today it is sitting at my collarbone, a straight, dark sheet. As I check my reflection, I see slight bags under my eyes and cringe at the wariness of my face. The March sunshine will do me well today. I sit back in my seat, reflecting on this mess of my life.

I have had a weird two years.

Two years, that's it?

That is all the time that has passed since I heard that horrible, life altering sentence?

"She will never be a part of my family."

Two years have gone by since I moved, broke up with Jared, moved again, befriended Jared, met Ethan, moved a third time, and now have moved a fourth time after breaking up with Ethan.

And I am about to move a *fifth* time in just under two weeks.

Why did I even bother taking my boxes inside?

I wake from my self-staring contest to my phone buzzing from beside me. I wince at the name I see on the screen, knowing I am about to hear how insane I am.

Again.

"Hi Beth."

"Get your boxes inside or are we just leaving them in your car for the next ten days?"

Her tone is unpleasant, but I say nothing about it. She has been with me through this all. It can't be easy to watch to your friend almost wreck her life every few months.

"My boxes are inside, safe and sound. I was just getting ready to back out of the driveway and come pick you up." I keep a smile in my voice.

"I don't understand what you are doing anymore, Trystan. I haven't for a while but what the hell is going on? Nebraska? *Again?*"

"I know. And I know I said it every time before but this time I have a plan. And this time I am doing this for *me*. Not to run away from Darla or to follow Ethan. I am moving this time with a plan for school and a job after and it's all on my terms and for me. Please, support me on this like you have every other time. *Please*, Beth."

Beth's responding sigh is answer enough that I finish leaving the driveway.

"I'll see you in fifteen, okay?" I ask.

"Yeah, yeah. See you in fifteen."

"You're going *where*?" Beth asks, almost choking on a chip.

"Jared wants to hangout before I leave again so I am meeting him at the L and we're going for a drive after this tonight." I keep my tone light and matter of fact.

Nothing to see here.

Beth and I decided we wanted tacos and margaritas, so we are sitting at the bar in On The Border. Neither of us dressed up for a night out. Both of us have zero make-up on, the messiest of buns, raggedy T-shirts, and black leggings. The chill in the March air has us wearing knockoff-Uggs. We look like cute, tired, twenty-one-year-olds.

The accuracy.

"Why are you guys meeting up?" Beth questions after a moment of silence.

Next to her at the bar, I turn my head and set my crossed arms in front of me.

"Is there a problem with me seeing him?"

She looks back at me, matching my energy.

"No, I'm just curious what you two will be doing. Just driving around aimlessly seems unlikely." She raises a perfectly shaped dark brow and smirks.

I roll my eyes in answer before taking a long sip of my strawberry margarita on ice.

"I will let it go," she says before turning to her own drink. "What is this big master plan you have for Nebraska two point oh?"

"Well," I begin. "I am signed up to take the CNA class at the local community college in town. That will start two weeks after I move there and so in the meantime and while I take the four-week course I will find a job and work."

"And where will you live?"

"My grandparents' house. My grandma is sick, as you know, and the additional set of arms and pair of eyes will be helpful."

Beth looks at me for a moment before taking a bite of her steak taco. Mouth full she says, "I guess this plan is more of a plan than the last times*ssss*."

I take her taco-free hand in mine and squeeze.

"Thank you for loving me," I say.

"Bleck!" She swats her hand away from mine.

"I'm serious."

She looks at me then, letting me speak my peace.

"You're my best friend. Through all of this... stuff you haven't left my side. You have been watching me run my life into the ground. You've witnessed me at my saddest and most miserable. You've watched me leave just to come back and you haven't ever said 'I told you so' or made me feel like a complete moron. I love you. Thank you for loving me through it all."

Beth wipes a rogue tear from her eye before saying, "I love you. Nothing will change that. I don't need to tell you I told you so because you already know. I don't need to make you feel bad because you do that for yourself just fine enough. I'll love you through anything. You keep me safe, my girl."

We hold hands for a long moment before I pick my drink up in my other hand, Beth following suit, and we clink them together as I say, "You keep me wild."

"So, when do you leave again?" Jared asks from the driver's side of his Continental.

"Like, twelve days I think." I take a sip of my Coca Cola I grabbed from the McDonald's drive-thru we swung through twenty minutes ago.

"To the same place we went for the Fourth of July that one summer?"

"That's the one. I'll live with my stepdad's parents. Go to school, get a decent job, find a place of my own. Do the *whole* thing this time," I say confidently.

I'm not faking the determination in my voice. This is it for me. I can feel it. I'm not running. I'm not hiding. I have a plan. I have a goal. I *will* succeed this time.

"Well, I'm glad I get to see you before you go." Jared looks over at me and smiles.

His smile is still my favorite.

Heck, *Jared* is still my favorite. Do I act on the things I wish I could act on? No. I don't reach over to hold the hand he has resting in between us on the gear shift. I don't ask him to park the car so we can fool around. I don't tell him I still love him desperately—even though I do. I keep that all to myself and give him the friendship that he can give me.

If I were to step back and examine me as a person, I think I would be confused. I don't know why I am still madly in love with this man. It's been years. I don't know how to stop myself. It was a dull roar while I was with Ethan, but it was like something snapped the second I crossed state lines when I moved back from Wyoming. I am still deeply and madly and unequivocally in love with Jared Dennis Barns. And there is not a damn thing to be done about that. I tried unloving him. I tried leaving—a few times. I tried doing some sort of forced proximity thing thinking if I saw him happy with someone else then maybe my heart would get a fucking grip. I tried moving on. But nothing has worked and I've resigned to just loving him anyways.

"Listen," he begins slowly. "I don't know what you have going on right now in your personal life..."

Yes he does.

He leaves that fairly open ended though, not asking but not really shutting down the option of discussing it all. I look at Jared, my brows raising in question.

"I don't want to put you in a bad spot or anything but I just-" he stops himself.

"You just what, Jared?"

I have a feeling I know where this is going but there is no way I am right because Jared doesn't cheat on Caitie.

Does he?

Would he?

Would I?

"I miss you," he says, looking at me while we sit at a red light.

He misses me? *Misses me,* misses me? No… No way.

"Jared, I need you to clear up what exactly is going on in that handsome head of yours."

Could I be the other woman? Could I handle it being *us* just one more time? Is the façade I put on that good that he has no idea I am still head over heels in love with him?

"I just miss you," he says again but this time he sets his hand on my thigh, rubbing his thumb there.

It's Jared. You would sell your soul for him.

And I do. I let go of my soul and my heart and my morals. I give it all up for Jared.

For him, I would lose it all, I did lose it all.

Nothing stopped us from having a few more "last times" over the next twelve days before I left.

CHAPTER TWENTY-NINE.

"**A**nd you just moved here from where again?"

"South Dakota," I say, nodding and smiling.

On the other side of shiny wooden desk sits the Director of Nursing for the local nursing home in town. She's... *beautiful. And terrifying.*

Susanne Harris, DON (Director of Nursing) and RN (Registered Nurse). Her mostly blonde hair is cut short to her shoulders and frames her face in a way that tells me she has had the same perfected hair style for years—if not decades. Her bright blue eyes sit under dark mascara-tinted lashes and her bright red scrub top shows off her small figure.

"And you moved here for what?"

Her voice is kind but firm, very much a leader.

"Well, honestly?" I hedge. "I had nothing else going on up there." I give a small shrug.

It's been six weeks since I have moved down here. Six weeks of waitressing and helping take care of my grandma while getting certified as a nursing assistant.

Professionally—I'm killing it.

I aced every test I had to take. I scored high as heck on my final. I made the other six ladies in my small class laugh daily. I did it all on my own.

Physically—also doing great. I've been so busy trying to stay busy that I haven't had time to binge or mope about anything that might be bingeable or mope worthy.

Everything else… Well… It's all fine.

It's fine.

Okay—it's a minor mess. Beth and I are good. FaceTime becoming a thing this year has proven to be a lifesaver. My parents and Mikey are good. I've been hanging out with a boy I met on the same dating app that I had met Ethan on. He's nice and funny, handsome, and good at keeping my *mind*, uh… satisfied. But he is definitely not long term and thank goodness for that because long term is the opposite of what I need.

And Jared… Well…

Not a single thing has changed there. We talk and *talk* regularly. We have plans to see each other at the end of the month, my brother's birthday party is over Memorial Day weekend.

So, things are fine. I may be *slightly* unstable—but things are fine.

"Are you single? How old are you?" Susanne flips through the papers filled with my information in front of her.

"Uh, what?" I laugh.

Susanne looks up at me, serious as a heart attack.

"Single?" she asks again before looking back at her papers. "Ah!" She taps her red polished index finger on what must be the answer to one of her questions. "Twenty-one!" Her bright eyes meet mine and she smiles a mischievous ivory smile. "My son is around your age. He isn't single," she says as she clicks something on her desktop computer and types on her keyboard. "But," she continues, "he has this friend that *is* single and quite handsome."

I start to object, "Oh, I don't know abou-"

She cuts me off and pivots her screen towards me.

"No, no! He is great. His name is Tyler Johnston. He's a few years older than you, grew up going to school with my son, works for a co-op."

Had to Google what a co-op was that night.

Susanne clicks through various images on Facebook before landing on one of this man named Tyler. His long, tan arms are covered in black swirling tattoos. His smile is gorgeous—bright and bold and big. Infectious. The picture itself is definitely a little aged, the quality is grainy at best.

I wonder what his laugh sounds like with a smile like that.

He has on a blue plaid button-up and dark jeans with a Busch Light bottle in his hand.

Questioning the sound of his laugh is all I need to convince me to say, "Yeah, okay. He's cute." I look up at Susanne and question, "Do I give you my number to give to him or?"

She smiles broadly and says, "Yes! That sounds perfect. He sells fertilizer to my husband so I will see him at some point in the near future and pass it along. Oh, how wonderful!" She claps her hands together. "Oh! You're hired. Did I say that?"

I had assumed so beings she was playing matchmaker, but the clarification is more than welcome.

The next few days are a blur. I completed orientation and then went to night shift at the nursing home. My grandma's health has been declining daily. Working two jobs and getting used to an overnight shift is proving to be a bit challenging.

I never realized how much I enjoyed standard sleep.

I have made some friends around here that make me feel less alone, but I don't go out of my way to really connect to them. I'm flighty and it turns out I also have attachment issues and those two things are weird together. I keep myself on lock, watering myself down. If they knew the thoughts that flood my brain in the quiet, still moments they would find out that I am some severely damaged goods. Working nights and adjusting to that, plus the emotional toll of everything going on with my grandma, and the going out with my new friends... I'm getting tired.

Okay—I've been tired.

And on top of all of that, Tyler texted me yesterday and asked if I would be out tonight at the bar. Seems like that's about the only thing to do around here for those of us twenty-one and over. I said yes and now here I sit, with people from my new job, standing at *The Pit* and waiting to officially meet Tyler Johnston.

"Trystan Harper?" a deep male voice sounds from behind me.

I turn around and am met with a broad chest. I raise my eyes and see a good-looking chin, a strong nose, piercing blue eyes, and a full head of luscious dark brown hair. He's got to be about six feet tall.

Seems I may have a type.

"Tyler Johnston?" I ask, holding out my right hand.

He takes mine in his and we look at each other for what feels like forever.

It's been two years since I broke up with Jared. I've been with other guys, obviously—I was engaged to one for a few months. But no matter who I was with or where I was, Jared's presence was still like a small echo in the back of my brain, in my heart, reminding me that I missed him in my very atoms.

But right here, right now, in front of this handsome man... As cliché as it is, it's like there is only him. There is no echo. There is still a small part of my heart that has those steel doors and locked chains—but that won't ever go away, I think.

Holy shit. Tyler is handsome. I take in his bright red Nebraska Husker's shirt, his thick tan arms.

"You don't have tattoos."

He gives me the most puzzled look. "What?"

"You had tattoos. In the picture Susanne showed me a few days ago. Tattoos covered your arms. You don't have tattoos now though." I bunch my brows in utter confusion.

"Oh!" he exclaims. "Facebook! That's where she showed you pictures!"

Still confused but with a smile I say, "Yes, and I still am not understanding."

"It was Halloween. Like two years ago. I wore tattoo sleeves."
DUH.

"Oh... That makes sense for the lack of ink tonight then."

"Is that," he lowers his voice, "a deal breaker? No tattoos?"

"What?! Oh, gosh! No! I'm so sorry, no. Not at all!"

Recover this fumble, stupid.

"I just was so confused and picturing one thing and here you are tattoo free and big, I mean tan, I mean, your arms..." I look up and meet his amused eyes. "You know what, I need another beer." I smile before I walk around him, gently placing my hand on his bicep as I go to the bar behind him.

I reach to grab cash out of my little black wristlet when Tyler steps up slightly half next to, half behind me and says, "I'll get this one."

I go to object, but the bartender has already taken his card and is walking back with our beers.

"Thank you, that was nice of you." I take a long drink. "I'm sorry if I sounded like a spazz. Obviously, I don't care if you do or don't have tattoos."

He laughs at my babbling, and I am instantly put at ease.

I am also instantly in *like* with Tyler Johnston.

Holy shit, I realize, *it's been a while for that feeling.*

Before leaving the bar to head home, our individual homes because I have learned my lesson in rushing these things entirely, Tyler walks me to my new-to-me little silver car.

Porscha, *yes spelled like that,* is her name. Is she a Porsche? No. She's a shiny Pontiac G6 and I love her.

"It's so cool how you can see so many stars here. Back home you have to drive into the hills or find a spot that is just right to see this many," I say to Tyler while looking up towards the sparkly black sky.

I feel him get closer, coming up behind me. I allow him to close the distance entirely, leaning his chest to my back.

He sets his chin on my shoulder, our ears touching, while he points to the sky and whispers, "That's the big dipper there."

I feign surprise, not telling him about my astrology phase in middle school so I know all about several of the constellations.

"That is so cool that you know that," I say as I twist around to face him.

We both smile at each other, him looking down, me looking up, and when Tyler leans in to kiss my lips, I don't stop him. The kiss is soft—he must moisturize. His face is smooth, and his hands hold on to me at my lower back. I settle mine on his biceps.

When we break apart, I look up at him from under my lashes and say, "Flex these for me." My smile feels big and true.

Tyler laughs at my random request but obliges.

"Alright, I'm sold," I say with a wink.

He tips his head back and laughs the most magically wonderful, full bodied, loud laugh I have ever had the pleasure of hearing. And I decide right then—that's it.

That is the laugh that I want to hear for the rest of my life.

CHAPTER THIRTY.

SUMMER 2014.

“A re you still going to see Jared when you’re back next week?”

I move the phone closer to me on my bed, balancing a bottle of red nail polish on a book called "Fundamentals of Nursing" from my grandparents bookshelf that's in my room.

“I'm not coming up there next week anymore. I can’t afford it,” I say to Beth sadly.

I'm trying to be okay with it—missing a milestone so early into living down here. And I'm doing *alright*. But man... The tears I cried when I told my mom a few days ago were plenty to get me by for the week.

“Oh, no. That sucks. Mikey will understand though.”

“Yeah, he doesn’t care.” I laugh. “He just wants to go bowling with his friends so as long as he has that, he’s chill.”

"Nice." Beth pauses before saying, "Okay, but... if you were coming up still, would you be, you know, seeing Jared?"

The way she said "seeing" has me rolling my eyes.

"No, Beth. I won't be screwing around with Jared here, nor there, anymore. Happy?"

"I just don't like how he is treating you or Caitie at this point. He misses you but he doesn't want to end things with her and be with you? It's bull shit."

She isn't wrong.

"It is what it is. Anyways, I'm seeing Tyler now. So, I told Jared the other day that I was done messing around with him."

How do you mess around seven hours away?

If you know, then you know.

"How did he take that?"

"It was over text, but I doubt he cared much, Beth. If he cared in general, in the way that would make a difference, shit would have been different." And while I may sound mildly bitter....I have great news.

I can, with absolute, undeniable, total honesty and certainty say that I am one hundred percent no longer in love with Jared Dennis Barns.

Do you know how long it has been since I was not in love with that boy?

I was 16 when I fell in love with him. Five years. I had been in love, head over heels, infatuated with him for five years. And even before then, I liked him immensely.

Now, don't get me wrong, I still love Jared completely. He will have a piece of my heart until the very end. My body will die, and my soul will continue to hold a place for him. He is, and will remain, my very best friend. Even if at some point we no longer speak—I will forever be in his corner, loving him the way that I can.

But I no longer feel this undying love for him in the way that was soul crushing and life altering.

And what a fucking relief that is.

After finishing up the phone call with Beth, her catching me up on her latest Fish-A-Plenty disaster date and me lecturing her on how she needs to tell me where she is going with random men *before* she goes with them, I make my way downstairs to see my family.

Everyone is here. All three of my aunts and their husbands, all of their kids. My two uncles, their wives and kids. Today has been an especially hard day for my grandma, the hospice nurse told us it would be best to start the goodbye's.

As hard as it is for everyone, I can't help but to feel relief for my grandma. And my grandpa and the rest of our family. It is heavy, caring for your loved one. Watching them wither away day by day, becoming less than they were with every passing week.

I have already said my parting words to her. Any time in the last two months that I have helped her to the bathroom, we would talk. Once it became too difficult to move her to the bathroom, I would use my newly acquired knowledge and license to assist her still. That kind of bond isn't something I feel the need to explain or use as an excuse but it's deep and it's enough for her and I. I don't think any of us are ready for her to be gone, her included. But I thank God that my life has led me here, to this point, to be able to see her more and be here for the things I can help with. Difficult as they may be.

In the last six months a lot has changed.

My grandmother passed away just before Memorial Day. Her funeral was beautiful, and the love felt from the community was plentiful.

I moved in with Tyler shortly after. I know, I know.

Moving so quickly again, Trystan?

And yes, but also no.

Things with Tyler are wildly... slow. It's like I have known him my entire life. The way our hearts and brains and souls love and live together is so harmonious and strong and stable. So, when it was time to move out of my grandparents' house... He suggested I simply move in with him. I said yes, and things have been so wonderfully sound since. I am at true peace for the first time in what feels like forever.

I still work at the nursing home, with no plans of that changing any time soon. I think I will eventually go to school for a bachelors in nursing. But for now, that part of my life is also really steady and enjoyable.

Beth has a steady boyfriend that I got to meet in August when I took Tyler up to meet her and my parents and Mikey. Hayden is great and I can't wait for the babies they will hopefully make some day.

My family adores Tyler. Craig doesn't get enough of nerding out over Star Wars and Lego's with him on FaceTime or when we visit. Michael loves to throw a baseball with him when we are there, and he bombards Tyler with a million questions about tractors over the phone. My mom gives him a hard time about random shit, which is as good as a golden thumbs-up from Tracy.

Tyler's family is… *wow*. I never knew potential in-laws could be so likable. His mother is an actual saint—that I am sure of. Like, mark a day in your calendar for her and celebrate it in her honor because the kindness and love and pure joy she emanates is powerful. His dad and sister are almost equally as wonderful, but no one can be as incredible as Laura.

Currently, at the store picking up some groceries, I move my phone from one ear to the other.

"You want to go to Australia?" I ask Jared. "Like, to visit right? That's far away, dude."

"To visit. To stay. I don't know. And far away is kind of the appeal, Tryst."

"Well…" I pause. It isn't my place, nor desire, to boss Jared around anymore. Or offer unsolicited opinions on his life. "If Australia is it for you and that's what it takes to get out of Rapid then I fully support that."

Neither of us say anything else for a moment. The silence between us is as comfortable now as it was five years ago, I think. We do this often—talk on the phone. Probably once every week, sometimes every other week. We text in between and just stay in general contact.

"Why did you break up with me?"

I physically flinch, nearly dropping the blue box of cavatappi noodles I'm holding. I set them back on the shelf in front of me and take a steadying breath.

"Why are you asking me that right now, Jare? Are you okay?" I say, my voice quieter than it was a few minutes ago.

"I was going through my closet, and I found a shoe box in there. I forgot I had it." He takes a moment and I hear a door close in the background.

"What are you doing?" I think I already know but...

"I just got home. Figured I'd go through it with you on the phone."

"Jared... I don't know what has gotten into you, and you know me, I love nostalgia. But are you okay?"

Jared has never been one to reminisce. He is stoic and kind and warm and likes the present. I can give a solid guess at what is housed inside the shoe box, and it is fully nostalgic.

"Remember those notes you'd write me when you were still in school?" Jared asks while giving a small laugh.

I could be a fortune teller.

I smile to myself. "Yes, I remember. Gosh, I was so bored in school. No wonder I almost failed calc my senior year."

That's not a joke. I really did. My teacher felt bad enough for me, my blatant effort in trying not being enough to carry me, that he passed me with the highest passing grade he could.

Jared sighs, "I kept them all."

He what?

"You what?"

"Every one. I put them in the box for the shoes you got me that first Christmas we were together. That first pair of white Vans. You remember those?"

"Of course, I do."

"I kept them all, Trystan."

I say nothing, giving him space.

"Why did you break up with me?"

I almost choke on the same lie I told him all those years ago. "The distance, remember?"

Jared scoffs. "I don't buy it. Because I read some of these when I found them. And not once, in any of them, did the feeling of distance being an issue come up. We had plans. A life waiting for us. A dog and a coffee table and pizza. Nebraska wouldn't have changed that. Not the first time, at least."

I don't know what to say. I don't think he's doing this, whatever *this* is, in a way that suggests he wishes things to be different between us. Our friendship is stable and something both of us have acknowledged as something vitally important to each of us. He's never expressed regrets when it came to us.

"I'm not dumb. And I wasn't then either. Tell me the truth, Trystan. Please."

"Okay, I guess we are doing this," I say more to myself than him.

I continue pacing the aisles, back and forth, up and down. No longer shopping, just walking. Working up the courage to say something I could have said then.

Maybe even should have.

What would my life look like today if I had told him the truth?

Would he have had my back?

Would he have chosen me?

Would we have survived him having to make that choice?

I never gave him the chance to answer that, I suppose. And that is on me.

"Trystan?"

"Yeah, sorry. You've caught me off guard here, Jare." I take a breath and push on. "I made that call and ended us that day because of what you said about your mom."

"What did I say about my mom?"

Of course, he doesn't remember—it wasn't life altering for him.

"You texted me that night saying that she had told you how happy you had been lately. Essentially—I left and you were better. That's what I took that to mean. She was better to you." My voice is sad, the feelings from back then still hurting. "I knew then, even before then, that at some point in time, whether it would have been the next week or when we got engaged or when we had a baby or whatever, I knew that at some point I would have had to ask you to choose—your mom or me." I swallow and take a breath, pausing my pacing in the aisle filled with cereal. "I knew I would have had to ask you to choose, and at that point... I didn't think you would have chosen me, Jared. So... I chose for you."

The silence we are suffocating in now is not one of comfort or companionable harmony. It is a silence from the depths of a dark place. A place where a nineteen-year-old girl was bullied by a fifty-something year old woman. A place where the boy that girl loved with everything she thought she would ever have—he didn't show up for her. A place where that boy knew deep down what was going on and instead of making a stand and doing something to fix it all, he chose to act ignorant to what was happening to the girl he claimed to love. No one is blameless in that place. We all fucked up in ways I can't even begin to dissect.

Maybe he did love me a whole lot, possibly more than I will ever know. Maybe to him he loved me with every atom of his own being. To him that might have been enough. Perhaps, if I had been willing to suffer his mother's comments and attacks and hatred for a few more years, I would have felt confident that he would have chosen me. Maybe I jumped the gun, it isn't like I'm not known for that by now. But maybe's don't change the facts—he loved me. But he didn't love me enough to help me while I drowned in the words and opinions of others right in front of him.

"Jare..."

"I don't know what I would have done, Trystan."

And that's okay—I want to tell him. I don't know what I would say either at this point. It's all over and done with for me. I had assumed it was for him as well. But then he found a shoebox of love letters and memories...

A moment passes before I say, "I really have to get this shopping done. Tyler is waiting at home for me and I'm picking up supper... Keep me posted about Australia, yeah?"

Jared clears his throat and says, "Yeah. I'll uh... yeah."

"You okay?" I ask softly.

"Always," he says.

Forever.

"I'll text you later Jared."

"Goodbye, Trystan."

Jared's voice felt like it held some extra weight at the end of our conversation. I tell myself to check on him later, make sure he's alright. It isn't my place anymore to try to understand the inner workings of his mind, his heart. We aren't together. He's still with Caitie—the girl he chose. And I'm with Tyler in my new life. But there is this weird feeling in my chest—an unsteady beat in that small part that belongs to Jared. It's like my heart once again knows something about Jared that my head just doesn't.

I don't like feeling like I'm keeping secrets from people. I can do it—keep secrets. Quite well actually, but I don't enjoy it. So, while Tyler and I eat the supreme pizza I picked up from Casey's Gas Station after I grabbed groceries, opting to not cook said groceries tonight, I told him about my chat with Jared.

Tyler knows all about Jared. My past isn't something I hide or shy away from. It is my life. It is who I was and why I am who I am today. It is why I love the way I love—wholly and openly.

So, Tyler knows who Jared is. He knows about his mom and the breaking up and the two years that followed. He knows Jared is still one of my very best friends and that that will never change. Tyler knows that I love Jared still and he understands that is a different kind of love than it was then, a very different love than I feel for Tyler now.

After supper Tyler settles on to the giant, light brown loveseat we have in the living room of our little home to play some video games. I give him a kiss before going to our room and laying down under the camouflage comforter that came with the man.

Hey, I hope we are good. Have a good Monday!

I click send and go to swipe out of my texts when I see a red circled "!" next to my text. I check the name to see if I accidentally tried sending it to the wrong person. When I confirm that it says "Jared" I freeze.

"What the fuck?" I mutter to myself.

I press and hold on my failed message, copying it and then pasting it in the new message box before hitting send again. When the same thing happens as before I sit up and cross my legs. I click his name and call him, hoping I'm wrong.

"The number you have trie-"

"No fucking way."

My shock takes center stage, irritation on the back burner. I try to call him again.

"The nu-"

I set my phone face down, fairly aggressively, in front on me on the bed. I decide to try again tomorrow. We aren't friends on Facebook or any other apps so finding him there and reaching out feels weird. I let it be for the night and try to sleep.

"Goodbye, Trystan," echoes in my head throughout my fitful night.

"So, he did block me then?" I ask Beth the next day.

"He must have if you can't see him, and I can."

"K," I pout.

"I'm sorry, babe. That sucks."

I called Beth this afternoon, both of us off today, to tell her about Jared and I's conversation yesterday, and then my failed texts and calls last night and this morning. Along with the empty social media searches, I can deduce now that Jared has left me entirely.

I'm sitting on the loveseat, my legs draped over one of the arms while my head rests on the other. I pull a piece of lint off my black leggings, needing to do something, anything.

I want to say I get it. I want to say I understand why he just *ghosted* me. I want to say I can appreciate his feelings, respect them.

I *want* to say all of that—to believe it. But I don't—I can't. Because I *don't* get it. I *don't* understand. And I *am* pissed.

Years. He has had *years* to ask me that question—to give a shit. And instead, he waits until now, until I am finally and fully moved on and in love and happy. He waits until now when there isn't anything I would change. He asks me a question, I answer honestly, and then he what? Bails? *Ghosts* me of all things? Decides that I don't even deserve a real goodbye?

"He fucking promised me, Beth. He promised he would let me say goodbye to him if it ever got to be too much for him." I am seething.

Unshed tears line my eyes and I force them to stay put. He doesn't deserve them anymore.

"I know, babe. I'm sorry. I don't know what to say beyond that."

I take some steadying breaths and close my eyes.

"He was my best friend and he just left me, Beth."

She knows that isn't a dig or anything to take away from her role in my life. He was my best friend. He was my friend before he was the love of my life. He was there for so many firsts. He walked with me through so many things that no one else will ever have the chance to see or do with me because they were that big. He was the first love of my life, and I his..

"Here's what you're going to do—nothing."

My eyes pop open at that, surprise and confusion mixing in my brain.

Beth continues, "He made his decision. It was what you thought it would be all those years ago—not you."

"I see we are going with tough love today, Beth. Alright." I sit up and cross my legs, putting my free hand between them.

"I think you need it today. He didn't choose you then and he didn't choose you now. It sucks, he's a big baby, and the lack of closure will hurt for a while." Her voice softens, "But you're going to be okay. He didn't love you enough, even now. And you, who puts one hundred and forty percent in to any and every relationship you have, doesn't deserve even a *friend* that won't put in as much as they can for you too. So, yes, it sucks. It really sucks because I know how much you loved him then and love him now. But this isn't on you. It's on him. Let him live a life without you if that is what he chooses.

I don't think for a second that he doesn't already realize how much he will miss you."

"What if he doesn't miss me?" I whisper, afraid that I am not someone he will miss.

"Impossible," Beth says confidentially.

"What if I imagined it all and he didn't even actually like me that much, let alone love me?"

Becasue what if that's the case? What if to me we were this big, eternal, bursting love that will live in on my heart and soul for the rest of forever? But what if to him... What if I was nothing more than just his first real girlfriend? The one his mom hated and drove away, and he just stayed friends with me to see how nice he could be?

Beth takes a deep breath, bringing my attention back to her. "You imagined *nothing*, Trystan Victoria Joann. I watched it all. I was there for everything, remember? I watched you two flirt for months before and years after. I watched you two make googly eyes at each other from across the room at work a whole year before you started dating. I watched him open doors for you wherever we went. I watched you look at him like his eyes held every answer to every question you ever thought. I saw the way he fell in love with you. The wondering way he would look at you when you laughed your real, full laugh. The way he would hold your hand every second he could. I watched him hurt for you, even if he didn't act on it, when his family started in on you. And you forget—I watched him break down after you broke up. Not up close, but I was still in town where you weren't. I was still around him in some capacity. And even if he was happy with Caitie then, even if his mom stopped being so horrible to him—I saw it. I saw the weight he lost. I saw the light dim in his eyes in the pictures she would post. I heard the way he laughed differently when I saw him out."

I stopped trying to keep my tears at bay at "googly eyes". I let them out and between a shuddering breath I say, "I wish he would have let me say goodbye."

"He loved you. Please don't doubt that. Don't gaslight yourself in hopes that you can make his actions make sense."

I wipe my wet cheeks and sniffle.

He loved me. I loved him. It was all real—the love and the joy, the good.

And the bad—his family, the fights, the losses.

But just like they were real, so were we—*Jared and Trystan.*

"Nothing can take away what we had."

We were good and pure—love and light.

Forever and always.

CHAPTER THIRTY-ONE.

a decade later.

SUMMER 2024.

"Yes, dear. I am aware. That is the sole reason I am in Target right now."

"Okay, keep that in mind before you grab one of everything that you think the girls need."

I set the bumblebee striped, long sleeve swimsuit back on to the wrack and roll my eyes.

"Tyler, I will be back in a bit. Let me know what kind of coffee you want and kiss my butt."

Tyler's laugh comes through the line, and I quietly giggle.

That laugh still fills my soul, even after ten years.

We hang up and I continue going through the little girls clothing area, as if my kids don't already have almost everything in here. We're in Rapid City this weekend for Mikey's birthday. He's turning twenty, which makes me want to be physically ill, so Tyler and I brought the girls up to celebrate their "uncle Mickey".

Elizabeth and Ann are seven and five and the literal heart and soul of my being.

Between the girls, Tyler and his busy season at work having come to a pause, and the hospital needing all of the overtime from us nurses this last spring—this trip is beyond needed. It feels good to not be working or cleaning this weekend. To wear clothes that aren't completely battered or bled on.

To be back home.

My ever faithful black leggings, white V-neck shirt, and hot pink linen button up serving as my just-in-case-I-run-in-to-any-one-I-know outfit makes me feel more put together than I am. My nearly-black hair with bright blonde peak-a-boos that reaches halfway down my back, is half up in a hot pink claw clip. Black Birkenstocks click on the white floor as I go through the store. I try to hold my chin high and keep my shoulders *not* at ear level, nervous to run into any old classmates and have to like, socialize properly or something.

I round the corner, walking towards the socks and sleepwear area when I am stopped in my tracks.

Breathing, beating, blinking—it has all ceased.

There *he* is. *He's here.* Alive and looking... like he's lived. Like he's happy and okay. Like he's everything I ever wanted for him.

He sees me.

I see him.

We lock eyes.

Gosh, the blue is so bright even from here.

I give a small, genuine smile and he... looks like he wants to die. Or vomit. Or both. And then he bolts.

He bolts?

He bolts.

I turn back, facing my cart again, my eyes wide and my pulse high now with embarrassment. I try to focus on a pair of fuzzy socks to calm my breathing, taking stock of them.

They're cute.

Mikey's girlfriend would like them.

They have baby penguins wearing Halloween costumes on them.

Why are there Halloween socks here right now?

$3.99 on clearance, huh that seems cheap.

Deep breath, Trystan.

In an alternate world, or 10 years ago, I'd react to him differently, I think.

I'd say something like, *"Why did you leave? Do you have any idea the things you missed? Do you have any idea how much I needed you still? How much you leaving me almost alone and without so much as a 'fuck you', affected me for months?"* I imagine my lip would start to wobble and my eyes would water as I told him, *"My grandpa died. My parents got divorced. Bear had to be put down. I got married and then immediately pregnant and then had a fucking miscarriage, Jared. You were my person. Even when or if you shouldn't have been, you were still my fucking person and you just left me to be alone and without you. You. The one person that knew me to my darkened, damaged core. I want to know why. I want to know why I wasn't good enough for a fucking goodbye."*

But this isn't that world or a decade ago and I'm no longer angry with Jared. I'm sad at the state of where we ended up. I wish I could still call him my friend. I love him still, that small part of my heart carries him it—*always and forever.* I root for him. I'm in his corner even if I don't have a single clue what that corner looks like anymore—even if he doesn't know that. I'm there.—cheering for him and wanting the very best for him.

I get ready to take a step forward, hoping for the ache in my chest to settle a bit, along with my heart rate.

It isn't a longing sort of ache now. It's more like... Like when you broke your wrist the summer you turned fifteen while playing soccer, right? And it hurt like hell? The most pain you had ever felt up until then. It was scary and you were mad at yourself for the accident. But life moved on and it healed. It got back to almost one hundred percent. Maybe even a full one hundred percent, just a little bit different. Not worse, not better. And for the most part it feels great. You learned how to function around the break for a while and then adapt to the small twinges after it healed. But every spring during a big storm, or every winter when it hits just below twenty-seven degrees, there's that *ache.* A brace at night or some over-the-counter medicine usually does the trick to settle it down—but it's there. It's always there. In the deep tissue and the scar from where the plates and screws got placed—the reminder doesn't fade.

My chest has that kind of ache.

Typically, it's dormant. Only showing itself faintly and accompanied with a small smile when a Gary Allen or Blake Shelton song from pre-Two Thousand and Twelve comes on the radio. Or in moments like right now—when I'm here, back home, getting a rare glimpse at the man I was so in love with once upon a time.

I take a deep steadying breath, gripping the red cart a little tighter. I close my eyes, exhaling as I picture the Halloween penguin socks. I pick my foot up to take the first step forward...

A hand grasps my elbow and before I know it, a familiar scent—*American Eagle cologne still?* It fills my nose as a take a deep inhale and feel the warmth of his chest on the left side of my face. He's got one arm wrapped around my shoulders and the other holding my head to him. Almost on instinct I've thrown my arms around his waist and I'm bunching the back of his shirt in my fists.

For a moment we just... *exist* together again.

Breathing, both a little shakily, we stand there holding one another. His chin rests on the top of my head as he moves his hand from there to my other shoulder blade, smoothing my hair on the way down. Jared takes a deep breath and I realize that I'm holding mine. I struggle to release it. It's like I know what is going to happen. I somehow know what this is already before it's even started. That's how it's always been with him—with us.

"I'm sorry."

That wasn't me.

He's sorry? He's got about seventy-four things he could be apologizing for, in my opinion, but I don't say that. We're not angry anymore. I wait for him to say which one he's shooting for. Maybe it's a blanket one? I tighten my grip on his shirt, a small bite of pain reaches my palms as my nails hit a little too hard. He grips me a bit more.

I realize then—Jared knows what this is too.

"I'm sorry I walked away," he says.

His voice is deeper, older, more worn.

"Then or now?" I ask myself inside my suddenly mushy, unusable brain.

"I didn't want to. I didn't need to add another hurt to the score. I don't know what happened in that moment, but I saw you and I saw you see me and I just..." He takes a much-needed breath before going on. "I panicked. I'm sorry Tryst." His last word ending in an exhale.

"Tryst"... I relax my body a little at him saying my name. It's been a decade since I've heard him say it. Has it been that long since he's said it out loud? Maybe even thought it? Thought about me?

I can feel that there's more, and conveniently for both of us I can't seem to find my voice quite yet. I silently nod against him.

I get it. I'd walk away too if I had at one point hated me, like I assume he did.

Does?

Did?

Jared's body tenses even more, both of us not saying anything for a moment. I hate that he feels stressed right now. I don't want that—I stressed him out enough over the years. Wanting him to feel settled and okay was the whole reason I did what I did. I open my mouth to say something, what I'm not sure, and he opens his at the same moment. My mouth closes, grateful for more time to try to get it together.

"I don't regret anything about you. Us. Except one thing."

Suspense strikes, threatening to take me out at the knees.

"I don't regret letting you leave. I don't regret not giving us more chances. I see how happy you are. I've seen it for years, truthfully. From afar... I've seen it."

That surprises me. I didn't think he had given me a second thought after he disappeared all those years ago. He tightens his grip for a moment and then releases just a smidge—a small hug.

"You have the most beautiful children, Tryst. I hope they *all* know how lucky they are to have you in their lives."

His emphasis on "all" lets me know who he included under that umbrella. And I appreciate it even more than he realizes. Not that I need his approval in the slightest to continue to be happy, but knowing someone I care for is happy for me just does something to my heart. I sink a little further into him.

"But, I do regret one thing. I'm sorry I didn't have your back more. I'm sorry I let my mother ruin a part of you, even temporarily."

I cringe at the mention of that horrible woman.

"I am *so* sorry I didn't stop her, Tryst. There's no excuse for it other than I was a coward and scared. And I ended up losing you for it. I'm just... You deserved better. From me. From her. And I'm sorry." He takes a big breath, like he's been harboring that apology inside of his heart for so long and now that it's out there he's a got a bit more room in his chest.

He lays the side of his face on the top of my head. I realize after several long moments of quiet that it's my turn.

Okay. I can do this. I can ask the one question I want to ask.

But first I need him to hear something...

"It wasn't your responsibility as a barely-adult to teach a grown woman how to not treat, what was essentially, a kid. She was mean—that was on her. I know you loved me—that was on *you*."

Jared gives a small nod on the top of my head letting me know that he heard me. I feel him relax just slightly. I fist my hands in his shirt once, twice.

Breathe.

"Why did you *ghost* me, Jare? You just... left me." My voice is barely above a whisper but by the slump in his shoulders I know he heard me. I try keeping my voice steady but fail entirely as I say, "And, no I wasn't alone—not completely. But your absence was felt, *greatly*, for a really long time. And I know you probably hated me, but I need to know why you couldn't have told me that. We told each other everything."

I resist the urge to look at him. This whole time we haven't made eye contact aside from when he looked at me like I was death incarnate.

"We made that promise, if it ever got to be too much, we would always say goodbye. You didn't say goodbye. Or you didn't let me say goodbye. Why?"

He's silent. But I can hear his heart, it's fast. And I can feel his breathing—also fast. And then it's slowing, like he's calming himself. I brace myself for impact. I don't want to hear how much he loathed me. How he couldn't stand to be fake with me anymore, couldn't be bothered to pretend to be friends with the girl that broke his heart. But I think I need the truth, even if it's that he hated me with every fiber of his being.

"I never hated you, Trystan."

I shudder a breath, relaxing slightly.

"I can't believe you thought I hated you," he says solemnly, shaking his head while it stays resting on top of mine. "I wasn't mad at you. Not for being happy, finding love, living *your* life for you for the first time in years."

"Then why? We had that last phone call. I remember it—it was good. It was easy and genuine, they all were. I laughed too loud in the grocery store and got funny looks. You told me about your Australian dreams. It got a little heavy, I know, but that never stopped us before from being close. What happened?"

We both take yet another deep breath. You'd think by now my pulse wouldn't feel like I've done burpees for seven minutes straight. But here we are—wildly beating.

"What happened was," he starts, "I found myself hanging up that night feeling like I was floating. Feeling light and happy and... loved. Even after the heavy shit, after the truth of it all came out. And I hated myself for a second because I was willing to see if you would want to throw away your current happiness—see if you'd choose me. Especially after you had told me all about the real reason you dumped me."

My breath hitches. The not so dormant ache in my chest is deepening. I try to blow it away with an uneven breath. It doesn't work.

"I loved you," he says quietly but deeply.

Ache.

"And I was so sorry for it because you loved him."

Ache.

"I didn't want to be selfish. That's all I was when we were young. I was selfish with your love and your grace and your kindness. I took it all—I took you for granted. I'm so sorry for that."

Breath's go deeper, grips hold tighter.

"That girl will never be a part of my family" rings in my mind, like I needed the reminder of the words that changed the trajectory of my life.

"I didn't leave you because I hated you. I let you go because I was still in love with you and I, for once, needed to not be selfish with you. I had to finally choose... and I chose you."

Ache.

Breathe.

Find your voice, damnit.

"I don't regret it. I see it in your eyes that you're loved, and loved *right*. I saw it in the way your smile met those perfect brown eyes—you're happy."

Don't cry. Not yet.

"I know you still love me, or that you did then. That you cheer for me, root for me. I know it's a different love then when we were kids. I know that kind of love now too because it's how I love you today."

He releases a quick breath. I think the inside of my bottom lip is going to start bleeding from me chewing on it. A tear falls, hitting his light gray T-shirt making a small dark spot. I close my eyes, not even bothering to will them to stop. I think I'd forgotten we're in public. People have had to notice. Target is busy today. I've seen some odd looks the few times I've dared to open my eyes. I can't see through the blur in them at this point, so closed they remain.

Everything just... stills. My breathing. His breathing. I'm almost positive my heart has even stopped.

I love that he knows how loved I am. I love that he knows he'll always be loved by me, even if it's from afar and not the same way it used to be. I never considered his ending our friendship to have been something he had done out of respect for my now husband and me. For the life I was creating for myself. It didn't occur to me that it might have been because he loved me...

And because of the hurt that had been causing him.

Ache. Ache. Ache.

We share yet another deep breath.

The worlds oxygen supply has got to be running low at this point.

"I'll love you for forever, Jare," I finally manage to get out.

There's a few more spots on his shirt by now. His grip is a little tighter and even after a decade apart, I know his breathing well enough to know my tears aren't the only ones that have fallen today.

"I'll love you for always, Tryst."

I don't want him to think I he can't leave if this is killing him, or that he has to like, care for me or something. So, I move to let go of his shirt, but he tightens his already strong grip on me.

"Just one more moment," he whispers into my hair.

Breathe in.

"One more," I respond quietly.

Breathe out.

And that's what we do. We continue to exist in each other's presence, just holding each other one last time. A few minutes pass. By now I can taste the salt from my tears, and I can feel him slowly loosening his hold. He presses his mouth into the top of my head, and I hug him so tightly, knowing this is the last time I'll get the chance. Once upon a time I had thought I would be hugging this person for the rest of my life. And now... All I have is this last time.

Just one more moment.

My chest aches still but it's different. It isn't less—it's not more. It's just... It's like when you chew a piece of minty gum and take a sip of ice-cold water. It stings but it's refreshing all at the same time.

One last moment with the boy I loved before anyone else—the boy I broke myself for. The boy who did the same for me a few years later.

He lifts his head off of mine and I loosen my grip. He rubs a small circle with his thumb on my shoulder. I place my forehead on his chest.

"Close your eyes. Count to ten," he whispers.

I do.

One. Two. Three.

Deep breath.

Four. Five. Six.

I am acutely aware of the loss of warmth Jared *was* providing.

Seven. Eight.

Nine.

Two more deep breaths for good measure.

Ten.

I brush away the tears from my cheeks before opening my eyes. I stare ahead at the now empty aisle I'm in. I turn back to my almost forgotten cart, grab the Halloween penguin socks, two pairs actually, and then I just...

Move.

I go back to my life. To my handsome husband. To my great kids. To my good job. To the hotel and to the life I love and wouldn't trade for anything.

To the home I've built and the life that I'll never be drowning in.

EPILOGUE.

two years later.

SUMMER 2026.

JARED BARNS.

H oly shit.

Holy fucking shit.

She's here. She's here with her husband and her kids. The taller one looks just like her—they're so beautiful.

Gosh, how long has it been since the last time I saw her in this same store? Two years?

Two years.

She looks so nice today. Her butt in those light blue jea-

Knock it off.

But that dark T-shirt…

Focus.

Should I duck around this corner? Would she see that and know? Do I even *want* to do that?

She's with her family, I should just play it cool and walk the other way.

Okay. That's what I'm going to do.

"Jared?"

She sounds so good. Fuck, I miss that voice.

I pivot from the end cap I'm standing by, various candles under a big red clearance sign now to my left.

I take a steadying breath before saying, "Trystan!" while throwing up a hand in a flat wave.

Get it the fuck together, dude.

"Hey," she laughs.

I always loved making her laugh.

Some things never change.

"Wow, what are the odds?" Her smile is wide and brilliant, her lips a bright red. "You look great," she says as she tilts her head to the side a bit.

She looks great.

I realize I haven't said anything after enough of a pause that the air has turned awkward. I shake my head and smile back at her, a genuine one—the only kind she deserves from me.

"You look good too, Tryst. It's good to run in to you." I stuff my hands in to my front jean pockets.

She backs her cart up the rest of the way before turning the front of it into an aisle lined with too many towel options. She takes a step forward before freezing, her smile only faltering slightly. Anyone else might not have noticed that.

I'm not anyone else though.

"Hey, I lost you back here."

The voice from behind me is one I have come to know well, and love deeply, over the last seven months.

Nic comes up to my side, sliding her bright orange nails along my bicep, while I turn slightly to meet her in the middle.

Looking between Nic and Trystan I tell Nic, "Yeah, I ran in to an old friend. Trystan, this is my girlfriend—Nic." I wave my hand between the two of them. "Nic, this is Trystan."

Recognition at Trystan's name flares in Nic's eyes and I pray that she is not one to react all weird when her boyfriend runs in to an ex-girlfriend.

"It's so nice to meet you," Trystan says.

Genuinely, of course.

There is about eight feet between the two of us and Trystan. I look to Nic, her eyes wide, her beautiful pink lips in an even bigger smile.

"It is *so* nice to meet you Trystan. I've heard really lovely things."

If I weren't already in love with Nic that right there would have sealed the deal. I grab her hand in mine, squeezing tight.

"Mom!"

A tall, skinny kid runs up to Trystan, grabbing at her shirt and smiling up at her with a crooked smile.

"Dad said to hurry up! He said to tell you that we don't need more towels so come on!"

Trystan smiles down at her daughter and brushes her light brown hair out of her eyes.

"Liz, don't be so rude." She winks at Liz. "These are my friends, Jared and Nic."

Trystan looks up and over to us and smiles, her bottom lip trembling the smallest bit.

"This is my oldest daughter—Liz."

"It's short for Elizabeth," says Liz very matter of fact, throwing her small little fists on little her hips.

I laugh at the display of sass, reminded of Trystan all those years ago. Young, pure, and good. And full of attitude.

"It's very nice to meet you Elizabeth," Nic says from beside me with a small laugh of her own, her arm now looped through mine and her other hand holding it.

Liz looks back up at Trystan, hands still on her hips, and says, "Let's go mom."

Trystan laughs at her daughter before looking at me and Nic again. Her beautiful brown eyes bounce between the two of us.

She smiles with closed lips and nods her head ever so slightly while she says, those eyes locked on to mine but then sliding to Nic's dark green ones as she says, "It was *so* wonderful to see the *two* of you. Be good, yeah?" she says with a wink before telling Liz to hop on the back of the cart and backing out of the aisle.

I watch Trystan go, Nic next to me. Neither of us speaks but she squeezes my arm and pulls me gently to turn from where she came.

"Let's go pick out some ice cream before we leave?" she suggests brightly.

I smile down at her and kiss her brow, her golden-brown pony-tail glimmering in the store lights.

Nodding, I say, "I think I want a brownie and cookie dough one."

end.

Acknowledgements

First, thank you to my husband for sitting through months of random outbursts with no context about I'll Never Be. Thank you for trying to comprehend the story I was trying to get out even when I gave you so little to work with. And finally, thank you for loving me. I love you.

To my kids, if you read this someday, way way way down the road, I hope you can see the pieces of me in it. I love you to bits.

To my book-writing Fairy Godmother, ABH. You are inspiration and kindness and generosity and intelligence. Your guidance and positivity and willingness to literally walk me through this process has forever changed me for the better. You have left a mark on my heart, and I appreciate you beyond words. This, INB, wouldn't be without you. Thank you, friend.

To my friends and family that have been hyping me up over this process, I love you all. Thank you for always being so excited about I'll Never Be.

To the group of people that read I'll Never Be before publishing, you rock. I appreciate the time you all put in to helping me get here. Thank you so much.

To anyone that reads I'll Never Be, thank you. I hope this story hits somewhere special in your heart. I hope that if you ever needed to relate to someone like Trystan, to know you aren't alone, you've found this and got what you needed from it. Keep on keepin' on. You are good and worthy and loved.

To "Jared", I'm still in your corner, buddy.

And finally, to this story... you're my favorite almost *always*.

Forever,

A. L. Fox

xoxo

About the author

A. L. Fox is a self-publishing indie author, though she feels weird calling herself the "a" word. She spends her days with her two small children and her farmer husband. She enjoys 70 degree weather and rain, Starbucks and Target, and laughing. A. L. Fox was born and raised in the Midwest and likes to think her writing will reach who it needs to. She plans to continue to create but has no real, big goals while doing so. She's thankful everyday for the chance to do this whole thing.

Her main goal: *bring joy to others.*

Also by

And Then I Saw You.

www.ingramcontent.com/pod-product-compliance
Lightning Source LLC
Chambersburg PA
CBHW031440160726
47994CB00005B/1809